PRAISE FOR THE SLOAN KRAUSE MYSTERY SERIES

Distinctive characters and fun anecdotes about beer and brewing help make this a winner. Readers will want to keep coming back for more.

— *PUBLISHERS WEEKLY* ON *BEYOND A REASONABLE STOUT*

Exciting and irresistible...this absorbing mystery will not let you leave it unfinished. Ellie Alexander is a formidable mystery novel writer.

— *WASHINGTON BOOK REVIEW* ON *DEATH ON TAP*

With its beautifully described small-town setting and seamlessly intertwined details about brewing beer, this cozy will appeal to beer lovers everywhere as well as readers who enjoy mysteries highlighting family relationships and independent female main characters.

— BOOKLIST

Likable characters, an atmospheric small-town setting, and a quirky adversary for the amateur sleuth. The engaging premise and pairings of beer and food should appeal to fans of Avery Ames's 'Cheese Shop' titles.

— LIBRARY JOURNAL

A delight for foodies, craft beer fans, and lovers of twisty mysteries with a touch of humor.

Charming...featuring a clever protagonist and talented brewer whose knowledge of the science and art of brewing beer is both fascinating and fun. The cozy village and the quirky characters who inhabit it are a delight, and the intriguing mystery will keep readers enthralled to the very end.

Ellie Alexander's prose bubbles like the craft beers her protagonist Sloan Krause brews—a sparkling start to a new series.

A concoction containing a charming setting, sympathetic characters, and a compelling heroine that kept me turning pages way past my bedtime.

Death on Tap is an entertaining sip of the world of brew-pubs and tourist towns. Sloan, a foster child turned chef, brewer, and mother, is an intriguing protagonist. Pour me another!

A 'hopping' good cozy mystery...Readers will enjoy listening to local gossip and tracking a killer along with her in the charming German-style 'Beervaria' setting of Leavenworth, Washington.

ALSO BY ELLIE ALEXANDER

THE SLOAN KRAUSE MYSTERIES

Trouble is Brewing

Death On Tap

The Pint of No Return

Beyond a Reasonable Stout

Without a Brew

The Cure for What Ales You

Hold on for Beer Life – Short mystery

Beer and Loathing

A Brew to a Kill – Short mystery coming May 2023

STANDALONE NOVELS

Lost Coast Literary

THE BAKESHOP MYSTERIES

Meet Your Baker

A Batter of Life and Death

On Thin Icing

Caught Bread Handed

Fudge and Jury

A Crime of Passion Fruit

Another One Bites the Crust

Till Death Do Us Tart

Live and Let Pie

BEER AND LOATHING

A SLOAN KRAUSE MYSTERY

ELLIE ALEXANDER

Published by
Sweet Lemon Press LLC

BEER AND LOATHING
Copyright © 2023 by Katherine Dyer-Seeley
All rights reserved.

Library of Congress Control Number: 2023902211

This is a work of fiction. All of the characters, organizations, and events portrayed in this novel are either products of the author's imagination or are used fictitiously.

Cover illustration by Kitty Wong
Cover design by Gordy Seeley

This book is dedicated to you. Without your unwavering support and encouragement, this series might have died off. But because of your emails, DMs, handwritten notes, and stopping me after book signings asking me to please, please, revive Sloan, I was utterly humbled and inspired. Sloan has always held a special place in my heart, and I'm so touched that she's left a lasting impression on you. I hope you enjoy her next story as much as I enjoyed writing it.

With love,
Ellie

CHAPTER

ONE

I PASSED BY THE BAR, precariously balancing a tray of black IPAs. Nitro hummed with the beat of drums reverberating off the shiny silver brewing tanks and bodies squished together around high-top tables. The crowd was somehow bigger than yesterday's, which seemed impossible. Our nanobrewery was as stated—*nano*, as in tiny. We brewed small batches of craft beer in our boutique space nestled in the Northern Cascade Mountains in the Bavarian village of Leavenworth, Washington. While some brewers dreamed of expanding and distributing their products nationally, I was quite content to keep things small.

Garrett Strong, my partner in crime, had opened Nitro just over two years ago after inheriting his Great-Aunt Tess's two-story Bavarian inn with its brocade façade, brown hickory balconies and spires, and signature lion's crest. While she was alive, Tess had used the old brothel as a boarding house and diner, but it had fallen into disrepair.

When Garrett took over, he renovated the building's entire interior. The front served as our tasting room and bar, with bright white walls and cement floors. The twenty-five-foot-high ceilings made the dining area feel expansive. A long

I

distressed-wood bar served as a divider between the dining space and our brew operations.

Garrett had kept Tess's commercial kitchen and small office mainly intact and transformed the rest of the open space in the back into our brewing operations. Our stainless-steel mash tuns and shiny bright clarifying tanks were housed in the back, where all of the brewing magic took place.

Recently we had taken on the task of renovating the four upstairs guest rooms that had been untouched for years. After much deliberation, we decided to transform the rooms into Airbnb suites themed after the key ingredients in beer—water, yeast, hops, and grain. We offered guests an immersive beer experience with personal brewery tours, special beer tastings, homemade breakfasts, and extra touches like leaving hop-filled sachets under their pillows.

Last summer's project involved building an attached deck on the side alley for more outdoor seating. There were always dozens of things on my checklist as brewery manager, but at the moment, my top priority was delivering this round of drinks without spilling them on the floor.

I squeezed past packed happy hour tables. The front windows dripped with condensation as the late afternoon sun trickled in. I breathed in the aromas of hops and chocolate. The chocolate was from my early morning baking session. And the hops were, well, obviously, from our newest line of dark and delicious winter beers. Midwinter in Leavenworth can feel sleepy, so Garrett and I decided to try our hand at hosting a variety of pub events—trivia and game nights, paint and pint nights, and hosting local bands.

Schools were on break for ski week, so we had brewed batches of special winter beers—peanut butter and chocolate stout, oatmeal spice cream ale, and my current favorite, our obsidian black IPA.

We partnered with Der Keller for the dark and moody IPA,

the legendary brewery that had put Leavenworth on the beer map and was owned by my family. Technically speaking, ex-family, but the Krauses didn't believe in the concept of ex-anything. That was fine by me. Otto and Ursula welcomed me into their loving family when I married their son Mac. If it weren't for them, I never would have found my way to Leavenworth or ended up running a successful brewery.

In my early years of learning the brewing business, Otto taught me everything he knew, often to Mac's displeasure. According to Otto, I had "ze nose," which meant I had an innate ability to pull out each distinct flavor in a beer. It wasn't a skill I had attempted to master, which irritated Mac even more. He had traveled to international brewing conferences and studied with world-class brewers in an attempt to hone his olfactory senses, with no success.

In hindsight, I wondered if that had been part of our problem. After we separated and now that our divorce was final, things had smoothed out between us like a crisp summer pale ale. Mac had found his role running operations at Der Keller, and I was content tinkering with unique small batches at Nitro while staying connected with the Krauses. Otto and Ursula had gifted me shares in Der Keller along with Mac and Hans, cementing my affiliation with them. It took a bit to sort out our future roles with the ever-growing brewery, but I was proud of the work we'd done. Our divorce could easily have gotten messy. We didn't let it. Mac deserved credit for that, too. We had learned that we were better as friends, and we had one amazing common interest in our son Alex. I knew that Mac would do anything for Alex, and I was grateful we had come to a place of mutual respect and caring.

Not that he still didn't irritate me every now and then. Especially with his constant obsession to try every new trick of the trade, like when he invested ten thousand dollars into tabletop Keurig-style brewing machines that he claimed could revolutionize the dining experience for customers. His vision was that Der Keller guests could brew their own beer while waiting for platters of German sausages and potato soup. However, he forgot to read the fine print, explaining that the tech systems took two weeks to ferment.

Classic, Mac.

I chuckled to myself as I dropped the obsidian IPAs off at a table near the dewy front windows and stole a glance outside. Snow came down in heavy clumps as if being tossed from the towering peaks surrounding our alpine village. Garrett's parents and sister were due to arrive this evening. I hoped that they weren't going to get stuck in the passes on their way from Seattle. Traveling to our remote location this time of year could be dicey. The passes often closed due to heavy snow and rockslides.

Garrett had been buzzing for weeks about their visit. I knew he would be disappointed if they couldn't make it. At that moment, a snowplow chugged past Nitro, leaving a trail of fluffy white powder in its wake. It was a good reminder that the roads were constantly being cleared.

Stay positive, Sloan.

I smiled and turned my attention to the tasting room. Kat and Garrett worked the bar, pouring pints and chatting with customers. People mingled in the brewery, where we had set up extra folding chairs for guests to listen to the band. We'd installed tents, heaters, and firepits in the front and on the side deck, doubling our seating capacity. Garrett had been worried that no one would want to be outside, but the opposite was true. Beer lovers bundled up in parkas and ski hats and huddled near the crackling fires while sipping on porters and sampling our beer and cheese pretzel fondue.

I was about to go check on the outdoor crowd when I noticed a familiar face. Hazel, a young doctor, was crammed against the exterior door that led to the back patio. She reminded me of a turtle with her puffy yellow ski jacket tucked over her head. "Hazel, I didn't see you there. You're shoved into that corner. Can I find you a better spot?" I motioned toward the brewery.

Hazel looked up from her laptop and stared at me with a blank expression. "Huh? Did you say something?" She yanked an earbud from her ear.

"I asked if you wanted me to find you another seat. You look kind of cramped at that table." I wondered how Hazel was able to get any work done with the noise from the crowd and the band. Not to mention the constant wind blowing inside anytime someone opened the door.

"Oh, sorry. Uh, thanks. No, I'm fine." She tugged off her hood and took out her other AirPod. Her shoulder-length hair frizzled from the static and cold.

"I'm impressed that you're able to focus with so much going on." As if to prove my point, a round of cheers and applause broke out in the brewery as the band finished their song.

She twisted the string on her ski coat around her index finger. "It's called being a resident. Medical school taught me how to tune out anything. When I was at University of Washington, I used to study at bars. They were open late, so I would bring my laptop and AirPods and stay until closing."

"Wow, that is dedication. We're lucky to have you here."

The band started their next set. Hazel's eyes drifted in that direction where a group of her colleagues, some of them still wearing their scrubs from their shifts, were gathered around one long folding table.

She slammed her laptop shut and then shook her head while still fiddling with her coat string. "I wouldn't say that, and I'm trying not to get attached because I don't know how long I'm going to have a job."

"Really? Why?" I couldn't help but wonder if that was why

she had stuffed herself at a high-top table near the exit instead of sitting with the other doctors.

Hazel had become one of our regulars. Nitro was located a couple of blocks off Front Street, near Waterfront Park and the hospital. Given our proximity, medical staff tended to stop in for a pint or two at the end of their shifts. We appreciated the steady business, and they appreciated that Nitro was slightly off the beaten tourist path. City code in Leavenworth dictated that every storefront in the village adhere to strict Bavarian design standards. Our German architecture, cobblestone streets, alpine mountains, and festivals brought a steady stream of tourism to town. Nitro's exterior matched the Bavarian aesthetic, but unlike some of the shops and restaurants that catered to tourists seeking German cuisine and tchotchkes like plastic cuckoo clocks and knee-high beer stein socks, we had opted to carve out space as the local hangout.

She clutched her laptop to her chest and bit her bottom lip. "It's a long and complicated story, and right now, I don't know if I'm even right about what I think I might be right about. If I am, then I don't even have the slightest idea what I'm going to do." She shot her head in the direction of the other doctors and then trailed off. "Never mind. You're super busy. I should let you get back to work."

There was something about Hazel's breathless tone that put me on alert. I could only imagine how stressful her schedule as a resident had to be. I wondered if the long hours and lack of sleep were taking their toll. My motherly instincts kicked in. "I'm never too busy to talk."

"No, I need to go. I should go check with Tad, our IT guy. He might be able to figure something out." She stuffed her laptop into a matching bright yellow messenger bag and pulled her hood over her head again. "Just forget I said anything. I pulled a double shift and haven't slept in over twenty-four hours. I'm probably just stressed, you know? I'm overworked and running on cheap coffee and fumes."

"Totally understandable, but my offer remains. If you ever need a listening ear, I'm always willing to listen. It's the tap tenders' and brewers' code. Pints on the house, okay?" I tried to meet her gaze, but Hazel stared at the floor. "You and the entire team at the hospital work so hard to keep everyone safe and healthy, it's the least I can do."

Hazel gave me a weak smile. "I appreciate it. We all love Nitro's end-of-shift free pint. Like I said, I'm probably tired. I need some sleep, and then I'm sure I'll feel better."

"Sounds like a good plan. If you change your mind, I'm here."

"Thanks." She bounced her leg on the stool for a minute before eyeing the exit and heading for the door.

I didn't know Hazel well. She'd been coming in at least once a week for a post-work pint since she'd arrived in Leavenworth last fall. Most of our interactions had been casual. I had given her a few recommendations on hiking trails and ski runs nearby, and we had chatted about beer and her research. The motherly instinct in me kicked into high gear as I watched her scurry out of the pub and out into the cold. Hazel was in her late twenties and practicing in a field with a high burnout rate. She didn't have family here in Leavenworth, and I wasn't sure what other kind of support network she might have at the hospital. I hoped she would take her own advice and get some much-needed rest.

As I returned to the bar, I made a mental note to check in on her over the weekend.

"Sloan, we're killing it out there and it's not even after five yet." Garrett flashed a smile and angled a pint glass beneath the tap handle. "How's the snow looking?"

I tried to ignore the fluttery feeling in my stomach that seemed to surge anytime Garrett was near. This afternoon, he looked particularly handsome in a pair of jeans, leather boots, and an indigo pullover sweater that brought out the flecks of gold in his deep brown eyes.

"It's coming down," I said, looking toward the front windows where the light was beginning to fade. I placed the empty tray on the counter and cleared some empties into the sink. "Have you heard anything from your parents?"

"No. They texted when they left Seattle, but I haven't heard anything since then. Do you think they'll shut down the passes?" He scrunched his face in concern as he tried to get a better look outside.

"I don't think so. The plow seemed to be moving fine. I'm sure they have the bigger plows on a constant rotation on the highway." I flipped on the switch for the twinkle lights that hung above the bar. Soon it would be time to light the votive candles on the tabletops. Once the sun sank behind the mountains, the village would be plunged into darkness.

He pushed a strand of wavy walnut-colored hair from his eye. "I hope so. It's going to be such a bummer if they get stuck."

"I agree, but I'm staying positive. Think good thoughts." I made a funny face and stuck out my index finger in a warning.

"You're always positive, Sloan," Kat chimed in, her dimples widening as she smiled. She assembled bowls of our pub snacks, Doritos, nuts, spicy popcorn, and chocolate trail mix at the counter. Kat was in her mid-twenties with bouncy curls, bright eyes, and a can-do spirit.

"I'm glad you think so, too. We have to stay positive, right?" I winked at her in solidarity. "Of course, Alex might not agree when I've asked him a dozen times whether he's finished his essay for his college applications."

"Does he know where he wants to go yet?" Kat tossed a couple of nuts into her mouth as she finished filling the bowls and then placed them on a tray so she could take them to the tables.

We had a small pub menu at Nitro that consisted of daily soups, meat, cheese and veggie plates, seasonal specials like shepherd's pie and mac and cheese, and rotating desserts sometimes infused with our beers. Snacking and savoring a frothy pint went hand in hand, so we kept tables stocked with bowls of chips and nuts. Additionally, we served a beer-inspired breakfast every morning to our overnight guests. I loved sharing traditional German recipes passed down from Ursula and experimenting with new ways to add a splash of hoppy brew to pancakes or a touch of porter to chocolate babka.

"He's still undecided," I said to Kat. "UW is top of the list because it's close, and he's been a Husky fan his entire life. He's not ruling out playing soccer at a small college, though."

"I saw you talking to Hazel. She'll probably tell him all the reasons he should be a Husky. When she was in here a couple of days ago, we were swapping our favorite Seattle spots." Garrett angled a glass beneath the tap handle to fill it with our obsidian stout. "But once my sister gets here, she can twist his arm for Oregon."

"Let the college battle begin." I reached for a towel to mop up a little beer splatter on the counter. "We should connect Leah and Hazel. They have a lot in common. Med school, residency, and they're about the same age. Hazel seems pretty stressed, and sleep-deprived. It might be nice for her to have someone going through a similar experience to talk to."

"I'm sure Leah will be down for that." Garrett set the pint on the counter and began filling the next.

There's an art to pouring a perfect pint. It was something I had taught Kat from the first day she started at Nitro. Simply placing a glass under the handle and letting the beer flow would result in a foamy pour. Instead, we angled chilled glasses and slowly released the tap handle. Once a glass was about three-quarters full, then we would shift it upright and top off the pint with a nice layer of foam.

"Speaking of physicians. There's a whole crew in the back that is due for another round of drinks. Do you want to go check on them?" Garrett asked. "Or you can take over the bar."

"I'm happy to check on them." I pointed to Kat's snack bowls. "Can I steal a couple of these, too?"

"Go for it." Kat swept her hand over the bowls. Her nails were painted like mountain tops with tiny green trees and snowy tips. "Take your pick."

I took a bowl of Doritos and mixed nuts and made my way to the brewery. Typically, our brewing operations were off-limits to customers, but we had opened the space for happy hour and music tonight. The 80s' cover band was cranking out the hits while a handful of people were dancing in front of the makeshift stage. The doctors were easy to spot amongst the growing crowd. Their scrubs and tennis shoes were a dead giveaway.

"I hope you're enjoying the music," I said over the sound of the band. "Can I get anyone another pint?"

"Such service," one of the physicians replied. It was Dr. Sutton, another one of our regulars. She was close to my age and quite stylish for Leavenworth standards. Her scrubs were made of a soft, silky material in terra cotta. She wore a matching pair of burnt orange oversized glasses and funky earrings.

"Only for you, Dr. Sutton." I set the bowl of snacks in front of her.

She handed me her empty glass. "If you don't mind, I wouldn't turn down another black IPA. I preach slow sipping when I'm talking to patients about beer consumption, but I have to admit that was so smooth it went down faster than I expected."

"Hey, come on, it's Friday. It's happy hour. Time to blow off steam," the man next to her said, finishing off the last drops of his pint. His navy scrubs were form-fitting. The slim design showed off his muscular physique.

"Isn't that what anesthesiologists do all the time, Dr. Ames?" Dr. Sutton shot her colleague a challenging look.

I couldn't tell if she was teasing or if there was real animosity between them.

"That's why they pay me the big bucks," Dr. Ames said, flashing a hang loose sign. "We have to stay loose, and Nitro helps me do that. Also, how many times do I have to tell you to call me Shep? My dad is Doctor Ames. I'm not that old and cranky." He shuddered and pointed to his now empty glass. "Can I get a refill, too?" His energy reminded me of Mac. He was attractive but held his body and my gaze in a way that told me he knew it.

"A black IPA for Dr. Sutton and Shep." I stacked their empties on the tray and looked at the rest of the doctors. "Is everyone having the IPA?"

"I had the stout," the man seated next to Shep said with a huff. I didn't recognize him. He wasn't wearing scrubs, which either meant he wasn't a doctor or had changed after his shift.

"Sloan, have you met Jerry?" Dr. Sutton asked as if reading my mind.

"No, I don't think so." I couldn't exactly shake his hand with the tray and glasses.

He waved me off. "Nice to meet you. Good beer."

"Do you work at the hospital too?"

"In a roundabout way. I work for BioGold, a pharmaceutical company in Seattle." He tapped the logo on his black jacket. "Dr. Sutton and I are doing a clinical trial together. I'm here to gather the latest data."

"That's why we stopped by Nitro," Dr. Sutton added. She pressed her hands together in a prayer pose. "We're celebrating some really promising news on a drug that could be a game changer."

"WE'RE GOING to make a killing on this drug." Jerry tipped his head to Dr. Sutton.

She narrowed her eyes and corrected him. "And save lives."

"Of course," Jerry agreed. "But there's nothing wrong with making some money while we save lives."

"Congratulations." I looked at both of them. "I didn't realize that Leavenworth was part of a clinical trial."

"Not just any clinical trial," Dr. Sutton corrected me. She glanced at Jerry, who gave her a subtle nod, signaling his approval for her to continue. "This is a revolutionary drug. It will completely change the course of treatment for patients with high cholesterol. Our data is showing that it makes LDL numbers plummet; that's the 'bad' cholesterol. We've been pinching ourselves all afternoon reviewing the first round of data."

Jerry shifted in his chair. He was older than both physicians by at least a decade, given his receding hairline and graying beard. "It's true, and the best news is that there haven't been any reported side effects."

"Hey, hey, let's pump the brakes for a second. We're talking super early data here," Shep cautioned, turning to the last member of their group, a young nurse, Ren, whom I recognized as a regular. "You want to jump in here, man?"

Ren didn't exactly fit his name, aside from his spiky red hair. Otherwise, the nurse was the exact opposite of a skittish hen. He was tall and bulky with a sleeve of tattoos running up his arm.

"Don't put me in the middle. I'm the nurse. I just care for the patients. I don't know anything about the data." Ren slunk down in his seat.

"I don't know data either, I just dial in the good drugs for our patients to take a nice little sleepy *sleep*, but I know enough to know that it's still early, and none of your research has been peer-reviewed yet." Shep cocked his head to the side as he stared at Dr. Sutton.

Dr. Sutton took off her glasses and cleaned the lenses with the edge of her scrubs. "That's just a technicality, *Dr. Ames.* You might not understand the nuances of this kind of research, given that your role is sedating patients while my role is keeping them out of the operating room to begin with."

"It's Shep," he snarled through a curled lip.

The faintest smile passed across her face. It was clear that she enjoyed getting a reaction out of him. "As I have mentioned in our team meetings, it's critical in a town the size of Leavenworth to maintain professionalism. We don't want to blur the lines. Many of our patients are here tonight. It's critical with this kind of research that we keep doctor/patient boundaries intact."

"You do you, but I'm not going by Dr. Ames." Shep shrugged. "I read the med journals. I know my way around a clinical trial, and I'm trying to make sure you don't get your hopes up too early. It would suck to think you have a breakthrough only to learn that the drug fails in the next phase of testing."

"It won't," Dr. Sutton snapped. She put her glasses on again and composed herself. "Sloan, we're boring you with medical talk when you have a packed house. Ren, Dr. Ames, and I will do your black IPA, and Jerry will take a stout. Can you charge this round to my credit card?" She reached into her purse to hand me payment.

I took her credit card. "I don't know a lot about clinical trials, but that's very exciting that this kind of research is happening in the village. Is Hazel part of your team?"

The briefest hint of irritation flashed on her face before she smiled widely. "Why do you ask?"

"She was here earlier working on research." I nodded toward the back door. "I was impressed that she's so dedicated to her work and that she could concentrate with all the noise and activity in the pub."

"Hazel was here?" Ren asked, sitting up in his chair and glancing around. "When did she leave? Did she say where she was going?"

"Not that long ago." I glanced at the digital clock next to the Nitro logo that Garrett had painted on the far wall. "Maybe twenty minutes. She mentioned trying to talk to Tad in IT."

Ren ran his hands through his spiky hair and glanced at the retro Swatch watch on his wrist. "You know, I totally lost track of time. You two have the next round without me. I've got to go meet someone." He took off without another word.

"Okay, I guess that's only two more beers," Dr. Sutton said to me. "Did Hazel speak with you about her research?"

Was it my imagination, or had her tone changed?

"No, she mentioned compiling data, but she didn't go into detail." I readjusted the tray.

"Okay, good." Dr. Sutton sounded relieved. "Technically, we shouldn't be talking about any of this. I'd appreciate it if you kept what we said between us. I suppose I got caught up in the excitement of the data."

"Of course. I won't say a word."

"And you're sure Hazel didn't elaborate either?" Dr. Sutton repeated. "I've found that residents can tend to be eager to share news that isn't public yet."

"No. Not at all." I regretted bringing Hazel's name up. "Mainly we talked about how exhausted she is. She mentioned working double shifts and her side project reviewing the data. I suggested she get some sleep to recharge. I know that you all work long hours."

"Excellent advice," Dr. Sutton smiled. "Exactly what I would have told her if she were my patient. I'm glad she didn't reveal any specifics. I wouldn't expect her to do that, but we do have to be careful at this stage of the trial, like Ren said."

"Yeah, we stand to make a killing off this medication," Jerry said. "We wouldn't want to let the cat out of the bag too early, as the saying goes."

Dr. Sutton cleared her throat. "I believe you mean that we're going save lives with this incredible scientific breakthrough."

"Yeah, that too." Jerry patted her shoulder. "You're going to be very popular at BioGold if things continue this way."

Shep muttered something under his breath that I couldn't make out.

Dr. Sutton shot him a warning glare. "Sorry, Sloan, we're doing it again. Shop talk. Don't let us keep you."

I was glad for a chance to break away from the conversation that had become more and more awkward. "I promise I will not say a word, but I will be back shortly with your beers."

I returned to the bar feeling more resolved to check in with Hazel and see about connecting her and Leah once Garrett's family arrived. Dr. Sutton and Jerry's research sounded promising, but the dynamic between them left me unsettled. I couldn't help but wonder if part of Hazel's skittishness earlier had less to do with being sleep-deprived and more to do with being involved in the clinical trial. It was probably because of my nomadic roots that I felt a kinship to Hazel and wanted to make sure that she knew she had a safe place at Nitro to land if she ever needed it.

CHAPTER
TWO

THE NEXT FEW hours passed in a blur as the sky outside darkened, and we filled dozens of tasting glasses and sent beer sippers out in Leavenworth's notorious winter weather to enjoy snowy pints around the roaring firepits. Even with the blowing snow and freezing temperatures, everyone seemed to be in good spirits. Cheeks were bright with color from the frosty air and frothy beers. Hats, coats, and scarves were piled on tables and the woodsy aroma from the firepits wafted inside every time the door opened. As the dinner hour passed and there was still no sign of his family, I could tell that Garrett was becoming more anxious.

He paced behind the bar and checked his phone for what felt like the hundredth time. "Still nothing. I'm getting worried that something happened. They should have been here by now."

"Maybe it's taking a while to get through the passes," I suggested. "You know what it's like if you get stuck behind a snowplow."

"Right. But Mom said they'd be here by four at the latest." He clicked his screen again. "It's after six. And I've texted all of them—Mom, Dad, Leah. No one has responded." He stared at his screen as if willing it to respond.

I understood why he was worried, but my role at the moment was to stay calm. "The other thing to remember is that's there's no service in the mountains, so try not to worry too much."

"When am I allowed to call Chief Meyers and have her send out a search party?" Garrett tried to keep his tone light, but I could tell from the tight wrinkles around his eyes and his death grip on his phone that he was more than just a little stressed.

"Listen, I'm not trying to downplay your concerns." I squeezed his wrist in a show of comfort. "I think we should give them another thirty minutes. If you haven't heard from them by, let's say, seven, then I think checking in with Chief Meyers makes sense. Actually, if it would make you feel any better, we could call the Chief, or I could run over to her office and ask if she knows about any road closures."

"Yeah." Garrett tapped his phone. "The Trip Check app is down so I can't get any updates from that either."

"Why don't you try to text Chief Meyers?"

He gave me a sheepish smile. "I already tried. She hasn't responded, which is another reason I'm starting to freak out."

I scanned the pub. Every table was full, but there was no line at the bar. Kat was circulating the tasting room, picking up empty glasses and dishes. Police headquarters were only a block away. I could run over and see if Chief Meyers or her staff knew of any road closures in the passes and be back to Nitro in less than ten minutes. "I'll tell you what. I'll head over to the station and ask. It will make me feel better, too."

Garrett smiled for real this time. "Thanks, Sloan. I know I'm not usually like this, but it's my family, you know?"

"You don't need to explain anything to me. I get it." I reached beneath the counter for my coat. "I'll be back in a flash."

I didn't wait for him to reconsider. Garrett had been my steadfast supporter from the minute we'd met. He had hired me solely on the recommendation of Hans, my brother-in-law. He did so without asking any questions about my marriage imploding or why I had opted to leave a high-level position at Der Keller to come to help him with his startup. Nitro had been a salve for my soul. I needed space from Mac and the entire Krause family to work out what was next for me. Garrett had given me that space. I was eternally grateful for our friendship and partnership. Without the distraction of hanging artwork on Nitro's originally barren walls and creating a pub menu, I might have sunk into a dark place.

Lately, we had grown even closer. Although we had both agreed to take things slow. I wasn't ready to jump back into a full-fledged relationship. We'd gone on regular weekly dates —to the movies, bowling, beer tasting in Wenatchee, snow-shoeing, hiking, and even casual dinners. Spending time with Garrett was easy and natural. The only glitch was that we usually ventured out of the village for dates because of prying eyes, mainly in the form of April Ablin. She was Leaven-worth's self-proclaimed welcome ambassador and made it her mission to know everything and anything going on in town.

Meeting his family was a big step, professionally and personally. I had a feeling that part of his stress over their delayed arrival could be because he wanted me to like them, too.

Outside, snow piled on both sides of the streets. The plow had created berms like miniature mountain ranges along Front Street. It was impossible not to be captured in the village's winter spell. From the beginning of the holiday season through mid-March, millions of twinkle lights illuminated the entire town. Golden light spilled onto the snowy sidewalks from the rows of antique streetlights. The Bavarian storefronts glowed

with more colorful lights. Trees were wrapped in tiny twinkling yellow and gold bulbs.

Slanted rooflines were coated in fluffy layers of more snow. The beer barrels that flanked each corner displayed four-foot-high pine trees adorned with German flags. Every storefront was designed to make visitors feel like they were visiting the Alps, with turrets, rounded archways, pastoral murals, and window boxes that would be cascading with flowers come spring.

Walking through the village this time of year felt like stepping into a snow globe. I didn't stop to admire the charming scene. Instead, I crossed the slippery street in front of the gazebo in the center of the square, where kids and families were sledding down the small hill in Front Street Park. I waved hello to a few familiar faces and headed straight toward the police station.

A wooden sign reading POLIZEI hung above the carved wooden door.

The station was more like a welcome center. Tourists stopped in during busy weekends for festival maps or for minor issues like first aid for blistered feet from hours spent dancing in the Festhalle. Chief Meyers had kept watch on the village for as long as I could remember, and in my opinion, there was no one better for the job. She cared deeply for our community and was able to hold firm boundaries when it came to anything that might put the village, its inhabitants, and guests in harm's way.

Inside the office was a reception area with posters about bear awareness and disaster preparedness. I shook snow from my coat and pulled a piece of hair that had come loose from my ponytail back into place as I approached the front desk.

"Is the Chief around?" I asked the deputy. He had been a few years older than Alex and had played on the high school soccer team before graduating and pursuing a career in law enforcement.

The deputy looked up from a game he was playing on his phone. "She's out on a call. Can I help you with anything?"

"We were expecting Garrett's family to arrive nearly two hours ago and were wondering if the passes have been closed," I explained.

The deputy put his phone down and typed something into his laptop and then turned the screen for me to see. "That's where the Chief is. There was a slide about an hour ago. Extreme winds, whiteout conditions. It's a mess. Everything is shut down."

"What kind of slide?" A wave of dizziness came over me. I clutched the counter to steady myself.

"Sounds like it was a small avalanche." The deputy turned the screen back around and typed again.

My heart rate sped up. "Do you know if anyone was hurt?"

He shook his head. "Dispatch called in for extra support. The Chief left about forty minutes ago, but I haven't heard any updates from her since."

"Okay, thanks. Can you call the pub if you get any news?"

He gave me a quick nod. "You bet."

My stomach swirled with anxiety on the return trip to Nitro. An avalanche in the twisty two-lane highway that was the only route into Leavenworth was never good. Not only could it shut down the road for hours while crews worked to clear the debris, but it could also be deadly. While rare, over the years there had been a handful of accidents caused by rockslides and avalanches.

Please let Garrett's family be okay.

I stuffed my hands in my pockets and exhaled.

"*Yoo-hoo*, Sloan? Sloan, is that you?"

A familiar singsong, saccharine-sweet voice sounded to my left.

Great.

I clenched my jaw and turned to see April Ablin sprinting

20

toward me. She wasn't dressed for the elements in her mini barmaid skirt, knee-high boots, and tights. Not that I should expect anything different. April's entire wardrobe consisted of gaudy Bavarian costumes that everyone else in the village only wore on special occasions—like festival weekends.

"*Guten Abend.*" She breathlessly butchered a German accent as she caught up with me. "Why are you moving so fast, Sloan? Geez, slow down. I had to practically sprint to run you down. You are just who I needed to see. I was on my way to Nitro to find you."

"What's up, April?" I didn't have time for one of her outlandish requests or comments on why I wasn't wearing a dirndl. April had a penchant for low-cut, tight-fitting barmaid dresses and garish makeup and for some reason, she was under the impression that everyone else in the village should be, too.

"Did you hear the news?" She flipped one of her dyed red braids.

She also had a tendency to spread gossip.

"What news?" I kept my tone as disinterested as possible. Encouraging April Ablin was like opening a tap handle and letting the beer flow.

"There's been an avalanche." She fanned her chest as if she were unable to handle the news.

I wanted to know how she wasn't freezing her derriere off in her skimpy skirt and no coat.

"It happened only about ten miles outside of town. I heard it firsthand. You know that I'm on the critical response team list." She practically gushed with excitement. "The authorities are going to be bringing buses of stranded travelers into the village. Isn't it great news?"

"Great news?" This was too much, even for April. "Are you being serious? How is an avalanche great news?"

"No, Sloan, don't be like that." She swatted the air. "The travelers. That's the great news. It's not even a festival weekend and we're going to have a packed house. I'm going from hotel to hotel and *guesthaus* to *guesthaus* to get everyone to prepare to roll out the red carpet for our unexpected guests."

As always, she over-emphasized the 'h' in "haus," so much so that her mouth hung open wide like she was preparing for a root canal.

"How many extra guests can you accommodate at Nitro tonight?"

"None. We're full."

"What?" April's nostrils flared. "Unacceptable. You can't possibly be full. Don't try and tell me your little band and game nights have brought in that many extra people."

I couldn't resist a smug smile. "They have. Business is booming at Nitro. You should stop by. And also, Garrett's parents and sister are coming for a visit. We've already blocked out two rooms for them. It's not as if we have a ton of space, to begin with."

April puffed her checks. "That's just like you to be contrarian for the sake of it."

"What are you talking about?"

"I'm doing the village a huge favor with this boost of tourism out of the goodness of my heart. We need to roll out the welcome mat for our stranded travelers. They've been through an ordeal, and now they can cozy up in the village and spend their hard-earned money at our shops and restaurants."

Nothing that April Ablin did was out of the goodness of her heart. I decided not to bring that point up now.

"I hope at the very least that you'll be sure to make space in the tasting room and at your little event for them. And, please tell me that you have something else to change into?"

"Nope." I pulled my hood over my head. "I better run. It sounds like we have some extra work to do."

I could hear April sputtering as I picked up my pace. I wanted to give Garrett the news before April's gossip spread

throughout town. If they were bussing people to the village, that had to be a good sign, but I knew that if there were even a small chance that his family could be in danger, he needed a friend by his side. He had been by my side through some tough, tough times, and the least I could do was to repay the favor. More than anything, though, I wanted his mom, dad, and Leah to be okay.

THREE

THE TENSION at Nitro was thicker than a fresh pint of Guinness for the next hour while we waited for news on Garrett's family. I took over the bar because every pint that Garrett poured foamed over the edge of the glass and spilled down the sides like a frothy waterfall. Not that I blamed him. Last spring, I'd had a harrowing experience when Alex had gone missing. His disappearance resulted in closing every entrance into town and sending squads of first responders in from Seattle. Nearly all of our friends and neighbors joined in the search. Thankfully we found him safe and sound, aside from the emotional trauma of being kidnapped and tied up for hours while waiting for help to arrive. There was nothing worse than the feeling of helplessness I had had during that chunk of time that felt like days. I could only imagine that Garrett must be in the same space, so I sent him back and forth from the kitchen to the tasting room and brewery to deliver bowls of our steaming black bean and spicy sausage soup and platters of beer and cheese fondue.

At least serving our guests gave him something else to concentrate on.

"How's Garrett holding up?" Kat whispered as she entered drink orders into the iPad that ran our point-of-sale system.

"He looks rough. I've never seen him ruin so many pints. Actually, come to think of it, I've never seen him ruin a pint. That guy can pour a perfect pint in his sleep. I think he's pretty freaked out. Have you heard anything from Chief Meyers yet?"

"Nothing. Not a word." I'd been refreshing the Trip Check app every few minutes to no avail and checking my phone for an update from the deputy. "I thought we might have gotten an update by now."

Kat lined up chilled pint glasses and drink tickets.

There was a common misconception that beer should be served in a frosted glass. That wasn't true in the world of craft brewing. Condensation from an icy glass can dilute a beer and mute its flavor and aroma. Conversely, serving a pint in a glass hot out of the dishwasher was equally taboo. Ultimately it was a matter of personal preference. Chilling a glass in the fridge would help keep a beer cooler longer, but wasn't necessary. At Nitro, we served most of our beers in glasses at room temperature. We did keep a selection of glasses chilled—not frozen—for customer requests and for our lighter beers like our pilsner and lagers. These styles of beer featured a smooth mouthfeel over flavor, which is highlighted best when served cold.

I poured a pilsner and set it on a tray while she rang up orders.

I was about to pull a porter when Garrett raced toward us.

"They're fine! They're here!" He waved his phone, his face beaming with light. "I just got the text. They're on the bus and they're safe."

"That's such a huge relief." I didn't realize I had been clenching my jaw.

"Leah says they should be here in about ten minutes." He tapped his watch like he was willing time to move faster. "They have to fill out some paperwork at the police station in order to get their car once the roads are clear. Apparently, the department of transportation will arrange to have any stranded cars towed into town. They might not have their car until tomorrow or even later, but they're here in the village and safe, which is the only thing that matters." He blew out a long breath of air.

"Now it's time to celebrate," Kat said, raising an empty glass. Her abundant curls bounced as she did a little happy dance.

"For sure. Or pass out." Garrett pushed a strand of hair from his face. He often wore chemistry goggles when brewing which I had come to learn were like a headband for him, keeping his hair out of his face, but tonight he was dressed to impress. Not only were his jeans and pullover sweater a big step up from his punny beer T-shirts, but it also looked like he had styled his wavy hair with a touch of gel.

I found him attractive no matter what he was wearing, but like earlier, my stomach flopped and my cheeks warmed as I watched him release the tension he had been holding.

I hoped I had dressed appropriately for meeting his family. I had opted for a pair of fleece leggings, boots, and a cashmere cream turtleneck sweater that brought out the olive tone in my skin. I hated to admit it, but I had changed twice earlier in the day before landing on the outfit. I might be the parent of a teenager, but my budding relationship with Garrett had me feeling like a nervous teen. For as much work as I'd done on rewiring the pattern of scarcity I had grown up with, there were still moments (like now) when it was hard to tamp down the memories and emotions of my youth.

These days I had enough inner confidence not to let a conversation or a stranger's opinion of me get under my skin. But meeting Garrett's family was different. There was a potential future path for us, and I was fairly sure that the bulk of my nerves was due to my growing attachment to him. I wanted to make things work with us. I wanted to give us a shot. Meeting his family was going to take our relationship to a new level. I was ready to get more serious, but I was also nervous about repeating mistakes from my past.

Focus, Sloan.

I tried to silence my inner narrative and stay in the moment.

"They must be exhausted." I pressed my thumb and index finger together to center myself and finished pulling the porter. "Their rooms are all set upstairs. Do we have plenty of soup left? Should I put something heartier together for them?"

"Let's see how they feel once they show up," Garrett replied. "I don't want you to go to any extra trouble."

I wiped the tap handle with a towel and set the pint on the bar. "I'm happy to help and I know the kitchen is stocked, so I can get creative if they're in the mood for something more substantial than soup and bread."

"Thanks." Garrett's voice sounded stronger. "Thanks to both of you. Sorry for being so freaked out."

"No need to apologize. I'd be weirded out if you weren't worried about your family being caught in an avalanche." Kat's good-natured grin and ruddy cheeks matched how I felt.

"Agreed." I nodded in solidarity.

We didn't have to wait long. By the time I finished pouring drink orders and Kat loaded them on the tray, the front door swung open and Garrett's family burst in carrying suitcases and gift bags, and leaving a trail of snow behind them.

He hurried to help them with their gear.

I placed one hand on my stomach and drew in two short breaths through my nose. It was a centering technique I had learned in therapy. I was sure that the Strongs were going to be as fabulous as Garrett, but I was a bit taken aback by nerves and I didn't want them to get the best of me.

As they approached the bar, I took one more calming breath.

"Mom, Dad, Leah, meet Sloan." Garrett motioned to me and then back to his parents. "Sloan, meet my family."

Garrett's mom wrapped me in a hug, instantly putting me at ease. "Sloan, I've heard so much about you. It's an absolute delight to be here. I can't believe we're finally getting to meet in real life."

She was the shortest in the family with buttery blonde hair, touched with a hint of silver, and bright green eyes. Garrett had obviously inherited his height from his father, who was well over six feet with gray hair, a gray beard, and a huge, playful smile.

He extended a hand. "Great to meet you, Sloan."

"Thanks so much, Mr. and Mrs. Strong. We've been so excited about your visit, but it sounds like you had quite the adventure getting here."

"Oh, please call me Penny," Garrett's mom said with a warm smile as she offered me a gift bag. "A little hostess gift for you."

"Yep, and I'm Bruce," Garrett's dad added.

"You didn't need to get me anything."

"Open it," Penny encouraged.

I peered into the bag to discover a Mason jar of honey.

"That's honey from Bruce's bees." She nudged Bruce in the waist.

"Ohhh, I didn't know you kept bees. I'm going to need to hear a lot more about that, and I can't wait to try the honey. Thank you so much."

Leah had finished introducing herself to Kat and turned to me. "You must be Sloan."

"Guilty as charged." I winked, placing the honey under the bar.

The resemblance between Leah and Garrett was unmistakable. She had the same jawline and thick wavy hair. Like her older brother, she was tall. She had a similar natural style and a fresh face, free of any makeup.

"What can we get you first? A beer? Food? Or do you all just want to go upstairs and lie down?" Garrett asked.

"A beer sounds wonderful." Penny studied the far wall where we had created a gallery of old photos of the building, Leavenworth, and a collection of black and white family portraits. "This space is even better in person." She placed her hand over her heart and then leaned into Garrett. "You've done your Aunt Tess proud."

"Thanks, Mom." A hint of redness spread across Garrett's cheeks.

"Is that Tess right there?" Leah moved closer to the photos to get a better look.

"What a tribute to your roots," Bruce added. "The design aesthetic is wonderful. Clean and yet inviting."

"That's credit to Sloan." Garrett motioned to me. "I was going to tape up some chemistry charts and call it good, but she found these old photos when we were cleaning out upstairs and decided to frame them to create a gallery wall."

"It's perfect." Penny beamed with pride. "Garrett's so lucky to have found you."

I brushed off her compliment. "The thanks is all mine. Nitro has been a lifesaver for me." I was about to change the topic and ask what I could pour for her, but she reached out to touch my arm.

"We have so much to catch up on, but I promise that *you've* been a godsend for Garrett and we can't thank you enough, especially after everything he went through with..." she trailed off when Garrett caught her eye and shook his head to signal her to stop.

"Uh, in any event, we're thrilled to be here and cannot wait to sample your beer." Penny recovered quickly and busied herself with reviewing the menu.

Garrett's face blotched with embarrassment. I was familiar with the look. I'd seen that same blotchy expression on Alex before when I would ask him if he had a crush on anyone at school, and he would scoff and make up an excuse to get out of the conversation as fast as possible. It was an unexpected reaction from Garrett. What did Penny mean by everything he went through? When Garrett arrived in Leavenworth, it had taken him a while to adjust to our laidback lifestyle where no one locked their doors and neighbors knew just about everything that went on in the village. At first, Garrett had been uptight about keeping our secret recipes in a vault and shuttering Nitro like a fortress at night. Coming from the competitive tech industry meant reprogramming his approach to fit the lowkey vibe of life in the Northern Cascades. Could there be another reason for his initial intensity? Was there more to his past that he hadn't told me?

I couldn't exactly blame him if he had chosen to keep details about his personal history private. My years in foster care had left me with thick emotional armor. Learning to guard my heart had been a necessary skill when I was younger, and a detriment to my adult relationships. I'd spent the last couple of years finding ways to carve out chinks in my armor. Leaving Mac had launched me on that journey and my friendship with Garrett had been a big piece in learning how to open up more.

Was Garrett more like me than I had realized?

Now wasn't the time to delve deeper, but I had to admit that watching Garrett's reaction to his mom's slip left me feeling uncentered. I thought we were growing closer. Was there a reason he hadn't opened up about his years in Seattle? Could my tendency to hold my emotions in be a threat to our deepening connection? If Garrett didn't feel comfortable sharing his past, did we have a shot at a future?

I pushed the thought away as Bruce asked me a question about the stout. It took a minute to shake myself back into the present before I launched into brewer mode, explaining how he should breathe in the aroma of the stout first and let the beer linger on his palate. "You should get notes of dark chocolate, coconut, ripe berries, and a touch of coffee with this one."

I could feel Garrett's gaze burning on me as I handed Bruce a tasting glass.

Before I had a chance to ask Bruce his thoughts, a loud thud sounded behind us. Was it the band? Was someone locked out of the back entrance?

"I'll be right back. Let that sit on your palate for a minute." I excused myself and went to see what was going on.

I headed for the brewery and realized that what I had heard was one of the chairs from a high-top table being overturned.

Hazel was on her knees searching the ground around the high-top table where I had seen her earlier. She had knocked over the chair and pushed the people who were now at the table out of the way.

"Is everything okay?" I asked, approaching her with caution.

"I can't find my flash drive," she wailed, looking up at me with panic in her green eyes. "It was in my laptop bag; I must have dropped it on my way out the door earlier. I can't find it anywhere. I know I had it when I was here."

I knelt to help her search.

"Oh, my God. This is bad. This is really, really bad." She scanned the floor. "I have to find it. That drive has vital information about the clinical trial."

"I'm sure it will turn up."

"No." She sat on her knees and rocked back and forth like an inconsolable child. "You don't understand. I *have* to find that flash drive. Like right now. Everything is riding on that data."

I modeled deep breathing for her. "Okay, well, let's go check at the bar. Maybe someone turned it in earlier."

"Do you think so?" Her ashen skin and sunken cheeks made me wonder if her long shifts at the hospital were causing more than normal stress.

"I was gone for a while. We can check with Kat and Garrett. If you dropped your flash drive here, I'm sure someone turned it in, or it will turn up." I extended my hand to help her up.

Her fingers were damp and clammy.

"Hazel, are you feeling well? Could you be coming down with the flu?"

She wiped her hands on her scrubs. "I'm fine. I just need to find that flash drive."

I led her to the bar. She threw her hood over her head again, like she didn't want to be seen.

"Has anyone turned in a flash drive?" I asked Kat, who was chatting with the Strongs.

"Not that I know of." Kat caught my eye and then studied Hazel like she was evaluating her mental stability. Kat might be in her early twenties, but she was wise beyond her years.

The news sent Hazel spiraling. She scouted the front exit and then quickly looked behind us like she was worried she was being followed.

Garrett must have picked up on the tension too, because he stepped forward and explained to his parents that Hazel was a doctor at the Leavenworth Community Hospital.

I took a minute to introduce Hazel to Leah. "You have a lot in common. You're both big skiers and Leah is a resident at OHSU. I thought maybe you could head up to the ski hill sometime this week and swap stories," I said, hoping to lighten the conversation.

Hazel mumbled a hello.

Garrett bent down to look through a box we kept for lost and found. "Nothing in here yet, but we can keep an eye out when we clean up after closing."

Hazel's eyes were so wide, I wanted to remind her to blink. "I don't know what I'm going to do. What am I going to do? Months and months of data from our clinical trial is on that drive. I'm dead. I'm done. It's over. It's all over."

Leah stepped closer. "You must have backups. The hospital

certainly has to have backups, right? I know at our hospital we have so many redundancies when it comes to backing up data that some days between chart notes and backing them up, I feel like that's all I do."

"Yeah, yeah, maybe." Hazel sounded noncommittal as she gnawed on her thumbnail. "Yeah, I can check with Tad our IT guy about that, but I don't know if he can help. The problem is that the flash drive had my own data."

"Your own data?" Leah couldn't conceal the confusion on her face, but she didn't say more.

Hazel pounded her forehead with her fist. "Look, I have to go. We should get out on the ski hill while you're here, but in the meantime, I really have to find my flash drive. Maybe I dropped it on the walk from the hospital." She turned to me. "If you find it, will you call me right away?"

"Of course. I don't know that I have your number."

She reached into her laptop bag and handed me a card. Then she gave one to Leah. "Text me if you want to get out on the hill tomorrow. I'm going to get a few runs in before my afternoon shift."

"That would be great." Leah tucked Hazel's card into her pocket.

Hazel hurried away.

"I'm worried about her," I said to Leah. "I think she's working too hard. She looks so pale and seemed really skittish when she was here earlier."

Leah nodded. "Residency is rough. We run on gallons of caffeine, little to no sleep, and grabbing a power bar from the vending machines in between rounds. That's one of the reasons I'm so happy to be here. I don't think I've had four consecutive days off in over a year."

"That sounds terrible." Garrett handed his sister a black IPA. "You know what helps? A frothy pint of Nitro."

She raised her glass. "I'll drink to that."

33

"Don't feel any pressure to hang out with Hazel." I wanted Leah to enjoy her time off.

"No, not at all." She took a minute to breathe in the aroma of the beer. Garrett had taught her well. "I would love to get out on the mountain, and to be honest it's easier to blow off steam and talk to other residents about the experience. We're living it, so we get it, you know? I'll text her tomorrow. I'm guessing I can rent skis at the lodge?"

"Yep. There are a number of rental shops in the village, too. We can get you set up with a pair, no problem. But if you want real downhill we'll have to drive for that. The ski hill is fun for shorter runs, cross-country skiing, and snowshoe trails, but if you want longer and faster runs we need to go to Mission Ridge."

"Oh, no, I don't want to get back in a car. I'm happy with the ski hill and cozying up in the village all weekend." Leah took a sip of her black IPA. "And plenty of Nitro pints." She clinked her glass with her parents'. "Doctor's orders."

We all laughed.

I felt relieved that the Strong family had arrived safe and sound. My first impression was one of kindness and warmth. I was looking forward to getting to know them better over the long weekend, and I was glad that Leah and Hazel might connect. I had a feeling they could both use a listening ear and a chance to vent about their work lives in a safe space. Little did I know that our safe village might not end up being that space.

FOUR

WE STAYED up until long past closing. Once the last of the guests had left, we pushed together three tables and set out a midnight feast—cheeses and sausages from the local deli, beer fondue sauce with chunks of freshly baked bread, and my famous chocolate stout brownies. The Strongs reminded me of the Krauses with their easy banter and ability to make me feel part of the family immediately. As a staunch morning person, the fact that I kept my eyes open and made what I hoped was semi-coherent conversation until nearly two was saying something. Penny and Bruce regaled me with stories about Garrett's early science experiments, which involved baking soda volcanos in their kitchen, launching test paper rockets from their roof, and building a full-scale replica of the Seahawks stadium. Leah didn't get off the hook either. They reminisced about how they knew she was destined to become a doctor from the time she bandaged all of the neighborhood cats' paws with strips from her pink tulle tap dance costume.

I finally begged off in favor of trying to catch a few hours of beauty sleep before I woke with the winter sun.

On the short walk from Nitro to my cottage, I reflected on the difference between meeting Mac's family and Garrett's.

With the Krauses, I had fallen in love with Otto and Ursula before ever meeting their son. The thought of belonging had a deep pull. Of course, it helped that when I met Mac the first time, my knees literally went weak. He was blond and muscular with a summer tan and an innate confidence that drew me right in. My friends used to call him the golden boy, and it fit.

In hindsight, even if I hadn't been attracted to Mac, I wondered if it would have mattered. What we lacked in our relationship, Otto, Ursula, and Hans filled. I had been so eager to belong to a family like the Krauses that I had overlooked a few glaring red flags about Mac and me.

Growing up in foster care had plenty of challenges, but I had envisioned that once I turned eighteen and could officially be out in the world on my own, it would be easier. The opposite was true. Young adulthood is the worst time to feel alone.

I'll never forget the emptiness of my last foster family sending me off with money for the bus, a peanut butter sandwich, and a bag of quarters for the laundry machines. There were no teary goodbyes in my dorm room when I moved in with one backpack full of clothes and a few keepsakes that were my own. There were no moms or dads holding back tears and imparting final words of wisdom. There was no one to help review financial aid forms or to list on my emergency contact sheet. I never received a care package or a postcard. There were no visits on parents' weekend or anyone to reach out to late at night when my anxiety would creep in. My late teens and early twenties didn't feel like a time of independence; they felt like a neon billboard flashing constant reminders that the only person I could rely on was me.

Meeting Otto and Ursula at the farmers market where I took extra shifts on the weekend felt like fate intervening. They would gush about my cookies and greet me with kisses on my cheeks and news about their son, whom they were sure was perfect for me. In many ways, he was. Mac provided me with stability and gave me a family. For that, I would be forever grateful.

It wasn't like Mac and I only had struggles. We had good years, too. He sparked my spontaneity with weekend trips to the Pinnacles and rafting trips on the Wenatchee. His gregarious personality drew people in. Because of him, my circle widened and my connections grew.

With Garrett, it was the opposite. We had met as colleagues, grown into friends, and now maybe we were heading for something more. Meeting his parents at this stage was a natural progression, but there was a tiny nagging voice at the back of my head warning me that I could be repeating a pattern.

I tossed and turned all night and woke up with a newfound resolve that I wasn't making a similar mistake. I had grown and evolved in the nearly two decades that Mac and I had been together. Self-awareness hadn't come easily. Part of my journey had been coming to terms with my piece in the dissolution of our marriage. I had faced my demons and come out the other side.

Plus, I was content with or without a partner. I wasn't alone. I had created and cultivated family, not just with the Krauses and Alex but with the longstanding friendships I had built in Leavenworth. I was complete. I wasn't looking for the Strong family to fill a missing void. I had filled those voids myself.

If I was proud of anything I had done in my life (aside from raising Alex), it was that.

I smiled at the thought as I tugged on a pair of snow boots and my puffy parka. It was doubtful that anyone would be awake at Nitro yet, but I wanted to get a start on breakfast.

Part of the immersive beer experience for our overnight guests was a farm breakfast served family-style around a shared table in our upstairs library. We had renovated the landing above the brewery with floor-to-ceiling bookcases stocked with a variety of vacation reads, comfy couches, a long dining table, and a self-serve coffee, tea, and hot chocolate bar. Strings of dried hop vines snaked the ceiling intertwined with Edison bulbs, giving the space an intimate vibe.

When the guest rooms were booked, which was most days anymore, excepting a few mid-week vacancies, I enjoyed putting my culinary training to use and finding new ways to incorporate our craft beers into sweet and savory brunch dishes.

After I was sufficiently bundled up for my walk, I packed some extra ingredients that I had purchased at the village market and stepped out into the cold. The clouds had lifted, leaving the snow-coated rooftops in sparkling white. Front Street reminded me of a gingerbread village that had been sprinkled with powdered sugar. I sucked in a breath of frosty air and caught a faint hint of cinnamon, nutmeg, and wood smoke. The spices were from the Gingerbread Haus, where the early morning baking team was already taking trays of soft cookies from the ovens. The woodsmoke was from the sausage shop where the grills would be fired up all day, cranking out sausages and brats for hungry shoppers and the après ski crowd.

A thin layer of ice that had crusted over the snow crunched under my feet as I navigated the slippery sidewalk. City crews were at the far end of town, near Der Keller, clearing the walk-ways, but otherwise, the village sat in a sleepy slumber. This was my favorite time. I drank in the peaceful calm of the crisp air, the pinkish morning light, and the quiet.

When I made it to the bakery, I couldn't resist ducking in for a latte. The display in the front windows was too tempting. Baskets of sourdough, rye, and cinnamon and raisin bread called to me, as did the trays of coconut chocolate macaroons, slices of Black Forest cake, and marzipan cookies.

To my surprise and equal delight, Ursula was seated at the

counter sipping a coffee and nibbling on a slice of cherry streuselkuchen when I stepped inside.

Her eyes lit up when she saw me. "Sloan, *Guten Morgen!*"

"Don't get up." I greeted her with a kiss on the cheek and cautioned her to stay seated. She had injured herself a while back and had to undergo hip surgery. Her recovery had been relatively smooth. As of late she had given up her walking cane, but I still worried about how steady she was on her feet.

"You're up bright and early," I noted, placing my order for a latte to go.

"Ja, Otto and Mac are meeting ze team from ze new distributor in Seattle and I decided to come along with zem for a morning pastry. You know I cannot resist a streuselkuchen." Her light blue eyes twinkled with merriment.

"But your homemade is the best," I whispered.

"It is only ze best when you come to bake it with me." The wrinkles around her eyes deepened when she laughed. Her white hair was trimmed in a pixie cut that framed her face. "Tell me, did Garrett's family arrive? I am looking forward to meeting zem soon."

"Yes." I filled her in on the avalanche and road closures. "Garrett was so worried, but they're all okay and I have a feeling will likely take their time getting moving this morning."

The barista handed me my latte. The intoxicating scent of cinnamon and strong coffee made me breathe in deeply.

"I'm going to make them your recipe for Schnecken this morning along with bacon and eggs and fresh fruit." I patted the bag of extra supplies I'd brought from home. "Well, I should admit that I'm going to try your recipe with a little twist."

"Does ze twist involve beer?" Ursula cradled her coffee mug, and then wrapped her hand-knit shawl tighter around her shoulders.

"It does. I think a healthy splash of our stout could work in

39

the sticky buns, but I promise that if the recipe flops, I'll take the blame."

She patted my arm with her petite hand. It was dotted in age spots and lined with purple veins. Her hands were so familiar to me, almost like they were an extension of me—an extra limb. A surge of memories rushed forward. Hours in her kitchen with her blue and white dishes and gingham curtains. These hands had shown me how to knead bread dough, rocked Alex as a baby, and wiped away my tears. Ursula was everything I had dreamt about when I had imagined what it might be like to have a mother, and more.

"You will make it wonderful, I'm sure." Her fingers were warm from her coffee mug.

I leaned down and kissed the top of her head. "Have I told you lately how lucky I am to have you in my life?" Tears of gratitude welled in my eyes.

"Ja, Sloan, you have, and I know zis." She clutched my hand tightly and met my gaze. "As I have told you a million times, you are ze daughter I always wished for and zat will never change. You are a Krause and you are stuck with us."

"I know." I squeezed her hand in return. "I just had to say it out loud again."

She dabbed her eyes with the corner of a napkin. "I'm glad you did. Now, when can we come by to meet Garrett's family?"

"Anytime. I think his sister Leah is going to go skiing later this afternoon. I haven't suggested this to Garrett yet, but I wondered about doing a late lunch at the lodge. Would you and Otto want to join in? Hans, Mac, Alex, everyone is welcome."

"Ja, that would be lovely. I will check in with zem and let you know."

"Great." I picked up my latte and took a sip. The bakery always added a touch of cinnamon and cardamom to their winter lattes, giving the milky coffee a lovely balance of sweet and spice. "Wish me luck on this baking adventure."

"It will be ze best. I'm sure." She blew me a kiss as I left.

I went straight to Nitro. As expected, the brewery and tasting room were dark and there was no sign of movement upstairs. I started breakfast preparations as quietly as possible. Not that there was much risk of waking anyone. The building was well insulated and solid. What was more likely was that once the coffee had brewed and my caramel rolls had begun baking the aroma wafting upstairs might rouse our guests.

Ursula's recipe for Schnecken started with making a nutty caramel base. I melted butter on the stove and added chopped pecans, brown sugar, and a generous splash of our stout. Once it had reduced into a thick sauce, I poured it into a large baking pan. Next, I warmed water and sugar to activate my yeast. While the yeast began to bloom, I melted butter in milk.

My thoughts turned to Alex as I incorporated the yeast into the milk and butter and slowly began adding flour, one cup at a time. He had stayed at Mac's last night. It was part of our arrangement. Most school nights Alex was with me and then he rotated to Mac's on the weekends. It helped that both Mac and I had agreed to be flexible and generous about sharing time. Plus, there was always the Krause family standing tradition of Sunday night dinners. Most weekends we all ended up at Otto and Ursula's, sharing plates of schnitzel and slices of German chocolate cake. That was fine by me.

There had been a few months when everything I thought I had believed about the Krause family had been called into question. Sally, my childhood case worker, and my aunt Marianne had believed that Otto and Ursula had fled Germany and changed their names to avoid ties with a family member who had served in the Nazi regime. In reality, they had taken on new identities when they had uprooted their lives and moved to Leavenworth for a fresh start, but there was no truth to anyone in their family being Nazi sympathizers. I had trusted my instincts and had been relieved when they were proven correct.

I was conflicted when it came to Marianne. Last spring when she had arrived unexpectedly in the village, she had finally been the source of answers to some of my questions about my mother and my fuzzy history. She had given me the gift of knowing that I had been loved. She and my mom had done their best to protect me, but she had also involved Alex in her plot to thwart a would-be killer, and she had vanished before I had had a chance to really dive into the truth. Marianne was my only family and I feared that when she had disappeared last spring, it might be for good. The rest of my questions about my parents and my past might forever go unanswered.

You might have to let it go for good, Sloan.

I sighed at the thought and concentrated on baking.

Once a dough had formed, I rolled it into a long rectangle and spread on a thick layer of a cinnamon, pecan, and butter mixture. Then I sliced it and arranged the slices in the baking tray. They would bake over the pecan caramel stout. Once they were golden brown, I would remove them from the oven, invert the pan, and serve them with the gooey mixture on top.

I slid the pan into the oven and opened a package of honey-cured bacon. While the rolls were baking, I grilled thick slices of bacon, scrambled eggs, and chopped fruit for a fruit salad.

By the time everything was ready, I heard footsteps and the sound of running water overhead. That was my cue that it was time to take everything upstairs.

Garrett appeared at the top of the staircase. He was wearing a pair of sweats and a Nitro hoodie. He massaged his temples like he was trying to force his eyes open. "How long have you been baking, Sloan?"

"Not long." It was a half lie. "I wanted to make something special for your family."

"It smells amazing, but you didn't have to go out of your way." He rubbed the corner of one eye. "I'll help you bring stuff up."

42

Within a few minutes, the table was set with one of Ursula's linen tablecloths that she had embroidered with blue and yellow spring flowers. The upstairs dining area was cozy with its bookshelves and soft lighting. Garrett and I had repurposed chairs from Tess's diner and used an assortment of her vintage plates and silverware. It gave the space a homey vibe.

I smiled as I watched everyone help themselves to coffee and my beerish take on Ursula's sticky rolls.

"This is the kind of vacation I could get used to," Leah said stirring cream into her coffee. "Thank you so much for making breakfast for us, Sloan."

"My pleasure." I passed the bowl of fruit salad. "You have to have the complete Nitro experience while you're here."

"I may never leave. This beats stale hospital cafeteria muffins." She helped herself to a roll. "Speaking of hospitals, Hazel already texted. She wants to meet at noon. Does that work for everyone's plan?"

Penny and Bruce nodded. "We want to check out the shops this morning anyway."

"The lodge is wonderful this time of year and they do a really nice lunch," I said, pouring myself a second cup of coffee. "I wondered if we might want to meet up after you're done skiing. I know Alex and the entire Krause family want to meet you all, too."

"And they have the best Irish coffee and German hot chocolate," Garrett added.

"Sold. I don't know what German hot chocolate is, but I know I need to taste it." Penny pressed her fingers together and frowned. "As long as that won't throw your schedule off here at Nitro. We don't want to get in the way."

"Mom, we talked about this. We picked this weekend because it's slow and Sloan and I have extra help coming this afternoon."

"Perfect. I can't wait to meet your family, Sloan," Penny said to me as she handed Bruce the platter of bacon.

My family.

My family.

She was right. The Krauses were my family, and I couldn't wait to share them with Garrett's family.

FIVE

THE MORNING FLEW BY. Kat showed up near the end of breakfast to help clean and prep for the day. We sent Penny and Bruce on an excursion through town, making sure to point out a few of our favorite shops on the tourist map of the village. Leah opted to read upstairs before going to meet Hazel at the ski hill.

In the summer we hired twins Casey and Jack, who helped in the pub and at events and festivals, but since they were away at college we had hired two local teachers who worked alternating weekends for extra cash and free beer. It was a win-win for us and for them. Having additional hands during the offseason made a huge difference. It freed Garrett up to tinker with beer recipes and allowed both of us time for the dozens of other tasks that came with running a nanobrewery. We had specific brew days, but there were always products to order, marketing to be done, and planning for the future.

We had asked them both to come help today. I wasn't expecting the tasting room to be busy, especially with the storm and road closures. It wasn't a festival weekend and odds were good that Kat could handle it on her own, but Garrett and I both felt better about having more staff than not enough.

The only thing left on my to-do list was starting a soup of

the day. Beer and soup are the perfect pub pairing. It hadn't taken much to convince Garrett of this when we put together the Nitro menu. From a profit perspective, soup was our most versatile item. Our soup of the day allowed me creativity in cooking and could be prepared in advance. Not to mention our soups were the most cost-effective item on our small menu. A big vat might cost us twenty or thirty dollars in ingredients, but we could serve each bowl for five dollars. The math was simple, but even more importantly, our guests loved the comfort of a bowl of white bean chili or chicken corn chowder with a hot pretzel and a cold pint.

With the frigid temps and threat of more snow later in the day, I decided on a recipe from Great-Aunt Tess's files for Goulash Soup. I began by dicing onions, carrots, red peppers, potatoes, and garlic. I fried off more of the bacon from breakfast and reserved a bit of the grease to sauté the veggies until they were soft and tender. Then I added chopped boneless chuck roast, beef broth, a healthy splash of our obsidian IPA, tomato paste, and a collection of spices like smoked paprika, caraway seeds, salt, and white pepper. Once the mixture came to a boil, I turned the burner to low and covered it with a lid. The goulash could cook low and slow all afternoon. When we were ready to serve it, we would top it with a dollop of sour cream and crumbled bacon.

Once our weekend crew had the bar ready to go and my soup was simmering on the stove, Garrett, Leah, and I left for the ski hill. I had texted Alex earlier. He and his squad, as he called them, were already planning to spend the day on the slopes, so he gladly agreed to a free lunch.

The ski hill was a short walk from the village. We zipped our parkas tight as we paralleled Highway 2 and passed the row of alpine hotels. Their style was distinctly Leavenworth with low-angled rooflines, shutters, decorative trim, wood and stucco walls, and curved balconies. Hotel Residence was my personal favorite. It sat across the highway from my cottage. Guests were treated to a full German breakfast every morning in the hotel's fourth-floor solarium, where a traditional alphornist would serenade while they took in views of Wedge Mountain.

"I can't get over that everything in town is so Bavarian," Leah said as we passed the outdoor skating rink next to the library. "I mean, G, I know you said that it was like this, but I didn't realize just how much."

"Do you call your brother G?" I asked her.

She chuckled. "It's an old nickname given to him when..."

"Hey, check out the golf course," Garrett interrupted her and pointed across the street toward my cabin. "See the deer down the hill from Sloan's cottage?"

"You live here. Pinch me." Leah stuck out her arm.

"I know, sometimes I have to pinch myself too," I answered truthfully. "And here's an insider secret just between us. If we *happen* to have some extra grain from the brewery lying around and it *happens* to spill on my back deck, the deer will come right up and nibble away. They'll let you get very close."

"Yes, let's spill some grain." Leah squealed with delight and grabbed her brother's arm. "Deer. Have I told you how much I love deer!"

"No. Really? I don't think you've mentioned it." He rubbed her ski hat playfully. "Although what Sloan is suggesting is highly frowned upon by the authorities. I can't believe you're suggesting such nefarious behavior to my little sister." He winked.

We stopped for her to snap a few pictures on her phone. I had them pose with the crystalized snowy hillside and the family of deer behind them.

It was clear from Leah's bright wide eyes and matching smile that she was excited to see the herd in the wild, but I had to wonder if there was another reason that Garrett cut her off.

We resumed our walk to the lodge, which was a little over a

mile from the main section of town. Ski Hill Road took us the entire way. We weren't alone in our trek up the long road. Families dragging kids and thermoses of hot chocolate in bright red sleds and groups of teens I recognized from the high school lugging snowboards joined the parade heading for the lodge.

"How sweet that everyone can walk up to the mountain." Leah waved to a rosy-cheeked toddler bundled under a layer of blankets and greeting everyone with a wave fit for a prince or princess. "It takes at least an hour to drive to Mt. Hood from Portland, and that's not factoring in dead-stop traffic and waiting in hour-long lines for the chair lifts."

I knew I was biased, but I had to agree that we were lucky to live in such a special place.

When the lodge and ski hill came into view, Leah let out a small gasp. "Okay, am I in a Hallmark movie right now? This is ridiculously charming. Come on, guys."

Red chair lifts dangled in the sky. Skiers in bright snowsuits flew down the hill, while youngsters carted discs and retro sleds up the sledding hill. The lodge had always reminded me of Hansel and Gretel. It was constructed from a combination of stone and wood with blue shuttered windows, three stories, and a snow-coated sloping A-frame roof. Its massive chimney puffed out ringlets of smoke.

"It's pretty awesome, isn't it?" Garrett ruffled his sister's head again. "I hate to say it, but I told you so."

"I think I was too little when we came to visit Great-Aunt Tess," Leah said. "I have a couple of fuzzy memories of splashing in the river and eating giant pretzels, but I don't remember Leavenworth being this idyllic. I totally get why you left Seattle now."

"I'm glad you're loving it." Garrett sounded relieved. "I thought you would, but I know you also had some reservations when I decided to make the move."

That was news to me. Garrett had never mentioned

anything about his family not approving of his decision to leave the corporate world and start a brewery. Although I could understand why they might have had reservations about him giving up steady income and benefits for an entrepreneurial lifestyle.

"Don't listen to the doctor. That was probably just the med school in me talking." Leah gave him an apologetic smile. "No, really, this is amazing. I guess I was expecting it to feel more touristy, but it feels like the village is one big family."

"Well, if you were here for Oktoberfest you might not be saying that," Garrett admitted. "But yeah, when there's not a festival going on, Leavenworth is a small mountain town where everyone looks out for each other, right, Sloan?"

"It's true, and the hospital is always hiring. Just to put that out there." I winked as we got to the parking lot. There were a number of cars and the ski van parked in the lot, but there were equally as many snow lovers on foot.

"Don't tempt me. I'm already writing my resignation letter in my head."

As if on cue, Hazel spotted us and waved us over her way. She was standing near the ski van talking with a guy I didn't recognize. "You made it." She looked ready for a day on the slopes in her yellow ski gear with a matching fuzzy yellow hat and white and yellow boots, but the deep purplish blush under her eyes made me suspect she hadn't gotten much sleep last night.

"I'm excited to get on the hill," Leah said with a grin.

"Are we done here?" the guy asked Hazel. He was dressed in a T-shirt, skinny jeans, and Converse shoes. Not exactly skiing attire.

"Yeah. Thanks for coming." Hazel shot him a look I couldn't decipher.

"Nice shirt," Garrett said, pointing out the guy's shirt that read: No I Will Not Fix Your Computer.

49

Hazel chuckled. "It's a joke. Tad runs our IT department at the hospital."

"Nope. Not a joke. I won't fix your computer." Tad tapped the lettering on his shirt. "It's my day job, not a hobby."

Hazel ducked her head, nodded apologetically, and then smiled up at him. "I know, I'm really sorry about this, Tad. I can't tell you how much I appreciate you meeting me here on your day off. I'm going to make it up to you. I promise."

"You owe me." Tad didn't return her smile. "I'm not making any promises about what I can or can't do with this." He tapped a laptop under his arm.

"I know. I get it. Thank you for trying. I'll check in after we're done skiing."

"Fine." He turned and headed toward a candy-apple red sports car in the parking lot.

I wondered how he'd driven the lowered, rear-wheel drive car up the ski hill.

Hazel watched him go.

"Did you find your flash drive?" I immediately regretted asking because her sunken eyes practically bulged out of her head.

"No. I'm trying not to think about it because every time I do, I want to puke. I retraced my steps last night. I went everywhere —the hospital, the coffeehouse, the village baker. There was no trace of it." Hazel patted the messenger bag she had clutched to her side. "I gave Tad my personal laptop. He's going to try and recover my files. It's really great of him to help me out. He's not even working today, but I think he could tell that I'm a stress case at the moment."

"I'm so sorry you couldn't find it. We'll keep looking at Nitro." I glanced at Garrett, who nodded in agreement.

Hazel shrugged as if she weren't concerned. She wasn't very convincing. "It's fine. I'm trying not to think about it. Getting a few runs in should take my mind off it. Otherwise, when I start my shift later, I'm going to have to come up with Plan B." She looked at Leah and motioned to the lodge. "You need to rent gear, right?"

Leah nodded. We followed them to the lodge and parted ways. They went to the attached ski rental shop while Garrett and I went to find a table in the restaurant. The interior lodge had two levels for seating with an oversized rock fireplace, a snack bar, and plenty of cozy spots on the main floor to curl up in front of its large windows and watch skiers and boarders navigate the ski hill. Upstairs were more peaked windows, a second fireplace, and collections of dining tables and couches.

"Where should we camp out?" I asked Garrett. We had agreed to get to the lodge first to reserve a spot for lunch.

Garrett assessed the empty dining room and pointed to a collection of brown leather couches in front of the fireplace. "I vote those couches."

"Good choice. That's my favorite spot." The couches were positioned around the fireplace and offered sweeping views of the ski hill. There were three large couches and two plush chairs surrounding a large coffee table, which should give us ample space for our party. I had a feeling that people would come in shifts, especially since Leah and Alex were both likely to spend the bulk of their afternoon getting in as many runs as possible.

I sat near the roaring fireplace, feeling an instant calm spread through my body at the scent of hickory woodsmoke and the rhythmic flames lapping up the chimney.

Garrett sat next to me and leaned back, crossing one leg over his knee. He glanced around to make sure no one was nearby before lowering his voice. "Listen, Sloan, I'm glad we have a minute alone. There's something I want to talk to you about."

My brief moment of calm evaporated. I felt my mouth go dry and my throat start to tighten. "Okay."

"Don't look at me like that. It's nothing terrible. I mean, it is in a way, but not like you might think." He paused and uncrossed his legs. He reached for a menu on the coffee table and rolled it into a tube as he continued. "I don't exactly know where to start. It's just something I probably should have told you a while ago and I guess too much time passed and then it's felt weird to bring it up."

The shaky quality of his voice and his lack of eye contact weren't bringing me much comfort. Reading body language was my superpower. It was a skill I honed at a young age. It helped when navigating being placed in a new home. Everything about Garrett's body language was telling me that he was nervous. Really nervous.

"I should have told you when we first met, but things were... complicated." He inhaled as if trying to get enough air and courage to continue.

Only before he could continue, Otto and Ursula crested the stairs. "Sloan, Garrett. It is good to see you."

"We'll talk more later," he whispered, tossing the menu on the table and standing to greet the Krauses.

What did he want to tell me? What could be so bad to have him shaking the floor with his bouncing knee?

It was hard to make casual conversation with Otto and Ursula, but I didn't have another choice. Bruce and Penny arrived shortly after. We ordered a round of drinks and starters to share.

"It's been so long since we visited, I can't get over how much things have changed and how much the village has expanded. Bruce and I counted at least twenty restaurants we want to try. I remember the last time we visited Tess, none of the shops and the restaurants off of Front Street had been renovated; only the main part of town had gone through a Bavarian facelift. It's so great to see so many new places popping up and the village thriving," Penny gushed about their morning shopping stroll.

"That's thanks in large part to these two. The Krauses have dedicated themselves to making Leavenworth the place to be for anything Bavarian." Garrett raised his water glass in a show of respect.

Otto scoffed. "No, no. We are lucky to have so many friends who care about making zis a destination for beer and for festivals, but we have only been a small part of ze changes."

"We had lunch at Der Keller the last time we visited Tess," Bruce added, catching Penny's eye. "Do you remember how we talked about that sauerbraten for days?"

"I'm not exaggerating when I say that was a life-changing dish." Penny placed one hand over her heart and closed her eyes. "Please tell me it's still on the menu."

"Ja, we would never even zink about taking it off ze menu because it is my favorite too." Ursula clasped her hands in her lap.

"Thank goodness. That solidifies our dinner plans." Penny sighed with exaggerated relief. "You must have known Tess."

Otto responded first. "She was one of ze very first people we met in ze village. She was wonderful. She welcomed us and supported Der Keller from day one. She would be so very happy to see what Garrett and Sloan have done with ze old brothel."

One fun fact that always got an eye raise from our brewery tours was that the Nitro building Garrett had inherited from his Great-Aunt Tess had originally been a brothel. Tess had converted it into a boarding house and diner in the 1960s.

"Did someone say brothel?"

I looked up to see Hans. He looked like a stylish lumberjack with his Carhartt work pants, gold and green flannel, and boots. His soft brown eyes held their usual hint of mischief, something he had most definitely inherited from Ursula.

I scooted closer to Garrett and patted the spot next to me.

Hans tugged off his coat and introduced himself to the

Strongs. "How's your stay so far? I heard that it got off to a rough start."

They told the Krauses about getting stuck in the avalanche as our appetizers arrived. We passed around chips and spicy salsa, tater tots with ranch dip, and mozzarella sticks with marinara sauce. The lodge was known for its classic pub grub, which no one seemed to mind, myself included. Conversation flowed easily as we sipped beers and munched on snacks. Leah and Alex tromped in together just as we were about to order lunch.

"Perfect timing and I see you two already met," I said to Alex. He took off his Seattle Sounders ski hat.

"Leah was tearing it up out there. We got to the lodge at the same time and I was telling her all of my friends were impressed, and then we made the connection." Alex went straight to his grandparents and hugged them both.

It warmed my heart to see that despite his growing independence, he wasn't afraid to show affection or make time to have lunch with his family.

Leah joined us. "You definitely downplayed the ski hill." She punched Garrett playfully on the knee. "It was great. Of course, maybe it's not having to wait in the lift line five times longer than it takes to do a run. I swear, skiing on Mount Hood is more like standing in line. Here we did a run and were on the chair again right away. It's amazing. I'm telling you, Leavenworth is magical."

Otto lifted his glass with slightly shaky hands. "We would say Leavenworth has captured you under her spell—or der Zauber."

"It's true." Leah bobbed her head.

Ursula nudged Alex and Leah to finish off the appetizers. Neither of them put up a fight.

"Did Hazel have to go to work?" I asked as I handed Leah a menu.

"No, she bumped into some colleagues on our way to the lodge and got talked into one more run. It was weird. She seemed really hesitant. I invited her to join us, but I think she felt pressured into joining her peers. Come to think of it, that's probably why she was acting off. There's a hierarchy in hospitals. As a resident, when your attending physician asks you to do something, even during off hours, you do it."

We ordered food while Alex and Leah told us about their runs. The afternoon was about as close to perfection as possible. That was until a piercing, banshee scream sounded outside, followed by more yelling and hollering. We all jumped to our feet and stared out the window. People around us abandoned their lunches to see what was happening.

Skiers and boarders screeched to a halt and clustered at the base of the hill.

My stomach dropped as people on the ski hill began waving for help.

I watched the scene unfold like a bad movie.

Something was wrong.

Really wrong.

A skier in a neon snowsuit stood and waved wildly toward the lodge. Even from this distance, I could tell that something terrible had happened.

CHAPTER
SIX

ANOTHER SKIER BURST into the lodge and immediately began yelling for help.

"Is there a doctor? We need a doctor!"

Leah didn't hesitate. She jumped to her feet and sprinted outside. Garrett and I followed after her while the others stayed. We were both trained in first aid. If Leah needed assistance, we could help if necessary.

Outside was utter chaos. The sound of screams and cries of onlookers crowded around the base of the lift sent chills up my spine. Families hurried to get little ones out of the way, while a swarm of skiers surrounded the area of the accident, or whatever had occurred.

The lift stopped. Everyone stuck on the chairs overhead peered down at us, trying to get a glimpse of the action below.

Leah pushed her way through the crowd. A skier was already on the phone with emergency services. "She fell from the chair," he screamed into the phone. I couldn't tell if he was trying to be heard over the panicked buzz of the bystanders or if he was panicking himself. "I don't know. I can't tell for sure but it's probably thirty, maybe forty feet." He craned his neck to get a better look at the empty ski lift chair.

"It sounds like someone fell from the lift," I said to Garrett, knowing full well that he had likely heard the same thing I had.

It was evident immediately that the situation was going to require more than our basic first aid. My lungs felt heavy and not just because we were running through heavy snow.

"That's terrible." His gaze drifted from Leah, who had begun directing the crowd gathered around the fallen skier, to the lift. "I don't know if that fall is survivable."

"Garrett, get everyone back. I need some space." Leah knelt over the victim and tried to push the crowd back with one arm.

Garrett sprang into action. "Okay, everyone, let's give the doctor some room." He managed to gain control of the situation with his commanding stance, yet his calm and measured tone. The skiers broke apart, moving a few feet away from Leah and her patient.

I stood a few feet away, trying to make sense of what had happened. Someone had fallen from the lift. How?

The brick red ski lift chairs suddenly took on a different appearance as they swung in the light wind. A halo of sunlight broke through the clouds as if Mother Nature were trying to spotlight the accident scene. My eyes couldn't focus. I shielded them with one hand, trying to block out the bright reflection on the snow.

Sirens wailed in the distance. That was a good sign that the ambulance was on its way. It shouldn't take long, although they would have to be careful navigating an icy Ski Hill Road.

I tried not to look at the accident scene. There wasn't any evidence of blood on the snow, but I didn't know if that meant that the skier could be in better shape than imagined or if that meant they had horrific internal injuries.

The kid who was still on the phone with EMS was right in his estimate that the lift had to be a good thirty feet above us at this slope of the hill. There was a solid base of snow plus the fresh powder from yesterday's storm, but was that enough to cushion such a treacherous fall?

The team of doctors from Nitro last night appeared and began to assist Leah, who was performing CPR on the victim. From my vantage point, it was hard to get a good look. They were lying on the ground but surrounded by the team of doctors who were at Nitro last night. Every once in a while, someone would move just enough for me to catch a flash of color. It looked like the victim was wearing a yellow snowsuit.

I felt torn. Part of me wanted to know who had fallen and the other wanted to completely close my eyes and do everything in my power to avoid getting a good look. It made me even more impressed with Leah's career path. I wasn't sure I could handle the image of seeing someone with a broken leg—or worse.

The sirens grew louder and I realized that the ambulance was already pulling into the parking lot. The crowd had tripled in size. People had come out of the lodge to see what was happening. Skiers finishing their runs congregated at the base of the lift, which still wasn't running. I felt bad for everyone stuck higher up the lift.

Garrett encouraged the crowd to make even more space for the first responders. They flew past us carrying a stretcher and gear and went straight to work assisting Leah and the other doctors.

"You okay, Sloan?" Garrett asked as he moved closer to me. Ski patrol had taken over crowd control now that the paramedics were on the scene.

"I'm fine. Well, not fine. I hope the skier is okay." I glanced above to see snow boots dangling from a nearby chair. "I guess I'm having flashbacks to when Alex was little. Mac used to take him on the lift every Saturday. I was always worried. I used to ask him and anyone at the lodge who would listen why the lifts didn't have safety bars."

"Why don't they?" Garrett sounded confused as he glanced from the victim to the lift.

"Right? I was told it was because it's an old lift and enhancing safety features would be too expensive. I'm surprised this is the first time someone has taken a fall. It seemed inevitable. I spoke at a few town hall meetings about raising funds to renovate the lift and lodge, but it's never gone anywhere. Apparently, the lifts have been grandfathered in since the ski hill is historic, and the powers that be claim that the slope isn't high enough to require extra safety precautions. So my strategy has been to lecture Alex more than I'm sure was necessary about not messing around on the lift. I've seen kids trying to get their chairs swinging wildly. It's really scary."

"It sounds like an oversight." Garrett blew into his hands to try and warm them. We had rushed to the scene without bothering to grab coats or hats, a decision I was starting to regret.

"Do you know who fell?" I peered around his frame. Dr. Sutton stood out amongst the first responders because she was pacing with her phone pressed to her ear.

Was she calling for more help?

He shook his head. "I couldn't see, but there are like six doctors assisting."

We waited in silence while Leah and the paramedics worked on their patient. It didn't sound good. Leah called out orders to protect the person's head in the event of a neck or spinal cord injury and continued to perform CPR.

Chief Meyers and two police officers showed up and immediately began questioning ski patrol and bystanders.

"Do you think that's standard procedure?" I asked Garrett as I shivered. I wasn't sure if I was experiencing mild shock or if the cold was getting to me. "Or could something more be going on?"

"I'm sure that the Chief is going to have to do an investigation." He stuffed his hands into his jeans pockets. "There could

59

be a lawsuit with an accident like this. I don't know who would be responsible. The lodge, maybe? If they find that the lifts were unsafe."

I knew that the lifts were closed during inclement weather and windstorms. There was a slight breeze this afternoon, but nothing strong enough to warrant a closure.

At that moment the EMS crew loaded the patient on a stretcher, and I got a better glimpse of the victim's clothing. The yellow snowsuit and white and yellow boots were identical to what Hazel had been wearing earlier.

My chest tightened. I placed my hand over my heart and said a silent prayer that it wasn't Hazel.

The crew balanced the stretcher as they navigated the base of the ski hill and headed for the waiting ambulance. Leah and Chief Meyers had a private conversation before she came over to us.

"Did you hear?" She used her hand to support her neck as tears welled in her eyes. "It's bad."

"Are you okay?" Garrett asked, automatically wrapping his sister in a hug.

Leah received his hug but was too numb to return it. "It was Hazel."

"Hazel. It was her?" My lungs constricted even more, making it hard to speak. "I was afraid of that when I saw the yellow snowsuit."

Leah nodded like she was trying to process. "Yeah. I was just with her. I can't believe it. She went for another run with her colleagues, and I guess she must have slipped off somehow. I didn't have time to ask questions. She wasn't breathing."

"Is she breathing now?" Garrett voiced what I was also thinking.

"No." Leah hung her head and collapsed deeper into his arms. "We couldn't find a pulse." She kept her voice low. "The police asked me not to say anything yet. I suppose there's an outside sliver of hope that the paramedics or ED team at the hospital will have better luck, but I think the fall was fatal. In my professional medical opinion, I don't think she's going to make it."

SEVEN

GARRETT HELD LEAH TIGHTER. "I'm so sorry you have to go
through this. First the avalanche, now this. I was hoping that
the weekend could be a good break for you. I was never anticipating that you would be in a position like this."

Leah leaned into Garrett's shoulder. "How could you know
that any of this would happen? And it's my job. I'm used to
seeing death up close. Not that it ever gets easy, but I have come
to understand that in a field where we work to save lives, it's
inevitable that we lose some, too. I guess I'm more shaken up
because most of the time I don't know the patients. I can't
believe it's Hazel. How could she have fallen off the lift?"

"Could she have had some sort of medical emergency before
the fall?" I asked.

Leah considered my question for a minute. "You mean like a
stroke or heart attack? It's a possibility. Like I said, the staff at
the hospital will have access to more equipment than we did
here, and if they can't do any more for her, I'm sure there will be
an autopsy."

"You sound like you already have another theory," Garrett
noted. It made me realize how well he knew his sister.

As a kid, I had often dreamed about having a sibling or siblings. What would it have been like to grow up with someone who shared your DNA and potentially a bedroom? In my family fantasies, my siblings and I were the best of friends who stayed up late reading under the covers with flashlights and sneaking down to the kitchen for midnight snacks. The thought brought me comfort on nights when I would wake with my heart racing from a nightmare and have to try to find a way to soothe myself back to sleep.

"I think she suffered a fatal injury upon her fall. She fell the wrong way on her skis. I don't know if she would have survived it, but the way she hit the ground with her skis," Leah paused and stole a quick glance at the lifts, "the angle of the fall and her unresponsiveness make me think that it was the impact from that height. I told the police the same thing. Dr. Sutton and I think his name is Shep agreed, too."

Garrett breathed deeply.

We all followed his lead.

The group of doctors were huddled together near where Hazel had fallen, Dr. Sutton and Shep along with Ren, the nurse, and Jerry from BioGold. They had all come skiing together. I couldn't pinpoint exactly why but something felt off about that.

Leah pulled away from her brother's tight grasp. "Dr. Sutton is waving me over. I'll be right back."

Garrett let her go but didn't move or say another word. We both just stood in stunned silence, lost in our thoughts and emotion. I wasn't sure how much time passed. We stood in quiet reflection until Chief Meyers approached us and finally broke the silence.

She tromped toward us wearing her standard khaki uniform with snow boots and a brown fur-lined coat. "Sloan, Garrett, I'll need to take each of your statements as witnesses. Who wants to go first?" She didn't waste any time getting to the point. It was one of the things I appreciated about her. Chief Meyers was kind and caring, but she wasn't overly effusive. She showed her connection to our community by her diligence and professionalism.

"Beer before beauty, or should I say beer and beauty?" Garrett tried to smile at his attempt at a joke, but his eyes filled with sadness. "Sorry, I don't know why that came out. Joking is my stress response, I guess."

Chief Meyers gave him an understanding nod. She flipped her spiral notebook to a fresh page and waited for one of us to speak.

"Yeah, I'll go first," I said to the chief. "Although I'm not sure I have much to share. We didn't see it happen. We came out to help once we heard the screams."

The chief tipped the edge of her wide-brimmed hat and pointed to a clear area a few feet away. "You didn't see the fall, but why don't you tell me verbatim what you saw when you got out here to help."

I proceeded to tell her exactly what I had heard and seen, starting from inside the lodge and leading up to the paramedics' arrival.

"Did you recognize anyone in the crowd that had gathered around the victim?" She held her pencil at the ready.

"Recognize anyone?" I thought out loud. "Um, yes, I did and I was just thinking about how odd it is. All of Hazel's colleagues from the hospital are here. Dr. Sutton, who is head of the clinical trial that Hazel was working on. Shep, aka Dr. Ames, is an anesthesiologist at the hospital, but I'm not really sure what his connection is to the group or the clinical trial. Then there's Jerry, whom I met at Nitro last night. He's in town from Seattle. His pharmaceutical company BioGold is sponsoring the clinical trial. And the tall, burly guy with the spiky red hair and tattoos is Ren. He's a nurse."

She made notes as I spoke, but her face remained passive.

"I think they were all skiing together. Hazel had been skiing with Leah, Garrett's sister, whom you just met. She was going to come to join us for lunch in the lodge, but according to Leah she bumped into the hospital crew, and they convinced her to get in a few more runs with them."

"Convinced?" She raised one bushy eyebrow.

"Those were Leah's words, not mine. I just mean that it wasn't a surprise to see the physicians."

The chief was noncommittal. "Mmhmm."

"Do you know how Hazel fell? Are there any witnesses?"

"I'm not at liberty to expand much at the moment," she replied through pursed lips. "I can tell you that we have multiple witnesses who have reported that Hazel was alone on the chairlift."

"I wonder what made her fall," I questioned out loud. "Maybe she dropped something and reached down to try and retrieve it? You know how much of a proponent I've been for safety bars on the lifts. I'm surprised it hasn't happened before."

"Agreed." She put away her notes and used her index finger to motion me closer. "This stays between us, okay?"

"Okay." The hairs on my arms stood at attention and not just because I was cold.

"I have an instinct about this accident that I don't like."

"What kind of an instinct?"

She made sure no one was listening and motioned for us to lean in. "I'm sharing this only with you and Garrett because of our history and because I could use your eyes around the village the next few days, but this information doesn't go any further, understood?"

"Absolutely. You can count on my discretion."

Garrett cleared his throat and nodded solemnly. "Me too."

"I know. That's why I'm sharing my theory with you both."

My breath puffed out cold air as I waited for Chief Meyers to say more. My teeth hurt from the cold and my legs had begun to tremble, but there was no way I was going back inside the lodge until I heard more.

"It could be that Hazel had a tragic fall. We'll certainly be exploring every possibility, but my instincts tell me this might not have been an accident."

"You mean, you think someone pushed her off the chair?" I rubbed my palms together for friction.

"That I'm not as confident about, with multiple witnesses who saw Hazel riding solo. Not to mention the lift itself." She shot her finger in the air. "Where would they have gone? The lift stopped immediately upon Hazel's fall."

I exhaled slowly. "How would someone have killed her, though?"

"That's what I intend to find out and I could use your help." She readjusted her hat and walked toward the group of doctors.

We waited for her to interview Leah. Once they finished their conversation, Leah came back over to us.

"How did it go, sis?" Garrett asked.

"Fine. She doesn't give a lot, does she?" Leah's gaze drifted to Chief Meyers, who was now interrogating Ren. "There's not a lot I can do, but I'd like to speak with the attending physician and Chief Meyers said that she would give me a ride. Is that okay with you? I'm going to go return my ski rental and then head into the village with her."

"Sloan and I should probably go find everyone. We can take your skis for you." Garrett nodded toward the lodge.

"Thanks." Leah stood on her tiptoes to give him a kiss on the cheek. "I'll find you guys later at Nitro."

We parted ways.

"I'm guessing you picked up on the same things as me." Garrett sounded as incredulous as I felt. "Chief Meyers thinks there's a chance that Hazel's accident wasn't an accident."

"She isn't prone to exaggerating, and I can't stop replaying how stressed-out Hazel was at the pub last night." I could hear that my speech was slightly altered from the cold. It was hard to get words out between my chattering teeth and numb lips. "She was so worried about finding the flash drive, which now has me wondering if there could be a connection."

"Let's get you inside, Sloan." Garrett put his arm around me and rubbed my shoulder, sending an instant shot of welcome warmth through my body "What kind of connection are you talking about?"

"I don't know," I admitted. "And I'm also stuck on how someone could have caused Hazel's fall."

We both looked up.

The lifts were running again to allow the skiers who had been stranded to get off and the police squad had cordoned off the area underneath where Hazel had fallen, as well as the entrance to the lift. I had a feeling that skiing was going to be done for the day.

"Maybe that's why they've closed this off," Garrett suggested. "They're probably looking for evidence on the ground."

"Right, but what? If Hazel had been shot or injured before she fell, Leah would have noticed a wound."

Garrett squeezed my shoulder tighter. "Yeah, I'm stumped, but like I said to Chief Meyers, we'll do anything we can to support her investigation."

"For sure."

We traipsed down the ski hill to return Leah's skis and regroup with Garrett's parents, Alex, and the Krauses. I wasn't eager to have to share the news about Hazel's accident. The situation was going to put a damper on the weekend, which was the least of my worries. I couldn't believe that Hazel was dead. She was so young and had so much life and promise in front of her. It was tragic and senseless and it made me more resolved to hold true to our promise to Chief Meyers. If Hazel's fall wasn't an accident, I intended to do anything I could to help see that her killer was brought to justice.

EIGHT

WE STAYED at the lodge for another hour. Everyone needed time to process Hazel's death and take comfort in our connection with each other. I was thankful for the warmth of the fire and a round of hot spiked apple ciders that Hans ordered for the table. Garrett snuck downstairs to return Leah's skis, and I sipped my cider and tried to stop images of Alex dangling from the ski lift from assaulting my mind. My anxiety had a way of taking my worst fears and running them in a constant loop.

Hans joined me on the hearth. His golden-brown eyes narrowed as he rested his drink on the edge of the coffee table. "Keep sipping that slow." He nodded to my mug.

I cradled it in my hands and took another drink.

"So, you want to talk about it?"

Hans might have chosen woodworking as his profession, but he easily could have opened a counseling office in his studio. He had a way of gently pulling information out of me that no one else had ever come close to.

"Am I that obvious?"

He ran his finger around the rim of his mug. "Nope. You've had a traumatic experience. I would expect anyone in your situation to need to process."

I smiled and chuckled. "You always know the right thing to say."

"Hardly. I only know how to listen." He pressed his hand on my arm.

I fought back tears. "I just keep thinking it could have been Alex."

Hans reached into the pocket of his flannel and removed a handkerchief. He was the only person our age I knew who carried a handkerchief and I couldn't love him more for it.

I dabbed my eyes and whispered so that Alex couldn't hear me. "I think some of it is tied to the fact that he's growing up and is going to be gone soon, but then I also feel guilty and terrible for being relieved that it wasn't him on the lift."

"That sounds like a normal reaction to me."

"You think?"

He firmed his brow. "I'm sure of it."

I folded his handkerchief and gave it back to him. "Thanks, I guess I just needed to say that out loud."

We drifted back into the conversation with everyone else and sipped our drinks. After Garrett returned from the ski rental shop, Otto, Ursula, and Hans left for Der Keller. Penny and Bruce opted to take a short nap at Nitro before joining them later at Der Keller. Alex and his friends headed to Mac's for an afternoon of gaming since the ski slopes would remain closed for the rest of the day.

That left me and Garrett.

"Do you want to take a snowy walk before we go back to Nitro?" Garrett asked after we had paid the bill and bundled up in our coats and hats.

"Sure. Where?"

"The cross-country trails." He tapped a map printed on the menus that showed the cross-country and snowshoe trails that originated at the lodge and intertwined for miles through the backcountry. "Too bad we didn't bring our snowshoes."

"My boots should hold up."

We left the comfort of the lodge for the tree-lined trails. The snow had been packed down by skiers and snowshoers, making it manageable. We were careful not to walk on the cross-country tracks and stayed to the side of the trail.

The trail we were taking looped away from the lodge and up a steep cliff with a sheer drop-off on one side and dense forest on the other. It would eventually connect with another system of trails that would take us to the top of the ski hill and then out into the Enchantments.

A group of cross-country skiers glided past us. Everything smelled of fresh snow and pine. These trails were magical any time of the year. In the summer they made for great hiking. We would pack lunches and climb the hillside for sunny views of the village. But in the winter, being out in the wilderness felt like stepping back in time. It was a strange juxtaposition between Hazel's brutal fall and the beauty and stillness of nature.

It was incredible how quickly any signs of civilization vanished as we trekked deeper into the woods, sun filtering through the pine and aspen trees. The only sounds were our feet crunching the snow, our heavy breathing, and the occasional pinecone falling to the ground.

"This is gorgeous," I said to Garrett as we hit a switchback and started to climb higher. "But do you have an ulterior motive, other than breathing space and some fresh air to cleanse our heads?"

"I do," he said between breaths. "It should be around the next bend."

I followed him, trusting that his reason would become apparent soon, and even if it weren't I appreciated being outside and taking a little break from the reality of Hazel's death.

When we crested the next switchback, Garrett stopped,

bent over, and put his hands on his knees. "Damn, I'm feeling the elevation today."

"That's a good climb." I sucked air in through my nose. My cheeks were hot with perspiration and it was hard to catch my breath, but I didn't mind. Exercise was just what I needed to break the cycle of spinning into worry about Hazel's accident.

"Sorry. I didn't mean to sprint up here." Garrett heaved his shoulders back as he gasped to get more air.

"No, it's good. Honestly. It feels really good to sweat it out, you know?"

He took a second to catch his breath and then returned to standing. "Yeah, I think that's why my pace was so fast."

"What are we looking for up here, or were you just getting some air?"

His cheeks were flushed. "No, but you're right, it does feel good to move. I came up this way because I wanted to see this vantage point." His eyes traveled to a clearing of trees.

We were above the lodge and the ski hill, looking down on the chair lift.

"I don't think I realized that the view was this good up here." I craned my neck to get a better perspective. Skiers looked like Alex's LEGO minifigures. The lift could have been constructed from the plastic bricks from this height too, but despite how small everyone down below appeared, it was incredible to have a bird's-eye view of the entire ski hill.

"A few weeks ago I came on a moonlight snowshoe tour, you were in Seattle with Alex for his University of Washington tour, and our guide had us stop here. He said it's the most underrated view in town. And he was right. It was amazing to see the lights from the village glowing down below."

"I bet it would be incredible at night." I could see partway down Ski Hill Road where skiers and sledders were traipsing back to town.

"We'll have to come ourselves sometime soon, but I wanted

to see the lifts from up here. I thought a higher vantage point might offer some insight into what happened to Hazel." Garrett's breathing had returned to normal.

"Good thinking."

We both studied the slope. He was right. Being higher gave me a new perspective.

"It's interesting," I said pointing to the spot the police had roped off beneath the chair lift. "The lift doesn't look as high as I thought."

Garrett's hands moved in excited animation. "Exactly. Right? That's why I wanted to get up here."

"But what does that mean? Is our perspective skewed or was Hazel's fall not as far as it seemed?"

"I'm not sure, but if it's the latter that opens up a lot more possibilities."

"And also seems like it could have been more survivable."

Garrett scrunched his eyes together in thought. "Yeah, okay, so here's one theory. What if Hazel's killer was on the lift with her? They could have hit or knocked her off by surprise, which made the impact of the fall worse."

"And then what? They jumped?"

"If you knew what you were doing, maybe. If they jumped at the right angle and rolled?"

"I guess, but Chief Meyers said there were multiple witnesses who saw Hazel on the chair alone, and wouldn't there have been evidence of impact in the snow? The killer's footsteps? Skis? Something?"

Garrett frowned. "Yeah. Good points."

"Although Leah did say that Hazel's skis made the fall worse. Let's go with your theory for a minute. What if the killer didn't have their skis and bindings attached? That would have made them much more mobile and nimbler when they jumped off. There still would have been a sign in the snow, though— their boots, etc." I paused for a minute to think.

73

Garrett stared at the scene of the crime.

"You know, when we showed up, Hazel's colleagues who invited her out for another run were standing right there." I pointed to a spot where the police were combing the snowy ground. "That could have been intentional. Think about how many people came running. There had to have been at least forty or fifty people gathered around Hazel. What if that was the killer's plan?"

"All of the footprints wiped out any evidence that they had jumped," Garrett agreed. "Maybe they stuck around. Maybe they called for help and flagged other skiers and snowboarders down as a way to shift suspicion from them."

"No one would guess that they were involved if they were on the ground and trying to get help. Yeah, I like it," I said, forming a stronger theory in my head. "But there's still one major hole in this theory. What about the witnesses who saw Hazel riding solo?"

"Could the killer have lied? If they were first on the scene, let's say one of Hazel's colleagues at the hospital." Garrett strummed his fingers on his chin. "What if they said they had seen her on the lift alone? They set the tone, and everyone agreed."

"Chief Meyers has talked about witnesses being unreliable. That could explain it. I mean it seems a bit far-fetched, but it's not impossible."

"That's one of the reasons that witnesses are always questioned alone." Garrett twisted his head to get a better look at the police who were still spread out across the ski hill. "We're naturally influenced by other people's accounts. We could have a very savvy and clever killer on our hands who orchestrated the entire scene."

"I wonder if that's what Chief Meyers is considering."

"It is telling that there's still a team of officers in the area." Garrett zipped his coat tighter. "Are you getting cold standing here? We should probably head back since we exerted so much energy on our climb. It doesn't take long for hypothermia to kick in."

My body let out an involuntary shudder in response to his question. "I guess so. I am a little chilly now that we've stopped, and I have another lead for us."

"What's that?"

"The police are keeping people away from the area where the accident occurred, but what if we go check out the other side of the lift?" I pointed a gloved finger to the far side of the ski hill. A small ridgeline paralleled the lifts and the parking lot. "I don't see anyone there. What if the killer took off that way after they'd made sure that there were enough people around to disguise their footprints and any sign that they'd jumped?"

"Good thinking, Sloan." Garrett didn't waste any time turning and heading down the trail the way we had come.

The downhill trek took half the time. When we made it back to the lodge, we skirted the kids' tubing slope and parking lot. Neither of us wanted to be obvious about what we were doing, nor did we want to interfere with the official police investigation, so we kept to the tree line and out of sight.

The far side of the lift paralleled a row of old-growth evergreens that provided the perfect cover for our search. A set of deer tracks dotted the snow, but otherwise there weren't any human prints. It made sense. There wouldn't be a reason for anyone to be this far out of bounds. There was no skiing in this area. There was only a narrow access road for the snowcat and a row of western pine trees that barricaded the ski hill from the parking lot down below. The ledge was slightly precarious. One wrong step and either of us could sink into a tree well or slip off the side.

"I don't see anything out of the ordinary. Do you?" I asked Garrett as I paid careful attention to each of my steps.

"Nothing." He sounded dejected. "Let's go up a little farther just in case they tried to make their escape that way. Just make sure you keep away from the ledge."

We were level with the spot where Hazel had fallen.

After climbing for another five minutes, there was still nothing. The snow was pristine. Not so much as a pinecone had cracked its sparkly surface.

"I really thought we were on to something," I said to Garrett with a sigh.

"Me too."

"What do you think, should we call it and go back to the pub?"

"Yeah. We can cut down through the tree line if you want."

We started down the hillside, paving our path through the semi-wooded boundary to the snow park.

"Maybe Leah is having better luck at the hospital," Garrett said, watching his footing and kicking a branch out of the way.

"I'm guessing that Chief Meyers will have toxicology reports run. That may give her a better sense of the cause of death. If Hazel were drugged, that would explain her falling off the lift. Come to think of it, I don't think we can rule out that Hazel might have been self-medicating. She was so stressed and frazzled. She has access to medication at the hospital and I'm sure it's not difficult to get peers to prescribe a strong sleeping pill or anti-anxiety medication."

"That's definitely something to consider. We'll have to ask Leah if Hazel was acting strange. You would think that if she had taken medication, Leah would have noticed." He paused. "Unless she took something after Leah left."

"Exactly. Maybe bumping into her colleagues was a trigger and she self-medicated. There's a possibility that she could have accidentally overdosed. But, as we both know, if Chief Meyers is on high alert that Hazel's death may not have been accidental, she likely has good reason for that theory."

"Which is why I thought we might have spotted a clue out this way." Garrett froze in mid-sentence and mid-stride.

"What?" I half expected to see a black bear blocking our path.

"Look. Right there." He slowly raised his arm and pointed at a tree about ten feet away. "Do you see that?"

I squinted. "Is that Hazel's bag?"

We kicked up snow as we raced toward the tree.

"Wait, don't touch it," I cautioned when we got close enough to confirm that the bright yellow bag was indeed identical to the laptop bag she'd had at Nitro last night and in the parking lot when she had given her computer to Tad. "We have to call Chief Meyers—this could be tangible evidence."

I PULLED out my phone and called Chief Meyers. I gave her a quick recap of our hike up the cross-country trail and finding what looked like Hazel's bag.

"Stay put, Sloan. I'm going to get in touch with the team after we end this call. Don't move or touch anything until they can retrieve the bag and take it into evidence."

I hung up and informed Garrett that we were on bag watch duty until the police showed up. It didn't take long. Within minutes the police had trekked down, recovered the laptop bag, and roped off the section of trees.

"You two are free to go," one of the officers said. It was clearly a directive, not a suggestion.

Garrett and I took the cue and loped back to Ski Hill Road.

"Okay, this changes things, doesn't it?" he asked as we passed a small vineyard and private homes designed in the same old-world style.

"It's quite a coincidence that her laptop bag would be stashed beneath a tree. Why would she do that? She had it with her when we met her in the parking lot. She gave Tad her computer, so it's nearly impossible not to jump to the conclusion that someone was trying to find her laptop, is it?"

Garrett shook his head as he pondered my question. "I guess there's the off chance that someone stole it looking for cash and then ditched it out here, but that's a stretch."

"Or if Hazel was intentionally knocked from the ski lift, her killer could have stolen it and then dumped it. But then again, Hazel wouldn't have been skiing with her laptop bag. We'll have to ask Leah. I'm guessing she left it in the lodge when they went out to do runs." I slipped on a patch of ice. Garrett caught me at the last second, sending us skating down the street.

His firm grip on my arm felt especially welcome at this moment.

"That was a close one, Sloan. We can't have you breaking a leg or a tailbone. The brew would suffer."

"Just the brew?" I gave him a flirty look.

"And me. Definitely me." His voice dropped to a hush as he leaned so close that I could feel the heat of his breath on my skin.

Just as our lips were about to touch, Garrett lost his footing. I clutched his waist and managed to keep him upright. We both collapsed in a fit of laughter. It wasn't merely from the physical tension between us, although I had to admit that his body had a magnetic pull. I had a feeling that our burst of laughter was also a way to cope with Hazel's death. Not that either of us found anything funny about the situation, but more that in the midst of unexpected tragedy, one way to cope with the weight of darkness was to sink into lightness.

A group of snowboarders not much older than Alex passed by, giving us strange looks.

Garrett reached for my hand and pulled me to standing. "Come on, Krause, let's go."

We were both lost in our own thoughts on the rest of the walk to Nitro. I couldn't stop thinking about the reason that Hazel's laptop bag had been left in the woods. It seemed clear to me it had to be because of her research. Could there be a connection with her missing flash drive? She had been convinced that she'd lost the drive. What if that wasn't true? What if someone stole it?

Everyone involved in the BioGold clinical trial had been at Nitro last night. Granted, Shep, Dr. Sutton, Jerry, and Ren had been at a table in the back of the brewery while Hazel had been sitting near the door, but that didn't mean that Hazel hadn't interacted with them earlier. Or maybe one of them swiped it while she went to the bathroom or to the bar for a refill. It was definitely possible that one of them had stolen her flash drive. The question was why?

Could her research notes contain something important? Something worth killing for?

Hazel had said that she was dead if she couldn't find the drive. I thought she was being dramatic, but what if she wasn't? What if she had been jumpy and skittish not from lack of sleep or working overtime, but because she knew she was in danger?

I made a mental note to ask Leah about the documentation process for drug trials and whether she had noticed what Hazel had done with her laptop bag at the lodge.

And what about Tad, the IT guy? He had been trying to help her recover the data at the lodge before we arrived. Could he have succeeded? Maybe he had found the data she was looking for and had returned to the lodge with her laptop. Could they have met up again before she fell?

Nothing quite fit together or made sense.

Another thought began to form. Could Hazel have been self-dosing? What if she had opted to test the efficacy of the drug and its side effects on her own body?

I scoffed at myself.

That sounded like the plot of a movie. Alex had me streaming too many thrillers and espionage shows.

"Are you stuck in a loop, too?" Garrett asked as we approached Front Street. Sandwich board signs were propped on the sidewalks announcing ski week deals. People queued for hot off the grill sausages at the München Haus.

"Am I that obvious?" I thought back to my conversation with Hans.

"No, but I am. I have to come clean that some of the scenarios I'm working through in my head are pretty far-fetched." He yanked off his Nitro ski cap and stuffed it in his jacket pocket.

"Same." I pushed the button on the crosswalk. "The clinical trial feels like a key piece of this, doesn't it?"

"Yep. Too many coincidences. Everyone at the pub last night was also there at the time of her death. I don't like that. Not one bit."

"Agreed." We waited for a group of teens who must have just come from the *das Eis*, the ice cream shop. They were swapping tastes of their giant waffle cones as they crossed opposite from us. Alex and his friends frequented the hand-churned ice cream shop year-round. At the moment, the thought of anything cold in my body gave me shivers.

"And I don't like that my sister is caught up in this now." Garrett stepped off the curb. We crossed Front Street and turned toward Blackbird Island. "She's supposed to be taking a break from her grueling schedule. I don't want her trying to solve Hazel's murder or spending any extra time with those people. I'm not sure I trust a single one of them."

Garrett was starting to sound as paranoid as he'd been when he first arrived in Nitro, but I couldn't blame him.

There was a critical piece of the puzzle we were missing. We couldn't do much about that in the short term, but I had a list of questions for Leah, and I intended to keep an eye out for anyone from the hospital who might happen into Nitro.

Back at Nitro things were running smoothly in the tasting room. Not that I expected anything otherwise. There were a handful of customers in the front and at the bar, but our overflow areas were empty. I didn't think that would remain true for long as we were nearing happy hour and since the ski hill was closed for night skiing, we'd likely see an earlier crowd meander into the pub.

Garrett checked in with our staff, while I went to assess where things were at in the kitchen. Kat was loading the dishwasher.

"Hey, we heard the news." She twisted her curls into a messy bun and wiped her hands on a dish towel. "Are you guys okay? We heard that someone fell off the lift. I can't believe it."

I filled her in on Hazel's fall and the aftermath.

"That's so sad." Kat couldn't hide her emotion. Her voice cracked as she reached underneath the sink for dishwashing detergent. "She was just here last night. I didn't know her super well, but she was always so nice to me and left a big tip. I can't believe she's dead."

I consoled her with a hug. She had become much more than just a member of Nitro's staff. Kat was like a daughter or niece to me. When she had first come to Leavenworth, I hadn't been sure if she would stick around. She had come to the village on a whim and to follow her celebrity crush, who turned out to be a real ass. I wasn't sure if she was trustworthy when she had begged us for something—anything—she could do in exchange for a place to crash until she could get enough money for a train ticket home.

She had surprised me with her work ethic. Her desire to learn and grow had been evident almost from the minute we had offered her free room and board and a small salary in exchange for her help in the tasting room and at events.

As time had gone on, Kat had become an invaluable member of the team. We had raised her salary and given her more responsibilities. She had thrived at each new task we had assigned her, from obtaining her food handlers' and liquor licenses to learning the art of pouring a perfect pint and cleaning and managing Airbnb rentals. Lately she had expressed an interest in learning more about the craft. Garrett and I were eager to involve her in brew days and teach her the ropes. It felt like coming full circle. Otto had taken me under his wing, welcoming me to Leavenworth with open arms and passing on his wealth of expertise in the craft. Now I had a chance to do the same with Kat.

"Do you want to call it a night?" I asked her, offering her a napkin.

She blew her nose and shook her head. "No, I'm fine. I'd rather stay busy. It's just really terrible to think someone young like Hazel could fall on a fun afternoon of skiing and be dead."

"I know," I said in my most conciliatory tone. "It is terrible. I understand why you want to work, but if you change your mind, will you promise to let me know?"

Kat made an "x" over her heart. "I swear."

"Okay, on that note, how is the food situation for the dinner rush?" I surveyed the kitchen. Kat had obviously cleaned after lunch because there wasn't so much as a crumb or empty dish on the counter.

"I'm glad you asked, because we went through the entire pot of your goulash soup. People loved it." She opened the fridge. "I think there are only two cheese plates left. When they closed the ski hill we had a rush. I came in here to put together more cheese plates, but what should we do about the soup? Take it off the menu?"

"Let me see what I can scrounge up. I stocked up for the weekend, so I'm sure I can put together a couple of new specials for dinner."

"Don't you want to be with the Strongs?" She closed the refrigerator.

"Leah is at the hospital and Penny and Bruce are resting upstairs. I think the plan is to go to dinner at Der Keller later, but like you with wanting to work, cooking will help me get out of my head."

"Let me know if I can help." Kat picked up a stack of chilled pint glasses. "I'm restocking the bar, but since there's a lull for the moment, I'm happy to chop or dice or whatever you need."

"I'll holler. First, I have to get creative." I opened the commercial refrigerator. I had to give Mac credit for my tendency to keep my home and professional pantry and fridge well-supplied. When we were married Mac would often invite guests to dinner with little to no notice. He would call and tell me that the group of hop vendors in town for meetings at Der Keller were in need of a homecooked meal. I would acquiesce and quickly figure out what I could pull together. I remember the look of surprise on Garrett's face when he commented on Nitro's kitchen being the place to ride out a future zombie apocalypse and I had mentioned my history with Mac. Garrett had been appalled that Mac had resorted to such outdated gender roles in our relationship.

There was truth to that, but I also owned my role in our marriage. I had been so desperate for a family I overlooked a number of issues that I wouldn't today. I also enjoyed putting my culinary skills to the test. It was a fun challenge to peer into cupboards and come up with a dish that would be ready to serve within hours. I had honed my ability to infuse soups, stews, and pasta with flavor but without spending the entire day laboring over a hot stove.

Tonight called for comfort. Everyone coming to Nitro would want to process Hazel's death. Our tight-knit community would be rattled and the best gift I could offer was a warm bowl of soup and a listening ear.

I gathered onions, celery, and carrots for my base. In a large Dutch oven, I added a healthy glug of olive oil and even more importantly, our seasonal IPA. The veggies would sauté in the beer and oil mixture until they were tender. While they simmered, I grilled chicken sausages in a separate pan and set them aside to cool.

Next, I added chicken and vegetable stock, fresh herbs, and cheese tortellini. I chopped the sausages into bite-size pieces and tossed those into the soup. I brought the soup to a boil, covered it with a lid, and then turned the heat down to low.

I had roasted butternut squash and whole cloves of garlic a few days ago and had fortuitously saved the leftovers. I puréed them in a blender until the mixture was smooth and creamy and then incorporated that into the soup as well. For a final touch, I whisked in heavy cream and a big handful of spinach. A roasted butternut squash, sausage, and tortellini soup served with buttered whole grain bread and a pint should hit the mark for comfort food.

I still had time, so I decided to try a dessert. My chocolate peanut butter stout pretzel beer bars should hit the spot. Plus, they were a quick bake. I made the crust first by pulverizing pretzels and mixing them with melted butter and brown sugar. I pressed the grainy mixture into a long, greased baking pan and placed it in the oven to bake for ten minutes. The next layer of bars would be a chocolate stout mousse. I took a large package of imported German chocolate out of the cupboard and broke it into pieces. Then I added our chocolate stout, a pat of butter, and a splash of heavy cream to a saucepan and whisked them over medium-low heat. I stirred in chunks of German chocolate, vanilla bean paste, and confectioners' sugar.

The rich scent of chocolate enveloped the kitchen. I breathed in the sweet aroma as I whipped the remaining heavy cream until it formed soft, fluffy peaks like the snowdrifts outside. The trickiest part of assembling the mousse was folding the whipped cream into the melted chocolate. It had to be done in small batches so as not to deflate and remove all the air. I used a silicone spatula to scrape down the sides of the bowl into the center, flip the chocolate and cream, and then repeat the process.

A ding from the oven signaled that the pretzel crust was ready, so I removed it and set it on the counter to cool while I worked on the final layer for my bars. I wanted a crunchy peanut topping to finish off the dessert, so chopped the salted peanuts we served in the tasting room. I wanted to caramelize them to make it more like a brittle. I greased a baking sheet, spread out the chopped nuts, and then sprinkled them with coconut, oats, and brown sugar. I melted more butter and tossed everything together. It shouldn't take more than a few minutes for it to crisp up in the oven.

Once the pretzel crust cooled, I spread the luscious chocolate mousse over the top and placed it in the fridge to chill. My nut brittle was the trifecta of flavor and texture—crunchy, salty, and sweet. I generously sprinkled it on the mousse and sliced the bars into four-inch squares.

Baking didn't make me forget about Hazel's murder, but it had been the antidote I needed to clear my head. A little reprieve from the running loop of imagining her falling from the chair would hopefully allow me to be more critical in thinking through potential scenarios of who might have wanted to harm her.

TEN

PENNY AND BRUCE woke from their nap as I finished slicing the last of the chocolate peanut butter stout bars.

"The heavenly smell of whatever you're baking roused me from my rest," Penny said as she glanced around the kitchen in search of the aroma.

"Sorry, I didn't mean to disturb your slumber." I ran the knife under hot water.

She shook her head. "Oh, no, I read for a little while and might have dozed off for a minute, but after the accident earlier...well, you know, it was hard to sleep."

"That's why I was glad to have something to do. It took my mind off of things, at least a bit." I handed her a plate. "Care to give me some feedback on my dessert creation? Honest opinions only."

"It looks so decadent. What is the crust?" Penny examined the chocolate bar. "Cookies?"

"Pretzels."

"With a nut topping." She fanned her face. "Be still my beating heart and promise me that you won't let Bruce in the kitchen. This is his dream. If he gets his hands on these, I'm afraid he'll eat every last one."

I chuckled. "Where is he now?"

"He went to see if Garrett needed help. I tried to explain that Garrett has been successfully running the brewery without any input from his old dad, but Bruce likes to tinker, and I thought it would be nice if you and I had a minute to get to know each other better."

A wave of unfamiliar nerves rumbled through my stomach. I suddenly felt like a thirteen-year-old girl. What was wrong with me? I was a grown woman with a soon-to-be college student son, a mortgage, and a thriving business. I shouldn't be nervous speaking to Garrett's mom, and yet I couldn't calm the swirling feeling in my stomach.

Was this another sign that I was more serious about him than I had allowed myself to believe?

Why would my neck feel splotchy and hot if I didn't care about her opinion of me?

"That would be great," I said to Penny, hoping that she didn't notice. "Pull up a stool. Would you like a coffee to go with the bar? I just made a fresh pot."

"Dessert before dinner? This is vacation, right?" She scooted a barstool to the counter and sat while I poured us coffee.

"Garrett speaks so highly of you; I feel like I already know you." Penny cradled her ceramic mug, one of the holdover items from Tess's diner. "I can't tell you enough how grateful we all are for you. You've been a tremendous help and deserve credit for making Nitro a success."

Flames of heat rose on the base of my neck as I sat across from her. "I wouldn't say that. Garrett's beer has been solid from the start. I was worried at first because there's a big range when it comes to homebrewing and it's not always easy to make the shift from brewing as a hobby to a profession. In fact, most homebrewers fail."

"I'm curious, why did you take a chance on Garrett?" Her

tone was casual, but I wasn't sure how much of my history he had shared with his mom.

There was no secret about my breakup with Mac, but I couldn't tell if Penny was fishing for information or sincerely interested in my backstory. In the past I would have likely closed up and assumed the worst. That wasn't my journey anymore. I bought myself a minute to respond by taking a slow sip of coffee. "It was a rough time in my personal life, and it felt like opportunity came right when I needed it."

Penny listened with genuine interest, leaning her elbows on the counter and maintaining eye contact.

"Hans pushed me, too." I smiled at her as I took another drink of the dark roast. "I owe him for that. He was convinced that Garrett was the real deal. He was right."

"I think it's because you two complement each other so well." Penny took a bite of the bar. She closed her eyes and savored the flavors. "Wow, this is incredible and exactly my point. Chocolate and peanut butter and you and Garrett. Perfect matches."

Was she hinting at something more than our professional connection?

I shifted in my chair, unsure how much to share.

"I hope I'm not making you uncomfortable," Penny said, putting her coffee down and placing her hand on her cheek. "I understand that I'm biased as his mother, but I think Garrett is an extraordinary man and he went through so much before he moved here. We worried that Leavenworth was an escape for him. That he was going to shutter himself in up in the mountains. That's one of the reasons that Bruce and I initially discouraged him from taking over the inn, but now I see we were wrong. It's obvious that he's very connected to the community here and has a network of support, including you."

What did Penny mean about everything he had gone through?

89

She continued before I could ask. "It's a relief to see him happy. Bruce and I worried that he might not find happiness again. Garrett can have a tendency to withdraw and retreat. That was true when he was young. He was content to stay home and play board games with us or tinker with science kits in the garage over going to parties and football games. I didn't mind that, of course, but you know as a mother, we worry."

"Yeah." I took another sip of my coffee, thinking of Alex. "We're in the middle of touring colleges and there's part of me that is so excited for Alex to get to go experience the world on his own, but the other part of me is absolutely terrified. It went by so fast. It feels like yesterday that we were changing diapers and teaching him how to ride a bike and now I'm supposed to just let him go and make his own mistakes. It's rough."

She shook her head in sympathy. "I wish I could tell you the worry goes away as they enter adulthood, and it does to some extent, but the more accurate description is that it changes. I worry about Leah working too much and I worry about Garrett being alone and remote up here. Although now that we've met you and everyone in town, I feel better."

"Why did you think Garrett would close himself off here? I know a thing or two about that, but Garrett has never struck me as the type."

"I'm sure you know about his past and what happened with Halsey." She twisted her gold wedding ring as she spoke. "We didn't think he would get over it. Bruce was sure that the heart-break was going to crush him. He closed himself off. He wouldn't come to family dinners or vacations. Leah was the only person he would talk to and even then, she would coax him out for a coffee or lunch and he would stay for an hour, say very little, and then disappear again. I will say that's when he threw himself into brewing. I think brewing saved him."

My mouth went dry. I tried to swallow but couldn't. Drinking coffee didn't help loosen the tightness that was spreading down my throat. Who was Halsey? And why had Garrett never mentioned her? I replayed early conversations when we first met. He had said that he needed a break from the fast pace of the tech world in Seattle and that inheriting his great-aunt's estate had come at the right time. Never had he mentioned a failed love or any sort of trauma that had led him to Leavenworth.

Why had he never talked to me about any of this?

Sweat beaded on my forehead.

Penny leaned in. "Are you feeling okay, Sloan? You look a bit pale."

"I suddenly got a little dizzy. I think finally sitting down after everything that happened today has gotten to me." That was true, but what I didn't tell her was that my dizziness stemmed from the fact that her son hadn't been honest with me. Memories of catching Mac with beer wench rushed forward. Not that concealing his past was the same as Mac's infidelity, but it felt like a betrayal. I had confided in Garrett. He had been a solid place to land in those early days. But he didn't feel like he could reciprocate?

I had thought we were growing closer, but now everything I believed about our relationship was in question.

"I shouldn't be talking your ear off right now. You probably were getting ready to go home and take a break." Penny placed her hand on my arm. "You've been through a lot today. Resting helped calm me down a bit. I wonder if maybe you should do the same."

"That's a good idea." I stood and dumped the rest of my coffee in the sink. "I think I'll head home for a while and see if I can nap."

Penny offered me a soft smile. "Hopefully you'll feel up for joining us later. We're planning dinner at Der Keller at seven and would love to have you, but I completely understand if you just want to call it a night."

I mumbled something noncommittal and left. I didn't stop to check in with Kat or Garrett. I couldn't. I didn't trust what I might say.

Instead, I trudged through the snow and wandered home in a daze. Once I made it to the cottage, I flipped on the lights, locked the front door, fell onto the couch, and burst into tears. Uncontrollable sobs came in waves. I couldn't move. It felt like I was paralyzed, except for the heaves of my shoulders and the salty tears streaming down my cheeks. Some of my emotion was probably a pent-up reaction to Hazel's death, but it was also because of Garrett.

Aside from Hans, he was the person I trusted the most. It was almost unbelievable that he would have kept something that clearly had a major impact on his life from me. Was it because I was too reserved? I thought that meeting him had been part of what had opened me up. But maybe I was wrong.

Had I misread our friendship and connection?

Had I done something to make him think I wouldn't be able to offer a listening ear or a shoulder to cry on?

I wasn't sure how long I had been on the couch. It might have been an hour or four. A knock on the door forced me to grab a handful of tissues and try to soak up my tears.

In my blur of emotions, I had left my cell phone on the entry table by the front door. I glanced at it to check the time and saw that I had five missed calls from Garrett.

It was no surprise to find him standing at the door.

"Sloan, Sloan, listen, I'm sorry," he sputtered. "Can we talk, please? There's so much I need to say."

ELEVEN

GARRETT STOOD in the doorway with wide, pleading eyes. He must have noticed my tear-stained cheeks because he shook his head in disbelief and raised one hand like he was about to swear an oath. "Sloan, can I please come in? We need to talk. I know that my mom told you about Halsey, but I want to explain, okay?"

I stepped to the side to make space to let him in.

I wouldn't have done the same for Mac. I wasn't sure if that was a sign of personal growth or if I just really needed to hear the truth.

"Can I make you tea or something?" Garrett looked toward the kitchen. "I feel terrible. I didn't want it to come out like this."

"I don't understand," I said ignoring his offer and moving to the couch. "Your mom didn't tell me anything other than apparently a woman named Halsey broke your heart, and your entire family thought that you would never get over it and that it was a terrible idea for you to move here. I'm so confused why this never came up."

He slumped in a chair near the fireplace. "I know. It's a long story."

93

"A story you didn't feel like you could tell me?" I hoped that my tone didn't sound resentful. I didn't feel resentful. I felt confused as I looped back into my old pattern of blaming myself. Why hadn't Garrett trusted me? Had I been too closed off? Or was it that I was too needy?

"No, Sloan. No, no. It's not like that." He got up from the chair and opened the fireplace doors. Then he started stacking wood.

"What is it like, then? You know my past. You know how many people have betrayed me; this feels like a pattern I keep repeating." I pulled a blanket over my feet, wanting to disappear underneath it.

"Sloan, no, don't say that." He tossed a piece of wood in the pile near the hearth and turned to look at me. "This isn't about you. I promise you that much. This is one hundred percent about me."

"But it's never come up. I've never heard the name Halsey. You've never so much as hinted at having a painful past. You certainly never mentioned that being the reason for coming to Leavenworth. I don't get it."

He broke pieces of kindling that I kept near the fireplace. "Yeah, I know. I'm sorry. It was too hard at first. You were dealing with Mac and I was genuinely glad to have your input on Nitro. Remember how clinical and stark everything was? White walls. Nothing warm or welcoming. That's because that's how I felt inside. I wanted to lock myself into a sterile environment I could control."

He wasn't wrong about that. Nitro in its inception was basically a big warehouse with some brewing equipment, tables, and a bar. The bare, bright walls were glaring and non-descript. I remember feeling like I was walking into a clean room at a lab that first day.

"If you think about it, you've never heard me talk much

about Seattle. Not friends, not work, not much of anything." He opened the flue and reached for a box of fireplace matches. "There's a reason for that."

That was also true. I waited for him to say more.

He lit the fire and sat on the edge of the hearth. "You know, I've never had friends come visit. Why? Because I compartmentalized my life. There was the time before Leavenworth and then Leavenworth. I kept it that way on purpose. That's one of the many things I've appreciated about our friendship. I sensed that you knew I had my reasons to keep Seattle in the past. I thought that was why you never asked. It was like we had a mutual understanding."

A new wave of nausea came over me. He hadn't ever said more than a few words about Seattle and most of the time what he had said revolved around brewing in his garage. How had I been so oblivious? I prided myself on being able to read people. It was another skill I had mastered in foster care, but I had clearly missed the mark with Garrett.

"I can see you calculating in your head, Sloan. And even if you're not conscious of it, I know without a shred of doubt the reason you never tried to go deeper, press me for details, ask about old friends or lovers, was because at some level you knew I had a wound. You recognized your own wound in me."

Swallowing felt like there were dozens of glass shards lodged in my throat. "No, I didn't."

"You did." He flipped the matchbox as he spoke. "I know you did because I know you. And I've tried a few times to tell you the whole story and then we either were interrupted or I ran out of courage. My parents assumed you knew because all I do with them is talk about you."

"This doesn't make sense. We've had so much time alone. Brewing together, our trip to Wenatchee, date nights, working together every day. You've been a sounding board for me with everything I've gone through with Mac and with Alex. It feels awful that you didn't feel like I could be there for you."

"I know. I mean, I know you must feel like that, but it's not true. You have been here for me. I *do* feel like I can talk to you about anything." He tapped the matches on his forehead as if trying to punish himself. "I know. Like I said, I've tried to bring it up, and then I've stopped myself. It's not your fault for not asking. It's all mine."

I thought back to a handful of conversations when it seemed like Garrett had wanted to say more. At the time, I thought he was nervous about offering feedback on my relationship with Mac. I assumed he had wanted to tell me to kick Mac to the curb and forget about him for good, but didn't want to offend me. Instead, he had been trying to work up the courage to tell me about his past. How had I missed that?

"I should have been honest with you, especially now that we've grown closer. I care about you so much, Sloan, and I don't want to lose you. I had planned to tell you everything and then my family decided to finally show up, and I've been on edge for the last week because I had a feeling it was going to come up. I feel terrible for giving you even the tiniest reason to doubt my sincerity. I know what you've been through. I know that Mac shattered your trust and I guess since it didn't come up when we first met, I've been freaked out that I would do the same thing to you. It was like too much time had gone by and then bringing it up felt forced and fake and like I might ruin this good—this great—thing that we have, and now I've done that anyway." He hung his head and ran his fingers through his hair.

I curled my knees to my chest. "Are you in a space to share now?"

He sucked in his cheeks and gave me a slow nod. "Yeah. I wish I had talked about this sooner, but I was engaged when I was living in Seattle to a woman named Halsey."

His mom had told me some of that—not that he was engaged, but I didn't want to interrupt him.

"We met at work. She was in marketing so we didn't work directly together because the company was huge, but we saw each other at work functions. I was a lot younger then. I was only a few years out of college and it was common for everyone to go out for happy hour and drinks after work. She and I ended up seated next to each other, and we got to talking and hit it off. Things were really good and easy for the first couple of years that we dated. It was nice to have someone who understood the industry. We definitely had that in common. I wasn't really brewing at that stage. I was into the craft beer scene in Seattle and starting to dabble in homebrewing, but I didn't have my own equipment or anything at that point. I would go to brew-your-own workshops that a few of the pubs put on."

I nodded to let him know I was listening, but I couldn't help wonder if this background information about brewing was a stall tactic. What about a breakup could be so hard to talk about so many years later?

"Halsey was very social. She loved to party. We were in our twenties and making decent money. This was also before the Seattle real estate market exploded so we were doing fine financially. I'd never been a big partier. I don't even mean drinking heavily, although that too, but I didn't really do the party scene in high school or college. It's not my thing. I don't love making small talk with a bunch of drunk people. I'm happy to sit and sip an awesome craft beer and chat with friends, but at the time it seemed good that Halsey was forcing me out of my geeky shell. She was anything but nerdy. She loved the club scene and fashion. You know me with my style." He tapped his Nitro hoodie.

The fire glowed behind him, casting an auburn aura around him. It made him look softer and more vulnerable.

"In hindsight, I should have seen the signs." He exhaled like he was trying to rid himself of the memory.

"Are you sure you want to talk about this? It sounds like it's still tender."

"No, I'm sure." He sat up taller. "You deserve to know my full past if we have any hope for a future."

Was that true? We were both grown adults. I had a long-term marriage, a child, and an entire life before I met Garrett. He knew pieces of my story, but he didn't know every detail. How could he? And I wouldn't want that for him or for me. We had connected at a time when we were different people than we had been in our youth. Wasn't that a gift? Was I forcing him to reveal something he didn't want to?

I stopped him. "Honestly, I'm not sure that's true. You're afforded privacy about your past if it's not something you want to share with me. I think I was rattled and upset by the idea that you didn't feel comfortable talking to me about things that might be hard, but now as we're here discussing this, I don't want to pressure you into revealing details that you want to keep buried. I get that. And we are adults after all. We're not teenagers. My god, I *have* a teenager."

Garrett actually laughed for a second. "I still don't know how that's possible. I swear you could be Alex's big sister."

"That's not my point, though." I tucked the blanket tighter around my knees.

A flash of seriousness crossed his face. "I appreciate that but I do want to share this with you. It's hard to talk about it but it will feel like a relief. It's something that has been weighing on me." He let out a long sigh. "As I was saying, Halsey loved the party scene and dragged me to every work and non-work event she could. I went along with it for a while. Well, too long. It became a point of tension for us. I told her to go out on her own and I was happy hanging out alone or attending a brewing workshop. That's when things started getting bad, and it's still hard not to blame myself." His shoulders slumped.

I had a feeling I knew where this was going. Halsey must have met someone else while she was partying without Garrett. It gave me new insight into his kindness about Mac. He had been in a similar situation, although that thought also made it even harder to stomach the idea that he hadn't been willing to be open with me.

"Mom says that holding onto guilt doesn't serve anyone, but all these years later I can't escape it."

"Tell me more about that." I tried to tap into some of the leading questions that Sally used to ask me in our therapy sessions. I understood where he was coming from. Mac might have been the person who strayed in our marriage, but I spent a lot of time blaming myself, wondering what I could have done to stop it.

"Because she wouldn't be on the streets today if it weren't for me." The tone of his voice was so low I wondered if I heard him wrong.

On the streets?

I sat up and blinked twice.

"Wait, on the streets?"

He dug his fingers into his temples. "Yeah. She's been living on couches and in alleyways ever since her addiction got out of control."

This wasn't where I had thought the conversation was going.

"Oh, Garrett, I'm so sorry." I kicked the blanket off my feet.

He forced a half smile. "It started with the heavy drinking. I should have paid more attention. I should have intervened sooner, but like I said, our whole crowd would binge a bunch of happy hour drinks and show up to work the next morning fine. Except for Halsey. The binging sessions went longer and longer. We were living together and there were a lot of nights when she wouldn't come home at all. She'd stumble into the office the next day wearing the same clothes and looking wrecked. That lasted for a while. We got into some wicked fights—I mean, not physical or anything, but I wanted her to stop drinking. It had changed. It wasn't fun any longer. I tried to tell her that her drinking was interfering with work and with our relationship, but she wouldn't listen. She pulled farther away. She started crashing on friends' couches most of the week. When she would show up at our place she was barely able to stand and was completely incoherent. It was about that time that I realized she was drinking in the morning, too. I found her pouring vodka into her to-go coffee cup and then getting ready to drive to the office. That was my limit. That's when I kicked her out."

Saying it out loud seemed to open the floodgates. He continued to tell me everything, barely taking time to breathe between sentences. I let him continue. It felt necessary. Cathartic. Like a release that had been dammed up for too long.

"She didn't seem to care. That should have been another huge red flag. She laughed it off, packed her things, and left. We saw each other around the office some. It was obvious that she was drunk. Not just to me. To everyone. HR intervened. They organized treatment for her, secured temporary leave, and tried to support her in the process. I didn't hear from her at all during rehab. I sent encouraging notes and offered to attend sessions, whatever she needed or that her therapists and doctors recommended. No one ever took me up on those offers. I guess that's another piece of my guilt. I could have done more. I should have done more."

I wanted to hug him. He looked consumed by his guilt.

He pressed his fingers into his temples. "Maybe if I had just shown up at the rehab center, it would have shown her that she did have people who cared about her and wanted to be there for her. I didn't. I did the minimum."

I knew he needed to keep talking, but it was nearly impossible not to go to him to comfort him. Instead, I nodded and murmured encouragement for him to continue.

"She came back to work after rehab." He reached for another piece of wood for the fire, lost in his own memories. "I thought she had changed. I thought she had kicked the habit. We had one really good lunch. It was the best I had seen her in years. It felt like the Halsey I had fallen in love with. She told me that rehab had been hard, but that she was committed to making it work and that she understood why I had kicked her out. It felt like a shift, you know?"

I nodded. "But it wasn't, was it?"

His eyes welled with tears. I reached out for his hand, unable not to offer him a tender touch.

"Within a couple of weeks, she was drinking again. I could tell right away. She had those glassy eyes and frizzy hair and bright red cheeks. I did a bunch of research into relapses and learned they were common. I wasn't sure what to do from a professional position. People at the office hadn't noticed her behavior, or if they had they weren't saying anything. After wavering, I decided I needed to report her to HR. That seemed like the best path to getting her help again." His voice caught as he continued. "She didn't show again. Not a single day after my meeting with HR. I still wonder if she knew somehow."

"What happened then?"

"I heard from a mutual friend where Halsey had been staying that they had asked her to leave. Apparently, she started using heavier drugs. That was their breaking point. After that, I lost track of her. Every once in a while a colleague or our old happy hour crew would hear from her, usually because she was looking for money or a place to crash. I always heard that she was in bad shape and almost unrecognizable. I thought people were exaggerating. And then one night I was on my way home and walked past a group of tweakers who asked me for cash. It took me a minute to realize that Halsey was one of them." He gulped air like he was desperate for oxygen and wiped a bead of sweat from his forehead with his sleeve. "The people who had seen her weren't exaggerating. She was gaunt. I mean like a toothpick. I could have pushed her over with one finger. Her skin was pocked with red, oozing sores. Her hair was stringy and thin. But the image that still haunts me is her eyes. They were vacant. I get that she was probably high at the time so didn't recognize me, but I tried to break through the drug haze and it was impossible. She was gone."

"Oh, Garrett, my heart is with you." I let out a long sigh. "It must have been so painful to watch someone you loved and cared about go through such self-destruction."

He bobbed his head in agreement but didn't speak. I had a feeling that it was because he was close to tears.

I pressed my hands to my cheeks. "I'm glad that you felt safe to tell me."

"I'm sorry for keeping this in." His voice was shaky. "I'm sorry for not telling you sooner. I never saw her again after that, but I used to wander the downtown Seattle streets looking for her. Part of me believed that if I could find her I could help her, but I realize now that she was already gone. It was a rough couple of years for me. Then when Aunt Tess died and I learned that I had inherited the building, it felt like divine intervention. Moving to Leavenworth was a clean break. It took a few months but I got over the urge to look down alleyways and dark corners for her. I stopped dreaming about her. I wasn't perseverating on her every minute like I had been in Seattle. That's the weird thing. I wasn't in love in her anymore. I'd fallen out of love with her long before I kicked her out. It was the guilt of not doing more, of wondering if I had done something—anything—else that she wouldn't be living on the streets now."

"You know that we can't change other people, addiction or no addiction, right? We are only responsible for ourselves."

He looked up and held my gaze. His eyes were glossy. "Yeah,

Sloan, I think I'm finally starting to believe that, thanks to you, which is another reason I'm devastated that I didn't tell you this sooner."

"I'm glad you told me now." I got up and went to sit on the hearth with him. The heat from the fire warmed my back as Garrett collapsed into my arms.

CHAPTER
TWELVE

WE SAT on the hearth together. Garrett released the tears he'd been holding in and I decided in that moment not to repeat the mistakes of my past, of closing off and building a fortress around my heart. The sting of Garrett not sharing this information with me sooner was already beginning to dull. I could make a choice to stay angry. I could decide to shut him out and leave behind any nagging worries about trust. Or I could be gentle with myself and with Garrett. I could meet him with compassion, which is what I opted to do.

"Sloan, you're being so great about this." He reached for my hand.

I linked my fingers through his and massaged his thumb. "Because I care about you and watching Halsey slip deeper into her addiction left a wound in your heart. You know my history with that. I can tell you from experience that it hasn't always worked out well for me, so I want to try this differently with you."

"I appreciate your honesty and I can tell you that there's nothing else I've kept from you." He made a weird face. "Well, that's not quite true. There is one other thing."

"There is?" My heart rate sped up.

He released his clasp and cradled my chin in his hand. His touch almost burned with intensity. I could smell his aftershave and sense the pull of his body toward mine. "Sloan Krause, I think I'm falling for you—hard."

He leaned in and kissed me with such softness, I found myself wanting more. My body pulled toward his. The anticipation was electric. His lips were like butter. I could taste a hint of something minty on his breath.

"Sloan," he groaned with desire.

At that moment his phone buzzed with an incoming text, causing both of us to startle. He hesitated, torn between ignoring the message and giving in to the moment.

"Go ahead," I said softly, pulling away. "You should see what it is." I tried to steady my breathing. The chemistry between us had already been palpable, but our conversation and deepening connection had made it explosive.

A flash of disappointment crossed his face as he reached into his pocket to check the message. "Damn, bad timing. Everyone is heading to Der Keller. They really want you to come, but only if you're up for it."

"I'm up for it." I laughed. "I think we could both probably use a beer, right?"

"Only if you're sure." He sounded hesitant.

"I would tell you if I wasn't."

He kissed me one more time and then snuffed the fire out. He closed the screen and reached for my hand to pull me to my feet.

We walked hand in hand through the festive village. Snowflake lights hung from balconies and twinkled in the oak trees. The high school jazz band was playing a free concert in the gazebo. The smell of roasted nuts and sweet mulled wine drifted from the streetside stalls, adding to the festive atmosphere. Families huddled together sipping warm drinks while listening to the young musicians.

The soft glow of lanterns and twinkling lights from the surrounding buildings served as our guide as we continued through the enchanting winter wonderland.

Der Keller sat like a shiny beacon at the end of Front Street. The biergarten was packed with snow lovers seated at the outdoor gas fire tables and heat lamps, sharing pints and schnitzel. Bundled twinkle globe lights and blue and white checkered flags were strung from the scalloped trim on the building's roofline.

The Der Keller crest, two lions waving German flags, was painted on the white exterior wall, welcoming guests inside.

Before going into the restaurant, Garrett stopped me. "I know we were interrupted, but I hope we can pick up where we left off soon."

"Me too."

"Look at the lovebirds." April Ablin's nasal voice killed the mood. "Are you coming in or are you just going to stand there with those dewy looks on your faces?" She held the door open. "You're letting the cold in."

"After you." Garrett motioned for me to go before him.

"What fortunate timing to bump into you," April said as she unbuttoned her coat to reveal her cleavage. "I suppose you're here for the announcement?"

"Announcement?" I looked to Garrett to see if he knew what April was talking about.

"Yes, the BioGold clinical trial announcement. Jerry reached out to the chamber to let me know that they've made a radical treatment breakthrough and have decided spontaneously to announce their initial findings here in Leavenworth. It should be great press for the village." She pointed to her plunging red, yellow, and black checkered barmaid dress with layers of frilly tulle. She had really outdone herself tonight, adding tiny German flags to the end of her braids. Even her eyeshadow was done in red, black, and yellow. "Didn't you get my email? I made it crystal clear that anyone in attendance tonight should arrive in traditional German attire. We have an image of Bavarian culture that we must uphold. Our public expects it."

What I wanted to say was that I doubted April's dress was going to hold.

"They're making an announcement about the trial tonight?" Garrett sounded skeptical. "Doesn't the timing seem unprofessional and downright cruel, given that one of their team members died earlier?"

April threw her arms up. "Don't ask me. I'm sure they'll offer a tribute and a moment of silence for her. Their research is going global. This is a win for the village. Do you understand the enormity of this moment? Leavenworth is going to be on the world stage in the medical community and beyond." She spotted a reporter and adjusted her dress again. Before sashaying over to the small group of press, she pointed to the far end of the restaurant. "Since you refuse to wear the village uniform, at least have the decency to hide in the back when they start to film."

Garrett and I watched as she inserted herself into the middle of the group. Sure enough, there were probably eight to ten reporters from various Seattle and Spokane news outlets with their cameras aimed at Dr. Sutton, Shep, Ren, and Jerry from BioGold.

"This feels really weird," Garrett said.

Neither of us realized there was someone behind us until they responded to Garrett's comment.

"Thanks for saying that out loud, man. It's really gross even for this self-absorbed bunch." We turned to see Tad, the IT guy from the hospital. He may have been speaking to us, but his eyes were laser-focused on Jerry. "I can't believe they called a press conference. Tonight. At a pub. Hazel is dead and no one seems to care."

"We care," I said. "I'm so sorry. Were you and Hazel close?"

My question made him tear his eyes away from Jerry. I followed his gaze toward the bar where German memorabilia was on full display—beer awards, German flags, posters, and Otto and Ursula's collection of pewter beer steins. Beertenders in traditional *Trachten* shirts and black suspenders were pouring pints and taster trays.

But Tad wasn't paying attention to any of it.

He rocked on his heels as he spoke like he was trying to soothe himself. "Hazel was great. She was great. Most doctors treat those of us in IT like we're second-class citizens. Not Hazel. She would go out of her way to check in with me. She would bring us coffee, and always thanked me for helping fix her laptop."

That sounded like my impression of Hazel.

"She didn't deserve this," he sneered.

Garrett caught my eye and raised one brow. "Deserve what?"

"Them." Tad glared in the direction of Ren and Jerry. He looked like he was about to say more when Dr. Sutton tapped her microphone.

"Everyone, if I could please get your attention, I'd like to introduce myself. I'm Dr. Sutton of Leavenworth Community Hospital." She ran her hands over her white physician's coat that she wore over a pair of flared slacks and a silky tangerine blouse. "I know the vast majority of you already know me and know about the amazing community resources available at the hospital. We reached out to the Krause family about hosting a quick press conference here tonight because we are committed to this community and want you to be the first to know about some groundbreaking research that has happened right around the corner."

There was a handful of murmurs from diners at tables and booths.

I wanted to ask Tad about Hazel's laptop, but Dr. Sutton

continued, pushing a pair of oversized peach glasses to the tip of her nose. "I'm sure you weren't anticipating cameras at your evening meal, and I promise we won't take up too much of your time and let you get back to your delicious dinners. The news that we're about to share simply couldn't wait. However, before we make our announcement, we ask you to join us in a moment of silence for our beloved colleague Hazel Andres, who died in a tragic skiing accident."

A hush fell over the restaurant and bar. Not a single fork clinked. No one so much as whispered as we collectively held space for Hazel's memory.

Garrett reached for my hand and looped his fingers through mine. Honoring Hazel brought another wave of emotion to the surface. It had only been a few hours ago that we'd found her body on the ski hill. It felt like days had passed.

Dr. Sutton resumed her speech. "Thank you for that. We intend to set up a scholarship in Hazel's name. We wouldn't be making the announcement we are tonight without her invaluable input. She might not be here with us physically but she is here in spirit. Our team will be brainstorming additional ways to honor her research and legacy in the days to come."

The restaurant remained silent.

"To Hazel." Dr. Sutton reached for a pint and raised it.

Everyone raised their glasses too, but no one spoke.

"This feels gross," Garrett whispered. "Shouldn't they have waited at least a day before making the announcement?"

"I would have." I nodded in agreement.

Dr. Sutton returned her glass to the bar without taking a drink. She began by thanking the press, the chamber, the mayor, and a long list of community partners.

"Could it have to do with the research?" I asked Garrett, trying to make sense of the bizarre press conference myself. "I don't know enough about how clinical trials work, but maybe once you have data you want to be the first to release it in case there are similar trials going on simultaneously?" I couldn't think of any other reason for the push to host a press conference.

"That could be," Garrett agreed.

"Now for the real reason we're here," Dr. Sutton motioned for Jerry to step closer to her. "Our research has been funded by BioGold in Seattle and Jerry, let me be the first person to thank you for your generous support. This partnership has led to one of the greatest treatment breakthroughs in over four decades. We are standing in front of you tonight to announce that our clinical trial has completely cured every participant with no adverse effects."

This news sent a round of chatter throughout the bar.

"The results have greatly exceeded our expectations and will have far reaching impacts on future treatments and break-throughs for similar disease systems." She paused as if expecting applause.

Shep, who was still wearing his scrubs, stepped forward and clapped. He intentionally flexed his muscular arms as he encouraged diners to join in.

Dr. Sutton took a bow. "Thank you. Thank you."

"Are you getting April vibes from her?" Garrett asked. "She seems to be taking most of the credit for herself."

Jerry raised a finger. "If I may add, Dr. Sutton is being humble in what she's sharing with you. The kind of results we've seen for this clinical trial is likely going to have Dr. Sutton in the running for a Nobel Peace Prize."

The crowd didn't need any encouragement to clap this time.

Garrett shrugged. "Okay, maybe I'm seeing this wrong. It sounds like this is a big deal."

I nodded, but my gut instinct said otherwise.

"Why don't you tell them what really went down?" Tad yelled, interrupting Jerry's speech.

Reporters swiveled their cameras onto him.

Dr. Sutton recoiled. She brushed her shirt and spoke with a calculated calm. "Our IT department, like the rest of our staff, has been overworked trying to verify the results. Tad, I know you've put in long, long hours and we so appreciate your piece in this." She clapped for him.

Jerry ducked away from the microphone.

Tad was only a few feet away from us.

Dr. Sutton invited April and members of the city council up to the microphone to speak.

Jerry threw his arm around Tad. "Hey, I owe you a beer."

"A beer isn't going to shut me up, man," Tad snarled. "I don't know how, but I know you killed her."

Jerry whisked Tad up to the bar.

"Did you hear what I heard?" Garrett asked.

"Tad just accused Jerry of murdering Hazel." I blinked twice.

"Things are about to get interesting." Garrett's eyes drifted to the bar, where Tad threw Jerry's arm off him. He stabbed Jerry in the chest with his index finger.

I couldn't hear what he was saying over the dining noise and music that had returned.

"Should we go find my folks?" Garrett asked, pointing to a booth on the other side of the restaurant.

"Why don't you go join them? I'll head up to the bar for a second and grab us drinks."

"And eavesdrop on Jerry and Tad's conversation?"

"As a partial owner of Der Keller, I can grab drinks from the bar faster." A blur of colorful waitresses in *dirndl* dresses balancing trays of beer passed by us. "See, that proves my point."

"Sure." Garrett gave me a knowing smile. "Take your time, though."

April posed for pictures that no member of the press seemed to be requesting as I passed by. Dr. Sutton, Shep, and

Ren were deep in conversation. Were they trying to get their stories straight about what happened to Hazel?

Why was Jerry the person trying to appease Tad?

Questions assaulted my brain.

I barely noticed that Mac was blocking my way to the bar.

"What gives, Sloan? Are you trying to dodge me?" Mac's blond hair glowed under the bar light. Since our separation he had been taking better care of himself. He had slimmed down and started drinking less. It was good to see him investing in his own health and well-being.

"No, sorry. I was in my head," I answered truthfully.

He reached out to comfort me. His response was almost automatic. Cellular memory from spending so many years together. "Hans and Alex told me about Hazel. I'm sorry."

Never would I have imagined that I would appreciate my friendship with Mac on that fateful day I'd found him with his pants around his ankles in the brewery. The evolution of our relationship was another piece of my personal growth that I took pride in. Mac deserved credit, too. He had spent the past couple of years doing some serious self-reflection. I think we had both come to the realization that we were better as friends. Yet there was no denying our connection, especially when it came to Alex.

Mac hadn't always been a great husband, but he was a committed and involved dad. Alex was living proof that when it came to parenting, we were great partners.

I had friends who hated their exes and refused to be in the same room together. That wasn't the case with me and Mac. It had been awkward at the beginning, but I truly cared for him and we had a shared goal of wanting to make things as smooth and normal as possible for Alex. I never worried about Mac throwing me under the bus. I was confident that he would back me up when it came to parenting decisions and I would do the same for him.

Sometimes I wanted to pinch myself. I almost couldn't believe that we had found a way to build a new family dynamic in divorce. It helped that we also had the support of the rest of the Krause family.

"How's Alex doing?" I watched Mac carefully. He had a terrible poker face.

"He's okay. Shaken, like the rest of us." Mac moved out of the way for a server. Der Keller's staff embraced the family's German heritage with their blue and white *Trachten,* lederhosen for the male staff, and dirndls and blue and white checked aprons for the women. "I can't get over the hospital staff holding a press conference tonight. Since Hazel is the person who arranged it, I assumed they would cancel."

"Hazel organized the press conference?"

Mac nodded and moved behind the bar. "Yeah. She called yesterday. The events team passed her on to me because she was having a hard time securing a venue."

None of this matched what April had told me or what Dr. Sutton had said. I followed after him, eager to hear more.

"She said she had breaking, important information about the clinical trial that needed to go public." He held a pint glass to the light to make sure it was free of any spots before pulling a pint. "She asked about using the event space, but we already have a bachelorette party booked there."

"Did she use those exact words—*needed to go public?*" I asked.

Mac nodded, tilting the pint glass under the tap handle. "Yep. I got the sense that she was almost desperate. I asked her why they weren't doing the press conference at the hospital and she said she couldn't, but didn't elaborate on why. Anyway, once I asked her a few more questions it was pretty evident that all she needed was a public space for about fifteen minutes. I told her she could do it at the bar and that we could give her a mic and reserve three or four of the bar tables for an hour. I wasn't going to charge her anything."

Why would Hazel have needed a public space? Something didn't add up.

"When Hans and Alex told me about her accident, I had our event team call the hospital. I assumed they would cancel. I didn't want to set up the mics and reserve the bar tables, but apparently, Dr. Sutton wanted to proceed. It is amazing that they've found a cure here in Leavenworth."

"Yeah."

"You have that look on your face, Sloan."

"What look?"

"*The* look." Mac scrunched his forehead. "You think something is up, don't you?"

"I don't know yet." That was partially true. I had made a promise to Chief Meyers and while Mac and I had come to a mutual understanding, he had never been the model of discretion. I didn't want to divulge anything that might interfere with her investigation since everyone seemed to be under the impression that Hazel's death had been an unfortunate accident.

One of the servers needed Mac's help with an order. "Be careful, Sloan," he cautioned as he got pulled away.

"I will." That wasn't a lie. I had no intention of putting myself in harm's way. However, I noticed that Tad and Jerry were still arguing at the opposite end of the long bar. I used the opportunity to pour a round of drinks and listen in to their conversation.

"I warned you," Tad said to Jerry, his face etched with anger. "Nothing is ever deleted. I'm going to find it and then you are going to pay for what you've done."

"That's not going to happen, son." Jerry squeezed Tad's shoulder in such a way that to anyone passing by it would look like a friendly gesture. I saw Tad wince and grit his teeth in response to Jerry's attempt to pacify him.

Tad threw Jerry's hand off and got up, nearly knocking over his bar stool. "This isn't over."

Jerry's tone was condescending and cold. "It is."

I hadn't finished pouring drinks. "I'll be back in just a minute to finish these," I said to one of the beertenders. Then I hurried to catch up with Tad before he left.

I caught him at the front door.

He stuffed stray hairs into his beanie cap and zipped up his coat.

"We didn't get to finish our conversation before the press conference started," I said. "I wanted to ask you more about Hazel."

"What about her?" He stared out at the patio like he was looking for someone.

"A couple of things. First, you had her laptop, right? Did you find anything on it?"

"I have it, yeah." He didn't elaborate.

I tried a different approach. "You just made it sound like you think there was more to her accident. I've been wondering the same thing."

"There was. She was killed and one of them did it." He didn't hesitate in his response. "I have to find the proof."

"What sort of proof?"

"Her digital footprint." He took a defensive posture and frowned deeply. "They all have such inflated egos. They think they can't get caught, but here's the thing, tech guys like me, we know all of their secrets. *All* of them."

"And you think their secrets have something to do with Hazel's death. Have you spoken with Chief Meyers?"

"Not yet. I have to find proof first."

"I think the police will want to assist if you really believe that there's digital proof. My question is proof of what?"

His eyes bulged. "You don't know? I thought she told you."

"Told me what?"

"It's a lie. They faked the numbers. The data is false. The drug doesn't work. It's a failure. Hazel knew it and was planning to come forward with the real data, which is why they killed her first."

CHAPTER
FOURTEEN

Hearing Tad's theory wasn't a complete shock, but even still I gasped and recoiled slightly.

If he were right and Hazel had found proof that the drug had failed, that gave everyone associated with the clinical trial a motive to kill her. Everything that I had learned and observed thus far lined up with that theory. Hazel had been acting so panicked about losing her flash drive at Nitro last night. What if the flash drive contained the real data?

It would also explain why Dr. Sutton, Jerry, and the rest of the research team had rushed to make the announcement tonight. Although I still was confused about Shep and Ren's connection to the BioGold trial. Ren had mentioned something about patient care. As a nurse, what was his role? And Shep had made it clear that he wasn't involved with the research at all. Then why were both the nurse and anesthesiologist constantly hanging around with Dr. Sutton and Jerry?

Would any of these healthcare providers who had sworn an oath to save lives have killed Hazel? That seemed far-fetched.

"I'm going to go to my office now." Tad used all of his weight to push open the arched wooden door, allowing a blast of cold air inside. "I have to get to the servers before they find a workaround. I'm sure that Jerry is calling in support from BioGold. They've got a team of tech staff. If I could only find Hazel's research notes."

"You really need to let the police know," I insisted.

"There's no time." His tone was harsh and filled with intensity. "You can tell them, but I have to get to the hospital right now. Jerry's a smart guy. He's evil, but he's calculating. He didn't outright threaten me, but I know he's going to seize every piece of material at the hospital in connection with the clinical trial. He told me so a minute ago. BioGold is in this for the money and they aren't going to stop until every single trace of Hazel's data is permanently erased."

Alpine air seeped through the door as he took off in a sprint.

The stakes were too high not to involve Chief Meyers. I called her cell. She didn't answer, so I left a detailed message explaining everything Tad had told me and that she could find him at the hospital. He could be in danger. What if Jerry wanted him at the hospital? Maybe Jerry already had BioGold staff waiting for Tad.

The more time I spent thinking about the investigation, the more convinced I was that Hazel had been killed. If she had uncovered proof that BioGold had falsified their research, the implications were huge. It would also explain finding her bag near the ski lift. The killer must have been looking for her laptop. When they realized it wasn't in the bag, they tossed it and took off.

Tad was convinced that Jerry had killed her, but what about the other doctors? Were they part of the conspiracy to announce a breakthrough that was actually a dead end? That didn't make sense. Wouldn't they lose future credibility when it eventually came out that the drug was a failure?

I didn't know enough about the process. Maybe it would take years for the truth to come to light and by that time they would already be established in the field. Or the other possibility was that Jerry could be blackmailing or threatening them.

I went to the bar to finish pouring drinks and then joined everyone at the table. Not surprisingly, the talk at the table was centered on Dr. Sutton's announcement.

"Sloan, can you believe ze great news?" Ursula said, making room for me next to her. "A medical advancement in Leavenworth. I never would have imagined it."

Garrett caught my eye across the table. I could tell he didn't want to get into a conversation about what we knew. I gave him a nod of acknowledgment and set the tray of drinks in the middle of the table. "Is everyone ready for another round?"

"I don't know what they put in the water up here in the mountains, but every beer that we've sampled has been better than the last," Penny said, helping herself to a classic German Kolsch.

"Dis we cannot tell you," Otto replied with a twinkle in his eyes. "It is our secret."

I hadn't seen Leah since Hazel's accident. She sat across the table from me, running her index finger around the rim of her pint glass in a continuous circle. I didn't want to make things worse by bringing up Hazel, but not checking in with her felt weird, too.

Bruce solved my dilemma for me. "Leah, you started to tell us about what you heard at the hospital before they made the announcement."

She looked up from her drink and stared at her father like he was speaking German. It took her a second to process his question before she responded. I was familiar with the out-of-body feeling that came with a shock like the one Leah had experienced earlier. "When I got there they wouldn't let me be involved. I understand that technically it's hospital policy, but I was the physician on the scene so I feel like they could have made an exception. They claimed it's because I'm a resident."

"What could you have done, honey?" Penny asked gently.

"Likely nothing. It would have been nice to speak with the attending physician. Often they'll ask for insight from the emergency team. The attending declined." She raised her hands in a helpless shrug.

"Maybe it's for the best," Bruce added. "You've already been through a lot."

Leah nodded but her facial expression remained uncertain. "It felt off."

"Off?" Garrett held his beer to his lips.

"For the last three hours, I've been playing it over and over again in my head." Leah caught Penny's pained grimace. "No, not because I'm distraught or anything, Mom. I've called deaths before. Don't get me wrong, it's never pleasant and since I had spent the day with Hazel this one hits harder, but it's more than that. The ER was locked down. Staff and a huge team of what appeared to be support staff surrounded the entrances. No one was allowed access to the operating room."

"Is that normal?" I asked.

"Not really." She stretched her neck from side to side. "We've gone on lockdown before at OHSU for threats. It felt like that. I'm not sure why. It wasn't police presence, which is usually what happens in a lockdown situation. This was the internal hospital staff. I'm sure they were given direction not to speak with anyone because I tried to get information from the charge nurse and a couple of other doctors and they responded with the same phrase, 'I'm not at liberty to share any details about the patient.'"

"Patient privacy laws, maybe?" Garrett suggested.

"Yes. HIPAA laws apply in every hospital setting. They don't typically apply to someone who has been part of the care team."

Penny sighed. "I suppose you aren't a staff member though."

"That's true. I can't explain it, but my best description is that it felt off. The only thing I can come up with is that the staff were on high alert because they knew they were about to make the announcement about the clinical trial." Leah didn't sound like she believed it.

Our server interrupted the conversation to take our orders. After he left, the conversation shifted to Der Keller's history. Otto and Ursula launched into delightful stories about their first ventures into craft brewing.

"You remember when you put ze entire bundle of rosemary in zat batch, Otto?" Ursula wagged her finger in her husband's face. "I told him zat you only need a tiny pinch of rosemary, but he wasn't paying attention and dumped a garden's worth of herbs in ze brew."

Otto threw his head back and laughed. "Ja, ja. It was ze worst beer I ever made."

"But you drank it." Ursula pointed to the wall of extensive medals and awards that they had accumulated over the years. "Zis is ze number one rule in brewing. You have to drink it."

Penny laughed. "Well, I'm happy to drink this."

I was glad for Leah's sake that the topic had lightened. When Garrett and I had time alone later, I had a feeling he would want to loop her in on what we had learned. Her instincts about the hospital's response after Hazel's death lined up with Tad's theory. I hoped that Chief Meyers would check on him soon.

The hospital was a busy place, but if Jerry or one of the clinical team had killed Hazel there was a chance that they could kill again.

I got wrapped up in a debate between Otto and Ursula about who could do the chicken dance better. They playfully bickered for five minutes until they finally got up from the table to demonstrate their dance moves. When the waitstaff noticed what was happening, they cranked up the polka tunes on the overhead speakers and everyone in the restaurant clapped along as the Krauses looped arms and did a little spin through the dining room.

They were my role models for aging. Otto tinkered with the brite tanks and came in to brew with the team at least once a week. Ursula was less mobile but managed a daily walk through the village and baked homemade German chocolate cupcakes for Alex's entire soccer team. Their bones and joints might have been less flexible. They didn't let that stop them. They danced like they were in their teens with bright smiles and radiant eyes.

If I could inherit anything from the Krauses, I hoped it was their zest for fully living in the moment and embracing the now.

They returned to the table with flushed cheeks as our dinner was delivered. The rest of the meal was enjoyable. Penny and Bruce gave us a glimpse into Garrett and Leah's childhood, including the origin of Garrett's love of punny T-shirts.

"He made his first shirt in the fifth grade with Sharpies," Penny said with a laugh. "Do you remember the pun?"

Garrett shook his head. "I don't think so."

"You were obsessed with dinosaurs then."

"Now that I remember."

"You got an old white T-shirt and drew a T-rex with a shopping cart and then wrote 'I love dino-store' on the bottom. Your dad and I were impressed."

Garrett chuckled. "I was ahead of my time."

Our food was delivered and everyone enjoyed a traditional German feast and lighter conversation. I couldn't stop thinking about Hazel and whether she might have learned something about the clinical trial that made her a target. I tried to stay present in the conversation, but I found my thoughts continually drifting back to the image of her lifeless body on the ski hill. It made me even more resolved to figure out who had killed her.

CHAPTER
FIFTEEN

AFTER DINNER, Otto and Ursula invited Penny and Bruce on a tour of the brewery and bottling facilities. We agreed to reconnect later at Nitro, but instead of going there first, Leah asked if we minded taking a quick detour to the hospital.

"You read my mind." I filled her and Garrett in on my conversation with Tad.

"See, I knew it. My intuition was right. Why would the staff have closed off the exits and not allowed anyone in that wing after they brought Hazel's body back from the slope?" Leah asked as we approached the wall of Der Keller merchandise at the front of the restaurant.

Merch was Mac's specialty. From hats, T-shirts, and sweatshirts to stickers, bottle openers, and sunglasses, he would slap the Der Keller logo on just about anything. And I had to credit him, because rarely did a customer leave the pub without a Der Keller beanie or engraved pint glass. Recently he had partnered with a couple of local artists to create sketches of Icicle Ridge and the ski hill. He had turned their illustrations into a colorful outdoor gear line for Der Keller. I always grinned when I spotted someone sporting one of the trucker hats or ski caps in the village. It was good see Mac putting his skills to use.

We grabbed our coats from the repurposed ski racks near the front door and bundled up for the short walk to Leavenworth Community Hospital.

"Did Hazel have her laptop bag with her when you were skiing?" I asked looking out to the bustling winter beer garden where conversation and laughter mixed with clinking glasses.

"No, she left it in a locker in the ski rental shop," Leah replied. "Why?"

"I think someone stole it," I said.

"I wouldn't doubt it. I don't trust any of the BioGold team. They're hiding something," Leah said as she tugged on a pair of striped fingerless gloves. "I don't know what, but I'm sure they're covering up something."

"How does the research tracking process work?" Garrett held the door open for us. "Did Hazel happen to talk to you about her role in the trial when you were skiing?"

"I don't know the specifics of this trial. I can ask my attending at OHSU. I know there are literally dozens of trials running at OHSU right now. Some of them are big and some have less than ten or twelve participants," Leah explained as we left the picturesque pavilion and turned onto Front Street. "Hazel didn't say much. She kept talking about needing to blow off steam. She was flying down the hill. She mentioned wanting to get nervous energy out of her body before tonight. She never said anything about calling a press conference, though."

We passed Front Street Park where kids were sledding and having snowball wars while their parents huddled in the gazebo drinking hot chocolate. The band had finished their set, but a few music students lingered with their string and wind instruments. They belted out a rendition of Louis Armstrong's "What a Wonderful World" while encouraging bystanders to drop funds into a hat. A handwritten cardboard sign noted that they were raising money for a trip to Carnegie Hall.

"Hazel didn't mention anything about the trial either?" I

asked, reaching into my jacket pocket for a twenty-dollar bill and adding it to their growing pile of cash. Alex teased me about carrying cash. His generation used Venmo but having physical money on hand was another holdover from my foster care years. I liked to know that I could donate to young musicians, buy cookies when the local Girl Scout troop set up a table in front of the grocery store, or most importantly, get out of any dangerous situation safely.

"Not specifically." Leah ducked out of the way of an errant snowball. A rosy-cheeked kid with bad aim shouted an apology and in return she pretended to try to peg him with a snowball of her own.

"We could join in," Garrett suggested. "Really blow off some steam."

"No, I'm good." Leah chuckled. "I really want to see if they'll allow me to take a look at Hazel's chart notes. There should be a new staff on the night shift, so I figure it's worth a shot."

"It's great timing because I want to check on Tad," I said, watching my breath puff out in front of us as we passed by the Nutcracker Museum. A collection of ski-themed nutcrackers filled the arched windows. The museum procured the bevy of wooden statues from the Ore Mountains in Germany, where each figure was hand-carved and painted.

"We can divide and conquer," Leah replied. "In answer to your question about the trial, Hazel said a lot without saying a lot."

"That sounds cagey." Garrett frowned, stepping around a beer barrel garbage can on the corner.

"Exactly." Leah tried to snap, but her fingerless gloves muted the sound. "It's one of the reasons that I immediately wondered about the response from the team at the hospital. I asked her if she was enjoying working on the trial and her direct quote was, 'It's been the most eye-opening experience of my career.'"

"That's a loaded statement," Garrett said.

"When I asked her a few follow-up questions, she shut down. She said she had signed a non-disclose agreement with BioGold and couldn't talk about any specifics. I wasn't asking for specifics, which is why I felt like she was trying to tell me something with her body language and word choice."

"I didn't realize NDAs were used in clinical trials," I said as we turned off Front Street.

"Only in industry-sponsored trials like this one. BioGold is funding the research, not the hospital, so they can't share study protocols or proprietary documents without getting BioGold's permission." Leah held up her finger. "This is where it gets interesting. Hazel basically hinted that she had made backup copies of everything. She didn't say why but it was like she wanted me to know. I can't put my finger exactly on how to explain it."

"That matches what Tad told me. I wonder if he's been able to recover her files."

"There's one way to find out." Garrett pointed to the hospital's giant wood-carved doors. Yellow light glowed from within. Its stucco base with light pine siding and fascia scrolling made it look more like a ski lodge than a hospital.

"I'm going to check in with the nursing team," Leah said as we entered the lobby. "Let's meet here in thirty minutes or text me if you're ready sooner."

The hospital had been designed to soothe the nerves of patients with muted soft colors and plush furnishings.

Garrett and I walked over to the volunteer welcome desk. Visiting hours were done for the night, so the station sat empty. There was a seating area for visitors with complimentary coffee and tea, overstuffed armchairs, and potted plants. Gentle music played in the background.

"How do we find Tad's office?" Garrett asked.

I glanced to our right where the entrance to the emergency

department had a much more serious atmosphere. A handful of patients waiting to be seen spoke in hushed tones as machines beeped and doctors and nurses moved with urgency. The main nurse's station was farther down the corridor with patient rooms on either side.

"Tad mentioned that his office is in the basement." I nodded to a stairwell next to the elevators.

"Do you think we're allowed downstairs?" His smile wavered.

"I don't see a sign saying no entrance, do you?"

He shook his head. "You're trouble, Sloan."

"We just have to look like we know what we're doing. If we look confident, no one will question us." I held my hand toward the door and gave him a playful wink. "And if anyone asks, we'll say we got lost."

"At Leavenworth Community Hospital?" Garrett made a face. "All three floors of it, including the basement."

"Too bad we don't have growlers with us. We could claim we were doing a beer delivery."

"Now you just might be onto something. Beer delivery."

We headed for the stairs. The tiny hairs on my arms stood at attention. I half expected a voice to stop us or someone to block our path, but no one so much as blinked as Garrett and I slipped into the stairwell. It was dimly lit with linoleum flooring and heavy with the scent of antiseptic.

Garrett froze. "Did you hear that?"

"No, what?" I whispered, blinking to get my eyes to adjust to the muted floor lighting.

"I thought I heard something slam down that way." He waved his arm in front of him, which must have sent the motion lights on because fluorescent yellow flickering waves illuminated the stairwell.

He cupped one hand over his ear and pressed a finger to his lips.

I glued my feet to the floor.

A giant bang caused the floor to shake and sent sound ripples through the staircase.

"Was that a gunshot?" I grabbed Garrett's arm.

Before we had left Nitro I had checked my phone. Chief Meyers hadn't returned my call, but that didn't rule out the possibility that she and her team were here in the building now. Maybe Tad was actually in danger. If Hazel had been murdered because of the data on her laptop and the killer knew Tad had her computer, we could be putting ourselves in their direct path.

"I don't think so." He shook his head, but he didn't make a move forward.

It was a good thing, because the door down below swung open and Shep ran up the stairs two at a time.

When he saw us standing in the landing, he toppled backward.

Garrett caught his arm.

"Thanks, man." Shep brushed off his tight-fitting black scrubs and offered Garrett a fist bump. "I didn't expect to see anyone here. You freaked me out. I almost took a tumble. That would have been bad. I'm the only anesthesiologist on duty tonight."

"Sorry," Garrett apologized. "We were on our way downstairs when we heard a loud crash."

Shep tossed a casual glance down the stairwell. "Really? I didn't hear anything."

"Weren't you just down there?"

He tapped his left ear. "I had my AirPods blasting. It's how I get in the zone. Couldn't hear anything except for the page that came in."

It was a reasonable explanation, but I wasn't sure I believed him. He didn't have earbuds in now and how could he hear a page and not a crash?

"Did you see anyone downstairs?" Garrett asked, trying to peer around Shep's muscular frame.

"Nah. I was doing my thing." He flexed his arm. A code sounded on the speaker system. Shep patted his chest. "That's me. Anesthesia calls. Gotta put a patient into a nice little sleep. See ya."

He vanished.

"Maybe we're overreacting?" Garrett sounded like he was looking for confirmation. "Should we continue on?"

"Yeah. Obviously there are other staff around, which means we're probably not in any danger and I want to check in with Tad."

"And find out what those bangs were," Garrett added as he proceeded downstairs.

I followed close behind, my boots squeaking on the glossy linoleum flooring. Unlike the warm vibe upstairs, the basement walls were painted a drab industrial green.

The basement level housed the lab, which was closed for the night, physician offices, an employee lounge, and administration. There weren't many people wandering the hallways but there were lights on in a handful of offices. Notifications sounded every couple of minutes, doctors and staff being paged, but there was no movement in the basement.

The long corridor smelled like industrial cleaner. Overhead lights flickered and buzzed, casting an eerie glow over the facility.

"Do you know where IT is?" Garrett peered into a dark window labeled LAB.

"What are you looking at?"

"Just checking." He squinted and pressed his face closer to the glass. "Nothing. It's totally dark. Should we keep going?"

"Yes, IT has to be down here somewhere." I scanned the signs on each door. "It looks like all the administrative offices are over there." My stomach fluttered as we crept farther down the hallway.

"There." I pointed to a door with a small window and the words IT DEPARTMENT above it. Unlike the rest of the administrative offices, a dull light was on inside.

I knocked softly.

No one responded.

I tried again, knocking a bit louder the second time.

Garrett stood on his toes and peered through the window.

"Do you see anyone?" My hands suddenly felt shaky. Maybe this wasn't a good idea. If the killer had come after Tad, they still could be in the room.

"No." He clasped his hands around his eyes and tried to get a better look inside.

"Tad, it's Sloan," I called. "We came to check on you."

Garrett knocked harder.

My chest tightened as I tried the handle. The door opened with ease. I looked at Garrett and mouthed, "Should we go in?"

He hesitated for a minute. "Yeah, there are two of us, right?"

I swallowed hard, wishing the confidence I'd had a few minutes ago would return.

"Tad, is everything okay?" Garrett asked in a booming voice as I pushed the door open.

We immediately knew that everything wasn't okay. Two large filing cabinets had been knocked over. Their contents were scattered throughout the room—an overturned desk, a chair that looked as if it had been thrown against the wall, papers, pens, even the contents of a garbage can had been tossed on the floor.

"Oh, no." My breath caught in my throat. "It looks like someone beat us here."

"And beat Tad." Garrett's voice was thick with emotion. His face blanched. "Call 911, Sloan."

It took me a second to register what he was saying. It wasn't until he had stepped over the debris and lifted part of the desk that I realized Tad was in the room. Whoever had torn the office apart had knocked out Tad. Or maybe it had happened when they flipped the desk over.

Garrett circled his hand. "Sloan, you with me?"

"Yeah, sorry." I blinked rapidly and forced my feet forward. "Is he breathing?"

Garrett dropped to his knees and assessed Tad. "Yes, but I don't think we should move him. He's bleeding."

I did a double-take. Sure enough, there was a gash on Tad's forehead, probably from the bloody stapler nearby. I tried to keep my emotions in check. "I'll run upstairs. That will be the fastest option, right?"

"Yeah." Garrett yanked off his hoodie and used the sleeve to apply pressure to Tad's wound. "I'll stay with him. Get help. Then call Chief Meyers."

"Right." I sprinted back down the corridor and upstairs to the emergency room.

"We need help now," I said to the medical receptionist checking patients in. She must have heard the urgency in my tone because she didn't hesitate. Within a few seconds, two nurses and a doctor followed me to the basement with medical gear and a stretcher.

By the time we made it back to Tad's office he was sitting up with Garrett's support. Blood dripped from a gash on the side of his forehead. The doctors opened their bag and began taking Tad's vitals, while one of the nurses slipped on gloves and took over applying pressure to the wound.

The other nurse tended to Garrett. She gave him antibacterial wipes and recommended he take a seat and practice slow breathing. I wondered if she was worried that he might go into shock. His skin looked dull, but his eyes were alert.

The medical team asked Tad a sequence of questions to test his mental agility, including the year, who was president, and what had happened to cause his injury. He was able to answer the first two questions without fail, but the third one tripped him up.

"I don't know. I was working at my desk. I had my back to the door and didn't hear anyone come in because I had my headphones on." He paused and searched the area for his headphones. "I don't know where they went. Whoever attacked me must have taken them."

"Did you see the person?" Garrett asked, carving his hands through his hair.

Tad pressed his hand to his other temple. "No. I only saw their feet. They hit me with something. I fell off my chair and hit the floor. I was sort of with it for a few minutes. I saw them frantically going through my laptop and the filing cabinet and then they knocked my desk on top of me."

"Was there anything about their feet that might stand out?" I asked.

"They were wearing black scrubs and black tennis shoes."

The doctor cautioned Tad not to move. "He might have a concussion. We need to get him upstairs for a CT scan."

They proceeded to transport Tad upstairs. I called Chief Meyers and left another message. When I hung up the phone Garrett stood up and paced from the desk to the door, his eyes wide with disbelief as they darted from the overturned desk to Tad's office supplies littering the floor.

"The killer must be getting desperate." He sounded like he was talking to himself as much as me. "That had to be the sound we heard—them knocking over furniture and ransacking Tad's office. I wonder if they found what they were looking for."

"I know. And there is someone who matches Tad's exact description. We just saw Shep coming from the basement wearing black scrubs and tennis shoes."

SIXTEEN

It FELT like déjà vu as Garrett and I waited in Tad's office for the police to arrive. It was only earlier this afternoon that we had done the same on the ski hill, and yet it was as if weeks had passed. I didn't want this to become a habit. My vision for the week had been showing the Strong family around the village, snowy adventures, and lots of cozy family meals around the fireplace. Never would I have imagined one murder and now what appeared to be an attempt at a second.

The police placed yellow plastic evidence markers around the room and posted caution tape over the door. We gave them our statements while they continued to secure the crime scene.

When I was finished answering their questions, I asked one of the officers about Chief Meyers' absence.

"She's in Seattle," the officer responded, not offering any further details. "We don't expect her back until Monday or Tuesday at the earliest."

Once the police cleared us to leave, Garrett and I went upstairs to find Leah and check on Tad's status.

"Chief Meyers must be following up on leads connected with Hazel's murder," Garrett commented, holding the stairwell door for me with one hand. The hoodie he had used to try to stop Tad's bleeding was in his other hand. The police had kindly bagged it in a blue evidence bag for him. "If she braved the mountain passes to get to Seattle, I wonder if she learned something important about BioGold."

"Or she's interviewing staff at UW," I offered.

"Or both."

Leah was waiting for us near the coffee station in the lobby. "What happened? I saw them rush a guy into the ED."

Garrett gave her the rundown. "They think he might have a concussion. The good news is that he was fairly alert and seemed to be doing okay, aside from the cut on his head."

"Head wounds bleed a lot," Leah said with authority. "Should we go talk at Nitro?"

Her wary glance told me that she didn't want to continue our conversation at the hospital.

"Absolutely, after you." Garrett motioned for her to go outside first.

Nitro was across the street and three shops down, so it didn't take long to get back to the pub. The minute Garrett unlocked the front door, I could feel relief flood my body

Kat and our other staff had cleaned and closed the pub for the night, which meant that we had the space to ourselves. Nitro's familiar, welcoming interior and the faint aroma of hops were like a balm for my soul. Hops are a natural relaxant. I often slept with a sachet of dried hops under my pillow. At the moment I could use a vat of hops to help calm my shaky nerves.

"Should I make some tea, coffee, hot chocolate?" I asked. "Or there's always beer."

Leah raised her hand in protest. "As good as your beer is, I can't do another, or I'll never sleep tonight, but a tea sounds great."

I let them get settled while I heated the tea kettle, gathered an assortment of teas, and discovered a few slices of my chocolate peanut butter pretzel bars. I brought everything out to the tasting room where Garrett had turned on the gas fireplace and Leah had wrapped her legs in one of the wool blankets we kept on hand for winter guests.

"Thanks for tea and dessert." Leah leafed through the basket of teas and opted for a packet of lemon chamomile.

"Did you learn anything on your search?" Garrett asked, pouring hot water into a mug and handing it to me.

I plunged a packet of peppermint tea into the water and cradled it in my hands, happy for the warmth of the mug and the fire.

"Sort of," Leah replied, blowing on her tea. "They wouldn't let me access Hazel's medical file. The lead night nurse told me that was police orders, not the hospital. When I explained that I had been the physician on the scene, she did grant me access to the ED chart notes."

"Is there a difference?" Garrett asked, rubbing his exposed arms. His Nitro T-shirt wasn't providing much warmth.

I stood to grab him a blanket while Leah answered his question.

"I was hoping to review Hazel's entire medical record, to see if there was anything that might have shown up as a red flag. Heart issues, prescription medication, that sort of thing. The chart notes are a glance at one moment in time. In this case, the day that she died. I was hoping for a broader look at her medical history, but I was able to see that there was no sign of a physical altercation or an injury prior to her fall."

Garrett shot me a look of thanks when I handed him the blanket. He immediately wrapped it around his shoulders and scooted closer to the fire.

"What does that tell us?" I sat and plunged my tea bag down into my mug.

"Not a lot," Leah admitted. "It basically means that she wasn't knocked out prior to falling off the lift, but there's nothing else conclusive. We'll have to wait for the autopsy and toxicology reports to come in before a cause of death can be determined."

"I guess we can at least rule out that the killer was on the ski lift with her when she died," Garrett said.

"Yeah." Leah nodded. "That matches eyewitness reports."

"I guess ruling out one possibility is better than nothing." I blew on my tea and wondered if there were any other suspects we could rule out. Dr. Sutton, Shep, Ren were all still on my list, and Jerry was at the very top.

"True, and now with the situation with Tad, there has to be a connection." Garrett broke off a piece of a bar with his fork. "Chief Meyers is in Seattle for the next few days. I wonder if she'll have one of her officers patrolling the hospital. If the killer attacked Tad while trying to find whatever evidence might be remaining on the hospital's computer system or Hazel's personal laptop, he could still be in danger."

"I'm sure the police have thought about that," I said. "What I'm stumped about is the filing cabinets and the rest of Tad's office."

"Why?" Leah asked, sipping her tea carefully.

"Hazel's missing flash drive has been at the center of everything since the beginning. The killer had to know that. Why would they even bother rifling through filing cabinets and paperwork if they were looking for the flash drive or her laptop?"

"Good question." Garrett savored a bite of the chocolate bar. "This is delicious, by the way. Leah, you should get in on this chocolate peanut butter action."

"You don't have to twist my arm." She reached for a piece.

"Do you know if the hospital keeps written records of the clinical trial data as a backup for the digital data?" I asked her.

She closed her eyes and held up her finger. "Sorry, I'm going to need a minute with this bar. Holy smokes, this might be the best thing I've ever tasted in my life. Sloan, will you marry me?"

"Gladly." I grinned. "I'm so happy you're enjoying it."

"Uh, enjoy is an understatement. I'm in love." She patted her heart and pretended to swoon. "No, this is seriously the most delicious experience of my life."

Garrett had polished off his bar and started in on a second. "Yeah, what she said."

"Okay, back to reality." Leah finished her bite. "I don't know if anyone keeps a paper record. Maybe, but I doubt it. Everything is done on the computer these days. I don't even recognize my own handwriting when I have to write a note."

"Tell me about it." Garrett nodded to the massive chalkboard menu behind the bar. "If I swapped out the rotating beers, it would look like a preschooler scratched a bunch of scribbles on the board. Thankfully, we have Alex for now. He designed the print menus for us."

"Really?" Leah reached for one of the bar menus. "He's good. Does he want to study graphic design?"

"Maybe." I stared at the fire for a second, wondering where Alex's next chapter would lead him. He had so many possible paths. "And political science, and journalism, and history. It changes every day. Last week he was talking about focusing on kinesiology and sports medicine."

"Ohhh, I should try to convince him to consider sports medicine." Leah's knee bounced on the floor as she spoke. "He's perfect. He's such an athlete with skiing and soccer, and UW has a great program."

"Go for it. Mac and I have been encouraging him to explore a variety of classes in his first year. There's so much pressure these days to declare a major and focus right away, but I think college is supposed to be about exposing yourself to new ideas and new pathways in order to find which one fits you best."

"You are an amazing mom, Sloan. That's good advice." Leah smiled.

A soft knock sounded on the door.

"I bet that's Mom and Dad." Garrett went to answer the door.

Leah leaned closer, while he went to let his parents in. "Seriously, I can't say it enough. I haven't seen Garrett this happy in a long, long time and I know it's because of you."

"I don't know that I deserve all the credit, but I feel the same. Nitro and your brother have been a godsend for me." I turned toward the door as Garrett greeted Hans.

Hans waved at me. I noticed his gaze lingered on Leah for a moment.

"Hey, speaking of brothers. I wasn't expecting to see you." I raised my tea glass to him.

Hans's cheeks were flushed from the cold. "I'm not crashing a party, am I? The lights were on so I thought I would say hi." He held a blue and white checkered bag with the Der Keller crest. "Plus, I have a gift for your parents from mine."

"That's so nice." Garrett shut the cold out behind him. "Can I pour you a pint?"

Hans shook his head. "I'm fine, thanks."

"I know what will tempt him." I swept my hand over the remaining platter of bars. "I made chocolate stout peanut pretzel bars."

Hans stabbed at his heart. "You're killing me slowly—death by chocolate."

Leah made room for him next to the fireplace. "There's also tea if that's more your speed."

They locked eyes for a minute. Was it my imagination or did Hans's cheek turn a burgundy shade of red? Leah absently checked her hair and shifted her seat to make more room for Hans.

"Tea would be great." Hans sat next to her and set the Der Keller bag on the table. "I left with marching orders to make sure to give this to your family tonight."

"What is it?" Leah tried to peer into the bag.

Hans picked it up and handed it to her. "See for yourself. It's the ultimate welcome to Leavenworth package from my folks."

"At least it isn't from April Ablin," Garrett said with a laugh. "You'd be stuck with a fake felt hats and cheap chocolates in the shape of cuckoo clocks."

Leah opened the bag to reveal Der Keller merch. Otto and Ursula had included hoodies, T-shirts, stein glasses, and stickers for all three of them. "That is so incredibly nice. I swear I feel like I'm living in some sort of Hallmark village the past couple of days."

"Minus the murder," Hans said, wrapping the string from his tea bag loosely around his finger.

"Minus that." She put a Der Keller hoodie on over her long sleeve shirt.

"It looks good on you. Blue is your color." Hans stirred honey into his tea.

Garrett caught my eye. He was picking up on the same vibe. I didn't want to get my hopes up but if Hans and Leah were attracted to each other, that would be my dream. My surrogate brother and Garrett's sister pairing up. What were the odds?

In all of the years that I had known Hans, he had dated very little. Part of it was a Leavenworth problem. With only two thousand permanent residents, there weren't a ton of options or a big dating scene in town. Not that April hadn't tried on many occasions to woo him. None of her attempts were successful, thank god.

He had dated a woman in Wenatchee for a short stint. When it didn't work out, Mac had asked him why and his response was because Wenatchee was too far away. It was an easy excuse. People commuted to Wenatchee daily so I had a feeling that was an easy excuse for not being interested in pursuing a long-term relationship. There had also been a few women he had met during festival weekends. They were visiting from even longer distances—Seattle and beyond. None of those had transformed into anything serious either.

If distance was an issue, then Leah's flirtation might not have much of a shot since Portland was even farther away than Seattle, but given that their knees were practically touching and their body language mirrored each other, I wondered if something more was blossoming between them.

I didn't want to get my hopes up, but it was fun to imagine. I genuinely wanted Hans to be happy. He seemed to be. He had carved out his own path quite literally, preferring to use his hands to create custom craft furniture rather than beer. But I also suspected that one of the reasons he had never left Leavenworth was because of his sense of responsibility to his family. While he wasn't involved in day-to-day operations at Der Keller, he played a major role in planning and setting a course for the future. He was also always fixing something, building a new hop trellis, or volunteering to pour at one of the beer fests.

"I'll have to thank your parents tomorrow." Leah placed her hand on Hans' knee as a show of gratitude. "They are the sweetest. Their accents are so great and they're adorable together. I can't believe they got up and danced around the bar."

Hans gazed at Leah's lips as she reached for her ChapStick. Then he sucked in a breath and turned to me. "Yep. That's them. Otto and Ursula refuse to let age slow them down."

"Are my parents still with them?" Leah lined her lips with ChapStick.

Their smiles seemed to grow wider with each passing moment. Hans scooted closer to her and Leah didn't move away.

I glanced at my watch. It was nearing midnight. Had the elder generation outlasted us?

"No. They took off a while ago. There's a comedy improv night at the festhalle. You'll never guess who is performing."

"Who? April?" Garrett asked.

"Nope." Hans stared at me and raised his reddish eyebrows. "Even better. A Krause."

"Not *Mac*," I said.

He nodded three times. "In the flesh."

"Why aren't we there?" I pretended to jump to my feet. "We have to see this."

"I had no idea he was doing it." Hans shook his head. His smile was unrestrained. "I stopped by on my way here, but sadly Mac had already done his set. In fact, your parents will probably show up soon. The event should be over about now."

While Garrett, Leah, and I had been trying to track down Leah's killer at the hospital, Mac had been on stage performing standup comedy. That was not anything I had expected to hear and I needed to know more—stat.

CHAPTER

SEVENTEEN

I HAD to wait until the next day to learn more about Mac moonlighting as a standup comic. Hans and Leah stayed up talking much later than I could handle. I left when Penny and Bruce got back. Garrett offered to walk me home, but I didn't want to pull him away from his family and my plan was to go straight to bed, which is exactly what I did.

When sunlight streamed in through my frosty bedroom window the next morning, I couldn't believe I had slept in. Of course, sleeping in for me was what Alex and his friends considered "the crack of dawn."

I didn't bother to make coffee at home, but rather got dressed and went straight to Nitro to make breakfast. I had already planned to make a large batch of sweet rolls. They were easy and always a hit with our guests. The only issue was that the dough took a little while to rise. I warmed water, added yeast and sugar, and set it aside while I made a strong pot of coffee. After I had added flour, more sugar, melted butter, milk, and a splash of beer to form the bread dough, I kneaded it by hand and covered it with a towel. I used the opportunity to wait for the first rise to savor my coffee and review everything I had learned about Hazel's death thus far.

It seemed like we could rule Tad out as a suspect. Unless he had staged his attack last night, which I highly doubted, that meant that the killer had come after him. The logical connection was that the killer was looking for Hazel's data. Could it have been Jerry? Tad told him exactly what he was going to do at Der Keller. He had been clear that he was determined to recover Hazel's files. Jerry could have followed him to the hospital, knocked him out, and taken off with the data before Garrett and I found Tad.

Then there was Shep. The anesthesiologist was the *chillest*, as Alex would say, doctor of the bunch. He didn't have a clear motive to want to kill Hazel. I needed to find out if he was connected to the clinical trial. Nothing he had said indicated that he had a connection to the research. But maybe that was intentional. Maybe he had been secretly involved, or maybe he had been tasked to keep Hazel quiet. I couldn't take his name off my suspect list. He had been at the scene last night and wearing an outfit that matched Tad's description of his attacker.

My thoughts drifted to Dr. Sutton. It was her clinical trial, so she had the most at stake. If Hazel had found anomalies in Dr. Sutton's research, it was certainly plausible that Dr. Sutton could be responsible for Hazel's death. Would she put her long, revered career at risk? She had been a lead physician in Leavenworth and a teaching fellow at UW for nearly twenty years. If the trial hadn't yielded the results she was hoping for, wouldn't she have the foresight to understand that was part of the process and go back to the drawing board?

The last person whom I had seen with the team of doctors and with Hazel was Ren. He had reacted immediately when he heard that Hazel had left Nitro the night before she was killed. Unless I had read him wrong, he had seemed worried and upset about her departure. The question was why? Was he concerned about her well-being? Could he have known that she was in danger? Or was his response because he was concerned that she was about to reveal something to him? And as the only nurse in the group, what was his role with the clinical trial?

I wasn't going to be able to figure it out on my own. Hopefully, after breakfast, I'd have a chance to drop by the hospital before we opened the tasting room. There were too many questions that I needed answered and the only way to do that was to go directly to the source.

By the time my rolls had baked to golden perfection, I began to hear movement upstairs. Kat arrived to help set up breakfast and prep for the day. I didn't join Garrett and his family but rather got a start on our soup of the day and housemade sausage rolls. One trick I learned from Ursula was to double batches of dough and set half aside without adding any extra sugar. That could be used to wrap savory sausages or as a traditional bread dough.

Garrett padded into the kitchen as I was placing a tray of sausage rolls in the oven. He wore a pair of soccer-style sweats and a pale green BOCK FROM THE DEAD hoodie. Bock was a style of dark ale. It was a classic Garrett pun.

Bock is a strong, malty German lager with a rich and robust flavor profile. It's often characterized by notes of toasted bread, toffee, and dark fruit, and has a relatively high alcohol content compared with other styles of lagers. It's typically brewed in the winter and its hints of sweetness made it a popular choice for those who enjoy a full-body beer.

"You're non-stop with the baking lately," he said, as he wafted the smell of baking bread toward his nose.

"It's called stress baking." I ripped off a piece of sweet roll that I'd saved for myself and smashed it into my mouth. "And it goes hand in hand with stress eating."

"Lucky us. Those rolls were amazing. My dad just polished off four of them. Mom is scolding him because she has a snowshoe hike planned and doesn't want him to slow her down."

"I can't imagine anyone slowing her down." Garrett laughed.

"Are you joining them?" I dusted a wooden cutting board with flour.

"That's actually why I came down. They would love for you to come along as well. I'm going to pack lunches and hot chocolate. Leah is coming. What do you say?"

"What about Nitro?" I rolled up my sleeves and began kneading the bread dough on the cutting board. There was something cathartic about digging my hands into the soft, pillowy dough.

"I already checked in with Kat and the crew last night." He took his phone out of his pocket to prove his point. "They're all good to cover again. I don't want to pressure you, though. If you don't want to come, it's fine."

"No, I do." I hesitated.

"I feel a 'but' coming on."

"It's Hazel's murder. I can't stop thinking about it and I have so many questions. I was hoping to swing by the hospital and see how Tad is doing. I also really want to talk to Ren. He was upset the night before Hazel died and I have a feeling he might know something."

"Go ahead. That's no problem. We won't leave for at least another hour or so."

"Perfect. I'll have Kat keep an eye on the sausage rolls and run over right now."

"We'll wait for you." Garrett refilled the coffee cup he'd brought from upstairs. "And Sloan, please be careful."

"I will." I made an "x" over my heart. "Back in a flash."

On my way out, I made sure that Kat knew to listen for the oven timer. I grabbed my coat and hurried across the street. Visiting hours were open at the hospital, so I asked the volunteer for Tad's room number. The reception desk was cluttered with get-well cards, flowers, and balloons waiting to be distributed to patients' rooms. The volunteer directed me upstairs to the third floor.

I took the stairs and came out into a hallway with soft beige walls and pictures of lush gardens and smiling patients. The air was scented with a mixture of cleaning agents and freshly brewed coffee from the cafeteria.

I found Tad's room right away. It was next to the nurse's station. I wondered if that was a safety precaution so that the nurses could keep an eye on him.

Tad was sitting upright in his hospital bed. A large bandage covered most of his head and he was hooked up to an IV and a beeping heart monitor.

"You look better than you did last night," I said.

He touched a bruise on his forearm. "It's a lot of bruising. The nurses say they're going to get worse before they improve."

"How are you feeling?" I asked.

"Not bad. My head is the worst part. I get dizzy if I stand up and my whole forehead is constantly throbbing."

"That doesn't sound good."

"I could be dead," he said without emotion.

His directness startled me. "I'm glad you're not."

"Yeah, I don't know if I thanked you last night. It's kind of fuzzy, but if not, let me thank you now." He motioned to the large window that offered a view of the snowy village. "Can you adjust the blinds? The sun is right in my eyes."

I pulled the blinds lower. "There's no need for thanks. Garrett and I were just glad we found you."

"You might have saved my life. I think Jerry was still there. He was going to knock me out for good if you hadn't come along."

I wondered how concussed Tad was. He wasn't making sense. "No one was in your office when we showed up. In fact, the entire basement was empty."

"I think he heard you. I've been playing it back in my head

this morning. I think my brain is trying to process what happened. I heard voices and footsteps, which must have been you and Garrett. That spooked Jerry. He must have taken off in the opposite direction right before you found me."

"Why do you think it was Jerry? Last night you said something about a person in black scrubs and tennis shoes."

"Yeah. That's right." He nodded, but then winced in pain. "Jerry killed Hazel and tried to kill me. The police are looking for him. They think he took off to Seattle to try and escape. Not a smart move. They're going to catch him. The officer they have posted at my door told me that the police chief is already in Seattle and she's working with their teams. It's only a matter of time before they make an arrest."

His confidence surprised me.

"I heard that Chief Meyers was in Seattle, but I had no idea they were so close to arresting a suspect."

"Not a suspect," Tad corrected. "A cold-hearted killer. Jerry didn't come out here to make an announcement about BioGold's successful research. He came here for one reason and one reason alone. To kill Hazel. He had to silence her, otherwise she would have gone to the press and revealed that the research is fraudulent."

"Were you able to recover her data last night before you were attacked?"

"No, but that doesn't change anything. Jerry killed her. I know it. He knows it. The police know it. Now they have to find him and put him where he belongs—behind bars."

"I hope you're right."

"There's no doubt about it. I'm right. Jerry did this to me." He touched his bandage ever so lightly. "He must have realized that I have Hazel's laptop. He had to get his grubby hands on it and erase any evidence of the fact that he blatantly faked the results from the trial. I'm sure that's why he tore my office apart. He was trying to make sure there wasn't a paper trail. The only thing that guy cares about is money. He saw that BioGold stood to make millions with the announcement of Dr. Sutton's breakthrough. Only it wasn't a breakthrough. It was a scam."

"There's one thing I don't understand. You said the person who hit you was wearing black scrubs, but Jerry was wearing jeans and snow boots at Der Keller."

"You didn't hear?"

I shook my head.

"The police recovered an entire bin of black scrubs in the laundry room. They think Jerry was trying to disguise himself as a member of the medical staff. He probably wore them over his street clothes, swapped his boots for tennis shoes, and then dumped them in a bin as he escaped."

I wondered what the implications would be for Dr. Sutton's trial if Jerry were arrested. Before I left, I asked Tad if he needed anything and promised him free pints at Nitro once he was up to it.

Tad's theory made sense. He had practically baited Jerry to come after him last night. Maybe he hadn't anticipated that Jerry would actually do it. Before I sighed with too much relief that the police were on track for finding Hazel's killer, I wanted to hear it from another source. Tad had taken a blow to the head. There was a chance that his injury was impacting his memory and judgment.

I returned to the lobby. Maybe Chief Meyers would get in touch today and be able to confirm Tad's theory.

As I was about to leave, I bumped into Ren, who was wearing the exact same set of scrubs and tennis shoes as Tad's assailant.

EIGHTEEN

"Ren, what a coincidence, I was hoping to talk to you."

He tapped his retro Swatch watch on his tattooed arm. "I've got ten minutes until my shift. Wanna walk to the cafeteria with me? I need a latte, or like twenty, to start my day."

I fell into step with him. "I see that black is the new blue when it comes to scrubs."

"Huh?" His shockingly orange hair was spiked in a full mohawk.

"Your scrubs. I've noticed a lot of staff have different colors of scrubs these days."

"You mean like the classic ceil blue? No one wears those anymore. Only the old-school docs."

"Black seems like a solid choice."

"These aren't even mine." He looked down at his nursing gear in disgust. "These are doctor's scrubs. I had to borrow a pair from the employee lounge. I hate looking like a boring doc. I like big 80s colors. It's my vibe, but *noooo*, now we have to look professional and wear classic black or ceil according to the chief of staff. Someone swiped my black scrubs from my locker. Who does that?"

I had a feeling I might know the *someone*. Could Jerry have taken Ren's scrubs?

"That's the sad state of hospitals these days. Stealing scrubs."

His story seemed to be in line with Tad's theory that Jerry was the attacker, but again I didn't want to get ahead of myself. There was also a possibility that Ren could be lying because he was the one who attacked Tad and he was trying to deflect suspicion. Until I had a chance to speak with Chief Meyers, every possibility was on the table.

"How are you holding up?" I asked as we got in line for coffee. I almost offered to bring over a cup of our Nitro French press. When Ursula had undergone hip surgery I was introduced to the hospital cafeteria coffee, which was glorified thick sludge. It reminded me of the trube we scraped from the bottom of the brewing tanks. I shuddered at the memory. "You and Hazel were close, weren't you?"

"What did you hear?" He stepped closer to me to avoid being overheard by anyone else in line. Then he licked his index finger and used it to smooth his mohawk straighter. "It wasn't like you think. I wasn't stalking her. I asked her out a couple of times. She said no. I dropped it. We're friends first, I told her. It wasn't like I was pressuring her to go out with me."

"I never said that." I was surprised by his reaction and admission that there were rumors about him and Hazel. What I didn't expand on was that I hadn't heard anything about him stalking Hazel.

"Why would someone start a rumor that I was stalking her? She texted me for help." He pressed his fingers toward his spiky hair like he was trying to keep it in place. It appeared well-gelled and firm from my perspective. "We were supposed to meet at Nitro. I showed up and didn't see her. A bunch of other staff from the hospital were there so I figured she was being nice and inviting me out with the group, but when I learned that she took off I had a bad feeling."

We moved closer to the counter.

"She was desperate for my help. Why would she show up at the pub and not wait for me?" He got his ID card ready. "I went to look for her. I couldn't find her anywhere. I called. I texted. She never answered and then the next thing I heard; she was dead."

It was Ren's turn to order. He handed the cashier his badge and asked for a triple latte and an apple cinnamon muffin. We stepped to the opposite side of the counter to wait for his coffee.

"Do you know what she wanted your help with?" I asked.

"She didn't say, but I think it had to do with work." He nearly knocked over a stack of to-go lids but caught them at the last minute. "She told me she found something that was stressing her out and she needed to talk to someone she could trust about it."

A rush of adrenaline pulsed through me and I wasn't even drinking coffee. "Do you know why she was stressed?"

"Come on, who isn't?" He motioned to the line of doctors and nurses. "This is a hospital. Stress comes with the job. If you can't deal with stress, medicine probably isn't for you. Hazel managed her stress well. At least she had until the past few weeks."

"Do you think she could have been self-medicating?"

"Hazel?" Ren scoffed. "No way. She barely touched coffee. She drank an occasional beer or glass of wine at work events but she's not like some of the other staff."

"Like who?"

"You've met Dr. Ames—Shep, yeah? It's pretty common in that field to dabble on the side, if you know what I mean."

This was another revelation.

He grabbed his latte and muffin. "I gotta head to the ED. Are you going that way?"

"Sure. I'll walk out with you." I waited until we were out of earshot to ask a follow-up question. "Do you think Shep has a drug problem?"

"I think Hazel thought he had a problem. There's been some chatter that she caught him stealing medication when they had a shift together last week."

This was a huge revelation.

"Do you think it's true?"

"Why would someone make it up? It fits Shep's personality. He struts around this place like he's some kind of god that everyone should worship." He pointed to his hair. "People call me Ren the hen. It's ironic, because Shep is the poser. He's flexing his muscles and wearing skin-tight scrubs to try and show off. The guy is the worst, and Hazel wouldn't have had the authority to do anything since she's—well, she was—a resident."

"Aren't there systems in place for reporting substance abuse at work?"

He broke his muffin in half as we walked. "She could have reported it to HR, but if it's true that she caught him, he would have known it was her. She might have been worried about retaliation."

"And you think that's why she wanted your help?"

"It's my best guess," he replied through a mouthful of muffin. "I've been at the hospital for a long time. I know how the system works. We were friends. She trusted me."

We made it to the emergency department.

"Before you go, have you heard anything about the BioGold clinical trial?"

"Are you referring to the news about the study? We got an all-staff email with the announcement yesterday." He chugged his latte.

"No, I wondered if you had heard any rumors about Hazel and her role on the team?"

He shook his head. "Nope. That hasn't come up." He stuffed the other half of the muffin in his mouth. "They don't tell me much. I'm a nurse. I check the participants' vitals and the docs do the rest."

"Thanks for filling me in. It's helpful," I replied with a smile. That much was true, but was Ren downplaying his role with the BioGold trial?

"Anytime." He brushed crumbs from his scrubs and pointed to the emergency room. "I should get going."

I left him there and returned to Nitro to get ready for our snowshoeing trip. I had learned two major pieces of information related to the case. Tad believed that Jerry was going to be arrested and Ren had revealed that Hazel caught Shep stealing prescription drugs, which gave him a clear motive for wanting her dead.

CHAPTER

NINETEEN

Snowshoeing turned out to be a much-needed distraction. We opted to trek along the Wenatchee River. True to his word, Garrett packed a backpack with sausage rolls, cookies, snacks, and a thermos of hot chocolate. We started our outing from Blackbird Island.

The icy waters of the river gushed beside us as we glided over snowy trails and ventured deep into the woods. A vast network of trails looped through the island and then continued for miles into the Enchantments. For the first mile or so we could see the village, but soon swaths of deciduous trees enveloped us, shutting out noise and providing us with a canopy of forest green.

I used my trekking poles to keep pace with the Strongs. Physical exertion was just what I needed. The wind on my face and the rhythm of my snowshoes making contact with the packed snowy ground became like a moving meditation. I was content to drink in the fresh mountain air and get lost in my thoughts as we ventured on the path.

We crossed frozen creek beds and passed wild deer. The sun backlit the Cascades, casting a tangerine glow on the surrounding peaks. I'd forgotten how calming it was to be out in the backcountry.

When we finally stopped for lunch at a clearing, all of us were winded with rosy cheeks and sweaty brows.

Garrett laid out waterproof blankets for us to sit on and unpacked enough food for a small army.

"I could really get used to this lifestyle," Penny said, unwrapping a sausage roll.

Bruce poured cups of hot chocolate from the thermos and passed them around our little circle.

"Seriously, do you guys ski and snowshoe every day?" Leah asked, munching on a handful of crackers.

"Not quite every day," Garrett responded. "But pretty close. Last week we finished brewing and on a whim decided to open the tasting room late since it was a Tuesday, and the three of us, Kat included, headed out for cross-country skiing up on the ski hill."

"Hans was telling me the same thing last night." Leah cradled her steaming mug of cocoa. "He said that most days he takes a mid-afternoon ski break. That's amazing."

"It's also surprising how empty the trails are," Penny commented. "We've passed far more deer than people this afternoon."

"The weekends can get busy, especially on the ski hill, but during the week it's really just villagers and the occasional tourist. As for the trails like this, they're very sparsely populated once you get past Blackbird Island and out of the main section of the park," I explained.

"How angry would you be if your good old parents looked at buying some retirement property here?" Bruce clapped Garrett on the back and winked.

"Are you actually considering it?" Garrett's face perked up. "I would love it."

"Me too," Leah added. "I could take the train up from Portland when I have a stretch of a few days off."

"You can do that anytime, sis." He lifted the lid on a container of German chocolate cookies. "Come to the Leavenworth side, we have cookies."

I recognized the Star Wars reference from watching the trilogy with Alex.

Leah took a cookie from him. "I know, but I don't want to take your guest rooms. I know that's part of your income."

"It's yours whenever you want it," Garrett said, handing me the tin of cookies.

I nodded in agreement. "What he said."

Leah laughed.

We enjoyed a leisurely lunch but were careful not to cool down too much. We still had to take the return trip. Hypothermia is an issue in the winter months, even on short adventures. Living in the mountains made me hyper-aware of the importance of safety when venturing out into the backcountry. I had learned in my early years of hiking Blackbird Island and the Enchantments with Mac that it was always better to be over-prepared.

Once we finished lunch and packed the leftovers, Garrett took the lead.

Leah hung back to snowshoe next to me. "Hey, don't say anything to Garrett or my parents about this, but when I was at the hospital last night, I had a brief chat with Dr. Sutton. I wanted to ask her about Hazel. I think she must have had the wrong impression because she ended up offering me a job."

"A job?" I dug my pole into the snow, following the tracks we had made on our way out.

"She mentioned that they're understaffed at the hospital and that she would personally put in a word with my attending physician at OHSU about a potential transfer. She needs research help and said that as long as OHSU was amenable, I could likely start in a few weeks."

"Wow."

"Yeah." She glanced ahead of us. "I didn't want to bring it up last night. I don't want Garrett to get his hopes up. And it feels weird. I told her that I wasn't looking for a job and I certainly wouldn't want to step into Hazel's position. That feels terrible. Dr. Sutton said it wouldn't be the same role. Hazel had already put in for a transfer to UW and was planning to leave at the end of the month."

There was so much to process. I didn't know where to start.

"Are you considering it?" I asked.

"I don't know. It's not a decision to take lightly. Moving wasn't even on my radar. I'm not sure. I don't know how I would feel about working for Dr. Sutton. What if she was involved in forging data in the clinical trial? What about my colleagues in Portland? I don't want to leave anyone in a lurch. And then on the flip side, being here has been amazing. I've felt more relaxed than I have in years, even with Hazel and everything that's happened. It's hard to ignore the lure of this." She motioned to the mountains and then to the crystal blue sky. "I love the outdoors. I never dreamed that I might live someplace where I could ski every day in the winter and hike in the summer. Plus I would be close to you and Garrett."

She didn't add Hans, but I wondered if he would factor into her decision-making.

"I might not be the best person to offer advice because I'm biased too. I would love to have you in the village."

"Do you think it's odd that Dr. Sutton is already hiring?" Leah kicked a pinecone from the trail.

"The reality is that the hospital has to maintain staffing," I replied, impressed by her pace. She was a strong snowshoer, much like the rest of her family. Even with my long legs, I was struggling to keep up. "It sounds like Hazel was already leaving, so Dr. Sutton may have already opened a role. But if not, I don't think we can judge her for replacing a physician. That's business."

"That was my take on our conversation, too." Leah ducked under a branch and then waited to hold it out of the way for me.

"Thanks." I grabbed the needly pine. "I'm here if you need a listening ear. I promise I will try my best not to influence your decision, although Leavenworth is the best place on the planet." I motioned around us. It was hard to come up with an argument against her move. Tiny ice crystals sparkled on the snow. The sound of the river gushing and a hawk circling high above in the cloudless sky made me appreciate how lucky I was to live in the middle of nature.

Leah grinned. "You won't get an argument on that. I'm just trying to decide if it's the best place for me."

"That's a very smart approach."

Garrett, Penny, and Bruce were still a few hundred feet out in front of us. I took the opportunity to ask her about the murder. "Did Dr. Sutton say anything else?"

"She shifted the conversation to hiring me, which was sort of a red flag. I got the impression she was trying to distract me, and to be fair it worked. Once we started talking about the role, Hazel didn't come up again."

"We have a photo opportunity up here," Penny called. "Deer, lots of deer."

We caught up with them and dropped the subject. The thought of having Leah in Leavenworth was more than exciting. I was already slightly dreading next year when Alex would be away at college. Having Leah in town would be a welcome distraction from missing him. There was so much to do and to show her, wine tasting in the Yakima Valley, climbing the Pinnacles, day trips to Seattle, Oktoberfest.

As for her conversation with Dr. Sutton, I was torn. It was logical that even while reeling from the unexpected loss of

Hazel, Dr. Sutton had to fulfill her duties and hire a replacement and additional staff. It was also possible that Dr. Sutton was responsible for Hazel's death and her conversation with Leah was an attempt to pacify her and avoid answering any questions.

Either way, I would keep the job offer to myself and do what I could to support Leah in making a decision.

I snapped photos of the Strongs posing with a herd of white-tailed deer and the Wenatchee River behind them. I couldn't believe how connected I felt to them in such a short amount of time. They already felt like family. If Leah moved to the village, my family would suddenly expand and I loved the thought of that.

CHAPTER
TWENTY

THE REST of the day was relatively uneventful. I left the Strongs at Nitro to meet Alex at home. We had a lazy Sunday dinner of soup, bread, and his favorite winter cookies, hot cocoa s'mores. Our tradition was to play a board game and have dinner in front of the fire.

"Did you hear about Dad?" he asked, stretching his feet over the end of the couch. It was hard to believe that not that long ago he used to curl up in my lap for bedtime stories and hot chocolate. Now the couch couldn't contain his growth.

"Stand-up comedy? I can't believe it, and yet I also can. Did you go?" I opened the Yahtzee box and set out score cards and pencils.

"Oh, yeah, we went. I brought the team. I wouldn't have missed it for anything." Alex had inherited the best parts of Mac and me. He had Mac's natural charm and ability to draw people in, and my introspection.

"You did? How was it? He was probably great. He's always been able to hold an audience captive with his storytelling." I tossed the dice in the plastic container so the game would be ready when we were done with dinner.

"True, and he didn't have a single dad joke. His set was tight." Alex pumped his arm in the air.

"I hope he does it again. I *have* to go."

"He will. He killed it. People were falling out of their chairs laughing." He stretched out a lanky arm to reach for another cookie.

"Did you know he was going to perform?" I had to resist the urge to reach over and ruffle his hair or smooch his cheeks. Times like this were fleeting. I wanted to fully be in the moment with him, and yet I couldn't crush the ache of knowing that at this time next year he would be gone.

He devoured the cookie in one bite and grabbed another. "We talked about it a while ago. He ran a couple of jokes by me, but I didn't know he had signed up until yesterday. It's pretty cool."

I loved the fact that Alex could talk about Mac with such pride around me. If we had done nothing else right in our divorce, at least we had established a sense of mutual respect and caring for one another that was hopefully reflected in our son.

"His set mainly focused on village life and what it was like to be raised by German immigrants in fake Bavaria."

"They always say you should write what you know, so that makes sense."

Alex sat up to take a drink of his hot chocolate. "I wish I knew what I wanted to do about school."

"Tell me more." I wrapped a blanket over my legs and got comfortable, hoping to signify I was ready to listen for as long as he needed.

"I'm so confused, Mom, and I feel like I'm running out of time." He picked up a Yahtzee scorecard and stared at it as if hoping that it might contain the answers he was seeking.

"Do you mean because of college application deadlines?"

"All of it." He tossed the scorecard on the coffee table,

162

picked a melty marshmallow from the top of his mug, and popped it into his mouth. When he was little he used to eat the marshmallows first and then claim that they disappeared to get a second round. Neither Mac nor I could resist his chubby cheeks and bright eyes holding a cup and asking for, "mow mawows."

"Here's the thing I can tell you with confidence." I sat up straighter and met his eyes. "You can't make a wrong decision. You can only go with your intuition and where you feel drawn. If you end up not liking it or changing majors or even taking a sabbatical to go travel for a year, that's fine. You're not locked into anything."

"But I am if I play soccer." He pushed a marshmallow into the chocolate again and again.

"Why?" I asked gently.

"If I commit to the team and don't like it or it's too much, I'll feel terrible about letting my coaches and teammates down."

"Are you leaning toward not playing?"

He licked marshmallow from his finger. "It feels like a lot of pressure all of a sudden. I always thought that's what I wanted. It was the dream. To play at the collegiate level, but now I'm not sure. What if I can't handle it? What if it's too much of a time commitment with my classes? What if I'm not good enough at that level?"

"What if you flipped your 'what ifs'?"

"Huh?" He scrunched his forehead and frowned.

"You come by this naturally. I have the same tendency to sink into catastrophic thinking. Those 'what ifs' that live in my head can take up a lot of space and be persistent in their efforts to rule my thoughts, but over the years I've worked on flipping them to positive 'what ifs'. Like what if playing soccer in college is the best experience of your life? What if you meet friends who will become your friends for life? What if you thrive in your classes and soccer is an outlet to balance your studies?"

"Yeah, yeah, I get it."

"Listen, I'm not saying that I think you should play soccer if that's not what you want to do. I have no investment in you playing or where you end up at school or otherwise, except in wanting you to be happy. What I'm trying to tell you is that there are no wrong decisions in life. It's choices. We are always at choice. If you make what seems like the wrong choice with college or soccer, that's okay, make another one."

"Mom," Alex sighed.

I noticed his eyes were becoming misty. I moved to sit on the end of the couch with him, letting his legs fall into my lap. "Is there something else, honey?"

He fought back tears. "I guess it's starting to sink in that I'm leaving."

I didn't bother to try to hold my tears in. "I know, honey. It's going to be a big transition and I'm going to miss you more than I can ever articulate, but it's also such an exciting time to be on a new adventure. You might get homesick. That's normal. And trust me, I'll get on a plane or a boat or a car or a jet ski—whatever it takes—to come to visit you and bring you stacks of hot chocolate cookies."

"These cookies, you promise." He sniffled.

"Cross my heart." I made an "x" over my heart to prove my point. "I have a feeling that once you've landed wherever you decide to go, you're going to quickly forget about me and Dad and Leavenworth."

"I won't forget about you guys." He sounded incensed.

"Bad word choice. What I mean is that you're going to be swept up in so many new experiences with new friends and people from all over the world. You're going to have interesting discussions in your classes and live in a dorm on your own for the first time. Maybe you'll study abroad for a semester or sign up for an internship. The possibilities are endless. It's bittersweet to be your mom right now." I sniffed through my tears and pressed my lips into a smile. "I'm so excited for you. Honestly, it's going to be such an incredible time for you. I don't want you worrying about me. I'm going to miss your face, but I'm going to be fine."

He leaned over to hug me. "I'm going to miss you too, Mom."

"I know." I massaged his cheek with my thumb like I used to do when he couldn't sleep at night.

"And you're sure you don't care if I play soccer?" He pulled away to watch my expression.

I put my hand up like I was swearing an oath. "Not at all. We want you to go to college wherever you're going to be the happiest. I can say with confidence that Dad will one hundred percent agree."

He wiped his nose with the back of his hand. "There's one more thing."

"What's that?"

"What if I want to go into the family business?"

"You mean brewing?" I was shocked. Alex had never expressed an interest in brewing. He started working at Der Keller for the last summer as part of the waitstaff and I knew that both Otto and Mac had given him an overview of operations.

He shrugged. "Maybe. I don't know. There's the brewing program at Central Washington University. I would get a Bachelor of Science in Craft Brewing. I've done some research into it and it's very science-heavy. You study microbiology, biochemistry, and sensory analysis. You know how much I love science. Plus I'd be in the heart of the hop and brewing industry. Getting an internship should be easy."

I chuckled and winked. "I might know someone to put you in touch with for that."

Alex smiled. "It could be a nice balance. I'd still be away but not so far that I couldn't come home on the weekends, and they have a soccer team. The coach emailed me and he sounds pretty chill. I don't think it would be the same kind of commitment as playing for UW, you know?"

"Wow, I had no idea you were considering it."

"I didn't want to say anything to you or Dad or Opa until I was sure. I still haven't said anything to them yet because I guess I just want a little more time." He drifted off and took another drink of his hot chocolate.

"I won't say anything. It's your story to tell, not mine."

That was twice today. First Leah. Now Alex.

"Thanks." He sat up and guzzled the rest of his hot chocolate. "This feels like something I need to decide on my own."

"I trust you, Alex. You'll know what to do. You'll know what feels right."

"I wish I trusted myself as much."

"It takes time, honey." I patted his legs. "You know how many mistakes I've made over the years. Although what I've come to learn is that none of them have been mistakes. More like opportunities to learn and take a different path. That's what I want for you."

"I'll work on it."

"Would it help to take a quick trip to Ellensburg and tour the campus? Garrett and I have some contacts there. Remember that farm-to-table beer weekend we did?"

He nodded.

"A few of the members of their team had graduated from the program and had great things to say about it."

"Is there a way we can do that without telling Opa and Dad?" He picked up a pencil and wrote his name on top of one of the Yahtzee scorecards.

I didn't want to get in the middle of anything between Alex and Mac, but this felt different. I understood where he was coming from in terms of Krause family pressure. Not that Mac or Otto or even Hans and Ursula would intentionally put undue pressure on Alex, but their reaction to the possibility of his attending the brewing program at Central Washington would be met with an abundance of enthusiasm.

"We could take a day trip," I suggested. "It's only a little over an hour. We could leave in the morning, tour campus, you could probably sign up to do an official tour or at the very least meet with professors or students in the program, and then we could be home by dinnertime."

"Really?" He perked up. "Would it be weird for you not to tell Dad?"

"Not in this case. I get it." I put my name on the other scorecard.

"Cool. I don't have class this week for ski week, but coach wants us in the weight room training Monday through Thursday. It doesn't sound like we'll have lifting or practice on Friday. Could we go then?"

"Sure."

He kissed the top of my head. "Thanks for the talk. I don't think I realized how much it was bothering me. Can we hold off on Yahtzee for a few minutes? I'm going to go email the coach now and see about a tour for Friday." He took his dishes to the kitchen and hurried to his room.

I stayed on the couch a while longer, content that Alex felt safe to confide in me and still slightly stunned by his revelation that brewing might be in his future. It shouldn't be such a surprise, it was in his blood after all, but I had never let myself explore the possibility that he might end up in Leavenworth long-term. That still could change and I would make sure that I didn't influence his decision in any way, shape, or form. He was right that this choice was entirely up to him. However, the thought of him returning to the village after college to work at Der Keller or Nitro was the stuff of dreams.

TWENTY-ONE

I DROVE Alex to school for his weightlifting session with the soccer team the next morning due to weather conditions. Another storm had rolled in overnight, dumping six inches on our sleepy streets. Once I had promised him that I would take Friday off for our trip to Ellensburg to visit Central Washington University, I left the car at home and walked to Nitro. I was glad I made the choice because on my way I bumped into Chief Meyers at the coffeehaus.

"Sloan, you were next on my list." Her khaki police parka was zipped up to her chin. The line for coffee and pastries already wrapped out the front door.

I got in line next to her. The village was bustling for a Monday. City crews cleared slippery sidewalks with snow shovels and the snowplow cut neat rows through the streets as it went down one side, made a U-turn and came back the other. "I hear you were in Seattle. Did you make an arrest?" I asked Chief Meyers.

She scowled. "No. Is that the rumor going around?"

I filled her in on what Tad had told me about Jerry.

"Interesting. Not true, but interesting." She silenced her walkie talkie. "I'll get that later. By the way, apologies for not returning your messages. I did receive them and sent officers to the hospital upon listening to your report."

"I figured."

"Any other developments while I've been gone?" Her steely eyes scanned Front Street. The bookshop owner was posting signage about an upcoming author talk and an employee at Bavarian Wares, a store that sold high-end German pottery, was blowing snow from the balcony.

"Sadly, no," I replied. I was hoping that she might have news for me, not the other way around, but I filled her in on everything else I had heard.

We made it to the front of the line and ordered our drinks. She didn't bother to attempt to make small talk while we waited for our lattes.

"Walk with me a bit," she said, once her coffee was in hand.

I fell into step with her.

"Too many ears in there." She surveyed Front Street as if anticipating eavesdroppers lurking around the corner. "We were able to make contact with Jerry as well as other executives at BioGold while I was in Seattle."

My coffee was too hot to drink, but I took a tiny sip anyway.

"I trust you'll keep what I have to say in confidence. My team is working in coordination with detectives in Seattle on the investigation. I'm sure you've heard that we were able to determine the cause of death."

I nodded. "She was drugged?"

"According to toxicology reports, yes." Chief Meyers was matter of fact in her response.

"Do you have an idea who did it?" I couldn't believe that anyone in our village of cobblestone streets with their midwinter glow would resort to murder.

"We're in the process of procuring more evidence and conducting further interviews with the suspects."

I could tell she was speaking in code. The problem was I wasn't deciphering her message.

"Were you able to find Hazel's data? Tad mentioned that he hadn't been able to recover her files before he was attacked." I decided if I continued to ask her direct questions, it might help trigger what she could tell me.

"That's one of the things we're working on." She paused at the Nutcracker Shoppe where two life-size nutcrackers guarded the door. It sat adjacent to the museum, so that visitors could spill in and bring home their own nutcracker souvenirs. "I can't divulge much, but it's not a leap to say that the clinical trial and Hazel's death are directly connected."

Her words confirmed what I had suspected all along, but hearing them spoken aloud brought a flood of memories of Hazel's body on the ski hill to the forefront.

"I know I asked you and Garrett to keep an ear open and I appreciate the information you've been able to glean. Now, I need to ask another favor." Her tone sounded serious.

"Sure, anything."

"This one is dicey, and I preface the request by saying that I don't want you or Garrett to feel any pressure. I know that you've been through some things in the past and if you're not comfortable with my ask, it's fine."

My neck tingled. What was she going to ask?

"We'd like to use Nitro for a stakeout tonight if at all possible." She placed both hands on her hips and waited for my reply.

"Yeah, sure."

"Not so fast." She put out both hands to stop me from committing too quickly. "It's not that simple. It's a bit of a setup and we'd be asking you and Garrett and Leah to play a role and close the pub for the evening."

"Okay."

She pursed her lips together in a frown. "I need you to be

aware that there is risk involved. We need to get the BioGold team in a contained space. The hospital isn't conducive to our end goal."

"Nitro is pretty self-contained," I agreed.

"Exactly. It's small. We can lock down the back exit with a couple of my officers and have another team posted in the front."

I could tell she was already mapping out her stakeout strategy in her head.

"Are you hoping to make an arrest?" It sounded like she was preparing in case the killer attempted to make an escape. I didn't need time to consider her request. If using Nitro would help bring Hazel's killer to justice, I was all in.

"Perhaps." She tilted her head to one side like she was weighing how to answer my question. "We'll have to see how it unfolds."

"What do you need from me?"

"I need to check on a few things at the office, then I'll wander over to Nitro and go over details with you, Garrett, and Leah. If possible, can you reserve the tasting room for a private party for at least an hour later this evening?"

"Do you have a specific time in mind?"

Her walkie talkie crackled again. "What works with your schedule? I don't want to inconvenience you. We figured tonight might be better since any weekend tourists will have returned home."

"Yeah, it's fine. It should be slow."

"Let me check with my team and confirm, but we can shoot for seven?"

"I'll post a note on the door and have Kat update our social media."

"Thanks." She tipped her coffee cup. "I know it goes without saying, but let's keep this between us."

"Of course."

We parted ways.

Chief Meyers ambled down the sidewalk toward the police station. I took a moment to consider the implications of what she had just told me. She must be close to making an arrest. She confirmed that not only had Hazel been drugged before her fall, but also that her death was directly connected to the clinical trial.

However, she had been evasive about Jerry. They hadn't arrested him in Seattle. Did that mean he was innocent, or was it that she hadn't been able to find enough tangible evidence to link him to the crime?

Tad was on the bottom of my list after he'd been attacked, but I supposed there was an outside possibility he had staged his attack in order to shift suspicion away from him. Shep and Ren were both wearing the same scrubs as Tad's attacker. Did that mean that either of them was the killer? It was a huge stretch to accuse someone of murder based on their work uniform.

Ren had seemed genuinely upset about Hazel's death, but he had also admitted to asking her out on more than one occasion. And I couldn't ignore the rumors about him being a stalker. Maybe his attempts at dating her had turned dark. He could have been stalking her, or she could have turned down his advances and he snapped.

Shep had been at the scene when Tad's office was ransacked. Garrett and I had bumped into him running upstairs at the same time as the loud crash we'd heard coming from the basement. He could have hit Tad and then sprinted away before being seen. If he had a drug problem and Hazel found out, that definitely gave him a motive for wanting her dead.

Finally, there was Dr. Sutton. She had the most to lose with the clinical trial results. She'd been quick to push for the press conference and to offer Leah a position. Was she simply doing her job? It seemed in poor taste to move forward with both, but then again she had a hospital and clinical trial to run.

I sighed, not feeling any closer to knowing who might have killed Hazel. Hopefully by day's end, everything would become clear. Nitro was about to be part of a stakeout. That was a first. Maybe justice would be served at the pub tonight.

TWENTY-TWO

CONCENTRATING on daily brewery tasks and baking was difficult knowing that within a few hours, a team of police officers and detectives would be taking over our space. As expected, Garrett and Leah were both game to participate in whatever Chief Meyers asked of us. Penny and Bruce had signed up for a wine-tasting tour that started in Leavenworth and then would take them to Wenatchee. They would be gone until later, which worked out well for our involvement with police operations.

"Does it feel like the day is inching by?" Leah asked after lunch. We were in the office brainstorming new flavor profiles for our upcoming line of spring ales.

"It's like molasses," I agreed.

Kat had the day off and we didn't need extra help, so it was just the three of us. Garrett had shown Leah each step of the brewing process. We were already beginning to think about spring beers. Since every batch took a minimum of two to three weeks to ferment, we had to be strategic about upcoming events and seasonal brews. The next big festival would be Maifest, but spring break, which started in March and lasted through mid-April, would see an uptick in visitors. We wanted to have a spring line ready to go by then.

The whiteboard in our shared office was a jumbled mess of potential options. My current favorites were for a blood orange wheat and a Belgian whit beer with pears and apples. Brewing in such a fertile part of the world meant that we had a plethora of fruits, berries, and hops grown right here in the valley.

"I can't believe how much legwork goes into each beer," Leah said, as Garrett made notes on the bottom section of the whiteboard. "And that you have so many beers going at once."

"That's one of the pros of a brewery our size. We can be nimble," I replied, making note of the trio of hops I had added to our spring pale ale. It would have notes of rosehips, lemongrass, and strawberries.

"The only con is that we don't have the same size tanks as a brewery like Der Keller," Garrett added. "Once the kegs are drained on this batch, that's all she wrote."

"Or don't you mean that's *ale* she wrote?" Leah teased.

"Well done with the pun." Garrett clapped her on the back. "I've trained you well, young one."

"Young one?" Leah pursed her lips. "Uh, that's Dr. to you, sir."

"Sorry, Dr. Strong." He wrapped his arm around his sister. "Now, come out to the brewery and we can show you the real work—cleaning, cleaning, and more cleaning."

"How many beers total will you brew?" she asked me as we walked out to the brewery.

"Good question. We always like to have a pale on rotation for our signature spring brew, along with a light pilsner, a golden."

"And you brew them all here?" Leah pointed to the stainless-steel tank next to her. "What's the difference between a golden and a pale ale?"

Garrett motioned to me. "Sloan, this is your territory. You want to answer that?"

"It's both of our territory."

"Not so," he said to Leah. "Sloan usually hosts our brewery tours and people leave with a doctorate in beer science."

"Nice." Leah grinned. "I'll afford you Dr. Krause, just not him."

I laughed before going on to explain that a golden or blond ale was in the same category as a pale. The style was light and popular for spring and summer easy drinking. A golden derived its name in part from its color. Low in IBUs and bitterness, golden ales tended to be crisp and refreshing with very little maltiness. They were perfect beers to drink next to a lazy river or pack for a day of hiking to see the wildflowers blooming.

"I wish you could be here to taste these when they're finished," Garrett said with a touch of melancholy.

"Maybe I'll have to plan a spring break trip." Leah caught my eye, but she didn't mention a move or a potential house-hunting visit.

The afternoon continued to slog on. Alex texted me to tell me that he was going to dinner at Otto and Ursula's and that he had arranged a campus visit and a meeting with the soccer coach for Friday. His motivation made me think that CWU must be a serious contender. I told him that I would block out the day and to say hi to the Krauses for me.

We put CLOSING EARLY signs on the doors and attended to the few customers that trickled in for afternoon pints.

Finally around six, Chief Meyers showed up with four police officers in tow. We waited for the last guest to leave before locking the doors and congregating at the bar to go over our roles.

"You're all sure you're okay with this?" She passed around photocopied papers of her rough sketch of Nitro, including the exits and where each of us and her team would be stationed during the stakeout.

"I'll do anything to help with the investigation," Leah responded solemnly, studying the paper.

The chief looked to Garrett and me for confirmation that we felt the same. We both nodded.

"Okay, good. I appreciate it and can assure you that you won't be in any danger during our operation. As you see, I brought reinforcements and there are additional teams posted outside the building." She used her index and middle fingers to point out positions, like a flight attendant directing passengers to the emergency exits.

"Are you anticipating a standoff?" Garrett sounded nervous for the first time.

"No. I'm not even anticipating violence." Chief Meyers reassured him. "Standard protocol. What we don't want is for the suspect to run and not have a team standing ready to apprehend them."

That brought me some relief. I knew that Chief Meyers wouldn't put us in danger. She had said as much earlier and she was nothing if not true to her word.

"What do you need us to do?" Leah asked.

"I'd like you to insert yourself in the conversation." Chief Meyers motioned to a high-top table in the dining room. "We'll have them sit together right over there, and we'll give you a cue. You'll join their conversation. Bring up the drug that killed Hazel. You can let them know that we informed you of the toxicology report since you were on the scene at time of death."

That was unexpected. Chief Meyers wasn't attempting to pretend like we weren't in the loop.

"No problem. Anything else?" Leah sounded a bit breathless.

"We'll be listening in." Chief Meyers turned to me. "That's where you and Garrett come in. We need to set up in the back. Leah, are you comfortable wearing a wire?"

"A wire? Like in TV shows?" Leah bit her lip but put on a brave face. "Okay, that's fine. I can do that."

"Television and movies get about one percent of police

procedures correct, but as a matter of speaking, yes. Our team will fit you with a listening device. We'll be in the brewery listening to every word."

"Yeah, count me in." Leah clutched the sketch and nodded.

"We'll need access to your Wifi, a table, and a couple of chairs," Chief Meyers addressed us. "Obviously the brewery is fairly private, but we'll want to be out of sight on the off chance that anyone might walk that way."

"We can set you up in the office," Garrett suggested, pointing to the brewery. "That's about as private as it gets and the Wi-Fi signal is very strong in there."

"Excellent." She flipped through her notebook for a minute.

"Is there anything else you want me and Garrett to do?" I asked.

"Act normal. Everyone has been told that they've been invited to a private event hosted by BioGold. They have no idea that we're going to be on-site or that they're being observed and we want to keep it that way."

"So we should serve them beers, food, the usual?" I asked.

"Exactly." Chief Meyers looked behind us toward the brewery. "We'll keep a low profile."

"Didn't you say that there were going to be teams at both entrances?" Garrett motioned to the front door.

"Yes, but they'll be posted in places that won't be visible, especially in the dark."

"Got it."

"My team will take it from there. Everyone go about your normal business, Leah, join them and bring up the medication. We'll listen and observe. Should we need to sweep in and detain anyone, we'll do so. Otherwise, we'll give you the all clear after they're gone."

It sounded easy enough, but I couldn't calm the jittery feeling in my stomach as Chief Meyers and her crew took over the pub. Were we about to have a killer in our midst?

TWENTY-THREE

CHIEF MEYERS and her team were out of sight when Shep arrived. He was the first to show up and made a beeline for the bar.

I wondered how Chief Meyers had gone about getting the BioGold team to Nitro. Shep hadn't come from work. He was dressed for the gym in a pair of compression leggings with shorts over the top and a zip-up warmup jacket.

"Where is everyone?" Shep glanced at the whiteboard menu and strummed his fingers on the bar. "I'll take a stout."

I reached for a glass and poured his beer. "You must have beat them here."

"That's weird. I was the last to leave the team meeting." He tapped his fingers on the distressed wood bar top like he was playing the piano.

Was it a nervous tick? Or did he need a fix?

"How is everything at the hospital?" I hoped that I sounded casual. Garrett had run upstairs to make sure the guest rooms were locked per Chief Meyers' orders.

"Fine." He pounded his fists on the long countertop. "The usual. Do you know what this thing is about tonight?"

"No. We were told you were having a private event. That's

as much as I know." I hope I sounded as casual and evasive to him as I did in my head.

"It's weird." His eyes darted around the tasting room as if he suspected that the police were staked out. "Do you know who set it up?"

I shook my head. "No."

"I bet it was Ren."

"The nurse? Is he part of the clinical trial?" Maybe if I pretended to be totally out of the loop it would put him at ease and get him talking.

"Yeah, we call him Renny-Henny. Have you seen that hair? He likes to play off that he gets bullied but you have to be desperate for attention to walk around with a spiky pumpkin head." Shep let out a cynical laugh. "He was Hazel's right-hand man."

"Right-hand man?" That wasn't a phrase I expected to hear from Shep.

"Her lackey. He followed her everywhere. He took notes while she did the hands-on research."

"Wait, he was the one documenting Hazel and Dr. Sutton's research?" I asked.

"Yep. It was just a way to be close to Hazel. He had a thing for her. I guess he figured if he weaseled his way into helping with the study, it would impress her."

"Did it?"

"Does stalking impress you?" he countered, running his eyes from my head to my chest. "'Cause you're not bad on the eyes. I'd be happy to hang around here more often."

I ignored his comment. "You think he was stalking Hazel?" Ren had told me that there were rumors circulating about him stalking Hazel, but he had insisted they weren't true.

"The dude was obsessed. He would wait by her car every night, leave flowers and chocolates on her desk, and trade shifts so he could have the same lunch and dinner breaks. Dr. Sutton told him to leave the team. Not that he was on the team to begin with, but she had to tell him that he wasn't allowed to help Hazel with any documentation due to security reasons. I'm sure that Hazel went to her for help."

"Was Dr. Sutton concerned about Hazel's safety?" I started rearranging pint glasses to seem busy.

"Without a doubt. She sent an email to all staff stating that no one was to access any of the study sites, documents, files, etc. without her written approval."

This was news. Could that mean that Dr. Sutton knew that Hazel was in danger when it came to Ren?

"Ren got pissed about it."

"He did?" I cleaned the inside rim of a pint glass.

Shep gulped his stout. The dark beer was meant for slow sipping. I wanted to caution him to take it easy, but I didn't get the sense that he did anything in moderation.

"He freaked out in the ED a couple weeks ago. I'm kind of shocked that he didn't get fired, but we've been short staffed for a while, so I guess anything goes these days. You can flip out on co-workers and your boss and keep your job."

I was about to ask him what he meant by "flip out" but Dr. Sutton and Jerry came in together at that moment and approached the bar.

"I see you started without us, Shep." Dr. Sutton shot a disapproving glance at his nearly empty pint glass. She pushed her pink paisley glasses to the tip of her nose to see the beer menu. As always she was wearing her white coat, tailored pants, and heels.

How did she manage the slippery sidewalks in those shoes?

"Perfect time for another round." Shep slid his glass toward me. "Fill her up."

"Would you like another stout?" I asked.

"I'd like about twelve, but I'll start with another." He raised his eyebrows at Dr. Sutton, who rolled her eyes.

Jerry hung back and waited for Dr. Sutton to order. Garrett came downstairs to help me. Not that I needed it. Serving three people took all of about two minutes.

Dr. Sutton motioned to the table we had reserved for them. "Shall we?"

The two plain clothes detectives were seated at a table a few feet away. Leah probably didn't even need to wear a wire it would be fairly easy to hear the physicians' conversation in the empty pub.

I went to check on the table with the police officers while Garrett poured Leah a drink as she got into position at the bar to await their signal.

"I think you know why I've asked you here," Dr. Sutton began.

Jerry cut her off. "Before we get into business, let's have a proper toast. To this team and BioGold."

He raised his glass. Dr. Sutton looked annoyed but she toasted him and Shep anyway.

"Now, as I was saying, there are a few things we need to get straight before the national press arrives."

"National press. Isn't that a risk?" Shep asked.

"National and *international* press," Dr. Sutton corrected him.

"Fine, but my point is that it's still early. Are we sure we're ready?" Shep asked.

I found it odd that he used the term "we" because he had been so adamant that he wasn't involved in the BioGold trial.

"We're ready," Jerry said with confidence, tipping his glass toward Dr. Sutton. "Thanks to this superstar. We're more than ready."

I couldn't very well stand next to the table after already taking the police officers' orders without looking obvious, so I returned to the bar.

"How's it going?" Garrett whispered.

Leah was seated across from him, scrolling on her phone.

"They're talking about getting things straight before more press show up," I told them.

"That could mean she's referencing their data, or it could mean they were all in on Hazel's death together," Garrett said, wiping the bar with a wet cloth. "And they're making sure that no one goes off script."

I opened a bag of Doritos and poured them into a bowl. "Are you still feeling okay about getting involved in this?" I asked Leah.

She pretended to sip her beer and reached for a chip. "I'm fully invested."

The plan was that when Chief Meyers was ready for Leah to join the conversation, one of the plain clothes detectives would come to the bar and order a bowl of soup.

Waiting for the signal was agonizing. If it was hard for me, I couldn't imagine how Leah must be feeling. Thirty minutes passed. I tried to act busy by shining the tap handles, wiping down the bar with our natural cleaning solution twice, and rearranging our pub menus. I wasn't sure I was very convincing. My palms were sweaty and my pulse remained elevated. I tried not to stare, but it was hard not to steal glances at the doctors in hopes of catching some small sign of an admission of guilt.

I wondered if there was a chance that Chief Meyers had already heard what she needed because none of the plain clothes detectives approached the bar to give Leah her cue. Part of me wanted to go into the office and check, but I didn't want to do anything to risk her operation.

At that moment, Ren stormed into the bar. He stomped his boots on the mat and went directly to the physicians' table.

Something didn't add up. If Ren had been banned from the clinical trial, what was he doing here?

Dr. Sutton asked my question out loud. "Ren, this is a private conversation that doesn't involve you."

"It involves me. I know exactly what you're doing." His oversized parka and heavy boots made him appear more intimidating. He towered over the table. His mohawk made him look even taller.

"I'm going to have to ask you politely to leave." Dr. Sutton shook her index finger at him.

He firmed his stance and planted his feet on the floor. "I'm not going anywhere. This is a free country."

"You are interrupting a private conversation and being quite rude." Dr. Sutton swept her hand in the opposite direction. "There are plenty of other available tables. I'm asking you kindly to leave us to our discussion."

"Or what?" He puffed out his chest.

Was that the behavior of a killer?

I couldn't decide whether Ren was unhinged. Maybe he felt wronged by Dr. Sutton and had come to get his revenge. Could this be why Chief Meyers hadn't signaled for Leah's help yet? Was she waiting for Ren to show up and instigate a fight?

Is that why the other two officers were seated right next to the table?

The other possibility was that Ren knew that one of the team—or all of them—had killed Hazel. If he had been taking notes and helping her with documentation, there was a good chance that he knew the results had been altered. Maybe he had proof and was here to confront them.

I was so focused watching Ren that I hadn't noticed that one of the officers was moving in our direction.

"I'll take a bowl of soup."

That was the cue.

Leah stood up and abandoned her beer. "Wish me luck."

CHAPTER TWENTY-FOUR

EVERYTHING HAPPENED IN A BLUR. Leah played her part perfectly. She inserted herself in the conversation, not allowing Dr. Sutton or anyone else at the table to dismiss Ren. I heard her mention Hazel and the medication.

Shep pushed back his barstool and jumped to his feet. "What? Where did you hear that? That can't be true. She fell. She fell." He shook his head again and again as he repeated "she fell" like a mantra.

If it were true that he had a prescription drug addiction and Hazel had caught him stealing from the hospital's supply, it stood to reason that he could have killed her with the same medication. Was his reaction due to the realization that he was about to be arrested?

"She was murdered," Ren spat as he spoke. "One of you killed her."

"No, she fell," Shep repeated. He unzipped his workout jacket and slung it on his barstool. "She fell, right?"

Jerry cleared his throat. "I don't know where you're getting your information from, young lady."

Leah wasn't fazed. "As I said, the police chief."

Dr. Sutton spilled her drink and tried to dab it up with a napkin. I seized the opportunity, grabbing a towel to mop it up.

"Thanks." She stepped out of the way for me to clean the spilled beer.

"Look, I'm sorry to hear that, but I don't know how this relates to our data," Jerry said. "The police are handling that investigation we're trying to move forward with a new treatment that will save countless lives. This is a case of the good of the one versus the better. Hazel is already dead. There's no point in dwelling on it when our research has the potential to radically alter healthcare."

It was a cold reaction, to say the least. He wasn't even trying to pretend to be upset by Hazel's death. In fairness, I had no idea how closely they had worked together, but even if they didn't know each other well, it was still a heartless response.

"Wait, wait, can we back this up?" Shep asked, pounding his forehead with his fist. "Hazel was drugged before she fell? That can't be true."

"The police have definitive proof," Leah responded. "The toxicology report showed high levels of the substance in her bloodstream. It was a fatal dose."

"But I saw the report," Shep replied. He took his warmup jacket off the chair and used it to mop sweat from the base of his neck.

"How?" Jerry asked.

"It came through her file." Shep blinked hard as if he were having trouble with his vision. Was he trying to sober up? "I saw it that night. I checked because I wanted—needed—to know the cause of death."

Leah shrugged. "Maybe you saw a preliminary report?"

"That's impossible." Shep's neck bulged and he tightened the muscles in his arms like he was refusing to believe Leah. "No, none of this makes sense."

"Because you killed her," Ren said stepping closer to Shep.

"Me? No. Hazel and I were friends. Why would I kill her?"

"Because she knew about your little habit." Ren balled his hands into fists like he was preparing to fight.

Shep flexed every muscle in his body and clenched his jaw. Then he rocked on his heels. "You know, too?"

"Hazel and I *were* friends. Unlike you."

"Dude, you weren't friends. You were stalking her. Everyone on staff knew that. You were so obvious about it."

Ren shook his head, his mohawk flopping. "Did I like her? Yeah. Was I stalking her? No. And I certainly didn't kill her because she found out that I was stealing prescription medication."

Shep threw his hands up. "No, dude, you've got it wrong."

Ren scoffed.

"It's true, okay, okay. Hazel did catch me taking a few extra pills. It wasn't a big deal."

"Not a big deal?" Dr. Sutton spoke up for the first time.

I started to back away from the table. I didn't want to be in the way or in the middle of any fight that might break out.

She grabbed my arm to stop me. "Could you be a dear, and get me a refill? Feel free to charge me for both."

"No problem." I took her empty glass and the towel to the bar.

"It sounds like things are heating up," Garrett whispered.

"I keep expecting Chief Meyers to pop out from the office and make an arrest." I peered toward the brewery but everything was still and dark.

"She's probably getting the entire conversation on Leah's mic."

"True. She might not have a murder confession yet, but Shep just admitted to stealing medication. I'm going to guess that's a fireable offense."

"And he's probably going to lose his medical license, too."

I poured Dr. Sutton a fresh pint. "Back in a minute," I said to Garrett.

"Take your time." He flipped through a stack of coasters. "I'm going to continue to make sure I have the count on these right."

When I returned to the table, Shep and Ren were still going at it.

"These are serious accusations being tossed around," Jerry tried to reason with them.

Dr. Sutton gave me a nod of thanks and set her beer on the table. "If you'll excuse me for a moment, I need to use the restroom. I think everyone should take a moment to take a beat, breathe, calm down, and when I return we can have a rational conversation about all of this."

Leah glanced at me with a look that said she didn't know what to do next.

"I think you forgot your beer at the bar," I said to her. "Should I bring it over?"

"Oh, I'll come get it."

She walked with me, keeping her voice barely above a whisper. "I didn't think things were going to blow up that quickly. Chief Meyers told me to bring up the medication and then make my exit. I couldn't figure out what to say next, or if I should stay to get everything recorded."

"It's okay. I don't think anyone would have scripted that interaction."

"Not me, but I hope that Chief Meyers is getting what she needs. Should I check with her?" Leah asked.

The officer who had ordered soup came up behind us. "I'm checking to see if my soup is ready?"

He and Leah stood at the bar. That was my cue.

"Let me go get it for you." I gave them a nod and went to the kitchen. The office door was still shut and there was no sign of activity in the brewery. That must mean that Chief Meyers wasn't ready to make an arrest yet. Maybe she hadn't heard what she was waiting for. Or maybe she had gotten exactly what she wanted, and she needed the group to disperse before making her next move.

I wasn't sure that the officer actually wanted a bowl of soup, but until the chief or any of the authorities staked out in the pub told me otherwise, I would continue to do my part to make it appear that it was a normal weeknight at Nitro.

As I entered the kitchen, a prickly sensation spread up my arms. I couldn't place why, but it almost felt like I was being watched. I checked around me. The soup pot was simmering on the stove and the dishwasher was running a load. Everything else looked normal and no one was lurking behind the island.

I shook off the thought and ladled soup into a bowl. I balanced it in both hands after replacing the lid and making sure the burner was turned on low.

As I was about to flip off the kitchen lights a voice startled me, causing me to slosh soup on my sweatshirt and the floor.

"Freeze. Not another step."

TWENTY-FIVE

SOUP SPLATTER BURNED MY FINGERS. I clutched the sides of the bowl and started to turn toward the sound of the voice, feeling a knife digging into my back.

"I said, not another step."

It was Dr. Sutton. She was holding a giant knife we used for cutting pineapple and squash against my spine.

"I'm not moving."

"That's right. You're coming with me. You're my ticket out of here." Her voice sounded oddly calm, which made it all the more unnerving.

I had no doubt that she would do whatever it took to avoid arrest, even if that meant harming me.

"Turn around slowly and put the soup on the counter," she commanded, firming her grip on the knife.

"I don't understand. *You* killed Hazel?" I did as she directed, while frantically trying to figure out my escape plan. I knew every inch of the kitchen and Nitro, which gave me an advantage.

I didn't trust that Dr. Sutton was acting in a rational manner. She might stab me with the knife, but if it came down to a foot race, I knew I would win. I was wearing snow boots.

She was in pink high heels. And I also was likely stronger than she was, but would that matter? She was armed with our deadliest knife.

"She got herself killed," Dr. Sutton's voice was monotoned. "If she had listened to me and done what was good for her and her future, she would be here now. But instead, she wanted to be a hero. Ha! Some hero. More like naïve. She needed to understand how research like this gets funded. The only way we get more money and are able to provide better treatments and hope for our patients is to show progress. So we massaged the numbers a bit. It happens all the time. I explained that to her. We make tweaks as we go but if you lose all of your funding, it's a dead end."

I set the soup down and wiped my hands on my jeans, acutely aware of the sharp blade piercing my sweatshirt. "That doesn't justify killing her."

"Doesn't it?" Her eyes were wild, like a deer trapped in the middle of a highway, frantically searching for an escape route that didn't involve getting mowed down by a speeding car.

Could I run to the stove and reach the soup pot? It was a risk, but if I could grab the pot, I could dump the scalding soup on her and buy myself enough time to make a getaway.

Where was Chief Meyers?

My head felt tingling and numb.

I needed to get out of the kitchen. Now.

"It's easy to make those kinds of judgments from the cheap seats." Dr. Sutton took two steps closer to me, while keeping the knife in front of her body. "You brew beer. I'm responsible for patients' lives. If I have to fudge a couple of Excel spreadsheets in order to save countless deaths, then I'll do it. I know how the game is played. Hazel would have learned that too if she had listened, but she had to be altruistic. You know she actually said she was the one saving people, not me."

Her twisted sense of who was right and wrong in this

scenario was another sure sign that she wasn't in a stable mental condition.

She poked me with the blade. "That way. We're going to head out the back door. Nice and slow. Don't try anything stupid and you'll be fine."

I took a tentative step forward.

She nudged the tip of the knife in my back.

My spine straightened in response. "What are you going to do now?"

"Head overseas. I have colleagues in France. I'll practice and continue my research there. Jerry will fund me, I know it. I'm BioGold's biggest success. He thinks I'm a rock star. And he's right. This kind of research demands hard choices."

Like Hazel, I thought to myself.

"Does he know about Hazel?"

"He does now, which makes him my accomplice. That's why he's going to fund me. If he doesn't, then I'll tell the police that he was fully in on it with me."

She was evil. Pure evil.

We walked past the rope that marked the space between the tasting room and brewery. I took a quick glance at the office, wondering if I should yell for help. Chief Meyers could hear me, but the tip of the knife digging into my sweatshirt told me to proceed however Dr. Sutton directed. Plus, I knew there was a team waiting outside. That gave me a leg up. Dr. Sutton had no idea that police were positioned at the back alley.

"Move. Let's go." She pressed the knife harder.

"I'm going." I wanted to stall, but there was nothing I could grab to use for protection. My only option was going to be outrunning her. If I could keep her talking until we got outside, I had my best chance there.

When we got to the back door, it was locked.

"Unlock it. Quickly," she demanded.

My hands were clammy with sweat. I fumbled with the lock.

"Stop stalling. Open it."

I brushed them on my soup-stained jeans. "I'm trying. It's not every day that I have a knife in my back."

"Oh, God, don't be so dramatic. If I wanted to kill you, I would cut your femoral artery right now. I need you alive to get out of the village."

Out of the village? Where was she planning on taking me?

I got the lock open and turned the handle.

A blast of cold air shot in my face.

It was just what I needed to react.

Without thinking, I ducked and darted to my left.

Dr. Sutton slammed the door behind us.

The back deck was dark. I had the upper hand in that Garrett and I had built the exterior patio last summer so I knew where the stairs were.

"Stop." She tried to grab my sweatshirt, but I yanked myself away and skidded across the slick, snowy deck toward the stairs.

The one thing I didn't know was how far away the police officers were. And had Chief Meyers heard us in the kitchen?

Were we about to be surrounded or did I need to sprint as far away from Dr. Sutton as possible?

I skidded into a stack of chairs and intentionally knocked it over, hoping it would block her path and buy me even another second or two.

"Help!" I yelled as loudly as I could. "I need help!"

"Shut up!" Dr. Sutton shouted back. "You're just like Hazel. You're going to make this so much worse and now I'm going to have to kill you."

I could hear her heavy breathing behind me as I clutched the icy railing and took the stairs one at a time. I couldn't risk falling. Otherwise she would overtake me and slice my throat in a matter of minutes.

"Help! It's Sloan," I called into the darkness.

Where was everyone?

A terrible thought took hold. What if Chief Meyers and the team stationed at this exit had already left? Maybe that's why the office door was closed and she hadn't made an appearance in the front. What if she had gotten what she needed with Leah's recording and they left from the back in order not to be seen?

If that was the case, I was in big trouble.

My heartbeat thudded in my head. A whooshing sound erupted in my ears. I was on the brink of having a panic attack.

I might be alone without anyone coming to help.

I tried again. "It's Sloan, help!"

Silence and the sound of my footsteps greeted me.

This was bad.

I tried to focus on the next thing.

That was a skill Sally, my case worker, had taught me early on. Don't get weighed down by every decision, just do one next thing. Make one decision and move on.

I could do that.

Do one next thing, Sloan.

I glanced behind me. Dr. Sutton was on the top stair. How had she managed to get around the stack of chairs that quickly? She was much nimbler than I imagined.

My feet hit the snowy pavement.

I had to make a decision on which way to go—now.

There was no time to waste. If she caught me, she was going to hurt me. That much was clear.

I decided on the right. That would lead me down the alley and then to Nitro's front entrance. I was pretty fast. Not as fast with an icy layer of snow coating the slippery cobblestone alleyway, but I thought there was a decent chance I could outrun her.

It was really my only chance. The other way led to the bakery, which was closed. I would have to run at least the entire block to get anywhere with people at this hour.

The glow of the streetlamp at the end of the alley was my only guide.

I reached out to use the side of the building to steady me as I took off, with Dr. Sutton right on my tail.

To my relief I heard voices nearby.

Was it the police?

As I reached the end of the alley the voices grew louder.

"Help!"

My voice echoed.

I didn't dare look behind me, but it sounded like I might have widened the gap between us. My breath burned in my lungs. Sweat dripped from my brow.

I burst out of the darkness and directly into Bruce and Penny, who were peering down the alleyway in surprise.

"Sloan, what's wrong?" Penny caught me.

I didn't have a chance to respond as I collapsed in Penny's arms. Flashlights blinded my eyes.

"We've got her," a voice called.

The two officers were upon us and chasing after Dr. Sutton, who had trapped herself in between both teams.

"It's over," Chief Meyers said as she stepped onto the back deck.

THE POLICE SURROUNDED DR. SUTTON.

Penny steadied me. "Sloan, oh my." She rubbed my arm in a tender show of comfort. "What happened?"

I told her and Bruce about the police stakeout. I wasn't sure any of my sentences were coherent. Dr. Sutton had not only killed Hazel, but she didn't sound like she had an ounce of remorse about ending the young doctor's life.

"How was Leah involved?" Bruce scowled.

My teeth chattered as I explained that Chief Meyers and her team had been posted inside the entire time. "Leah wasn't in any danger," I assured him.

"But you were." He rested a hand on my shoulder. "I don't like that, but I'm glad that they've arrested Dr. Sutton. I can't believe a doctor committed to saving lives would do something like this."

Shivers erupted throughout my body. Penny held me tighter. "Should we get you inside?"

The back lights came on, flooding the patio and alleyway with a glaring brightness. I closed my eyes tight, in part to try and adjust to the light but also to shut out the realization that I could have died.

Sirens and two additional police cars sped down the street and came to a halt a few feet away from us.

Chief Meyers had Dr. Sutton in handcuffs.

"This is ridiculous. Do you know who I am?" Dr. Sutton hissed. "Do you know how much money the BioGold research is going to bring into this town? Take these off me immediately."

Chief Meyers didn't respond to Dr. Sutton's tirade. She simply motioned for a police officer to take her to one of the waiting squad cars.

"That woman is delusional," Penny said, still rubbing my forearm.

My body shuddered in uncontrollable waves, but I didn't want to go anywhere until Chief Meyers gave us the okay.

"I don't know if we should leave until the chief says it's okay," I said through my chattering teeth. Suddenly it was like every muscle in my body had seized.

"You're freezing, Sloan." Penny massaged my arm faster to try to create friction.

"Hold on a minute." Bruce took matters into his own hands. He walked over to the porch, said something to Chief Meyers, and returned to us, pointing around the corner. "Let's go get you warmed up and something hot to drink. The police will come find you at Nitro."

I didn't resist.

It was nice that Bruce and Penny were being so thoughtful about my well-being. It made me appreciate them even more.

Inside, the plain clothes officers had revealed their identities and had Shep, Ren, and Jerry at individual tables waiting to be questioned.

The warmth from the cozy dining room and the gas fireplace was a welcome relief, but I couldn't stop the quivering as we approached the bar.

Garrett and Leah jumped off their barstools.

"We heard Chief Meyers take off out the back but they wouldn't let us follow her," Garrett said,

Leah studied my face. "You need to sit down."

I tried to protest, but it wasn't worth it. My body collapsed onto the barstool.

She checked my pulse. "You look a little ashen, but your pulse is okay. I'm going to get you some tea and something sweet to eat."

"I think I'm okay," I started to say.

Penny pulled out a stool and sat down next to me.

"Mom, keep an eye on her. Doctor's orders." She went to the kitchen before I could stop her.

Garrett took the stool on the other side. He struggled to speak. "Sloan, we were so worried when you didn't come back from the kitchen."

"It all happened so fast."

"Was it Dr. Sutton?" Garrett reached for my hand and massaged my palm.

Bruce brought over a blanket and wrapped it around my shoulders.

I let out a long breath. The shaky feeling was subsiding a bit. Everyone was being so kind, not that I expected otherwise, but I was starting to worry that maybe I looked a lot worse than I felt.

"She came out of nowhere. I got the soup and the next thing I knew there was a knife in my back." As I said the words it was hard to believe they were true.

Garrett laced his fingers through mine. "I'm so glad you're okay. It could have been a lot worse." The soft, husky tone to his voice made my eyes mist.

I held his hand tighter. The heat from his touch made me melt into the stool.

Leah returned with a cup of tea and a couple of cookies.

"Drink this slowly and eat a cookie. It will help, I promise." She reached for my wrist to check my pulse again.

It wasn't like I'd been in the elements long enough to become hypothermic, but I did as she directed, holding the tea to my lips with my quivering hands. The spicy flavors of apple and cinnamon instantly warmed my throat.

"They got her, right?" Garrett asked. "It sounded like a lot of sirens out there."

"Yes, the arrested her." I tried to stop my hands from trembling so I could take another sip without spilling tea all over myself.

"But she was chasing you," Penny said, wringing her hands together.

"She was." I told them about Dr. Sutton hiding in the kitchen and coming after me with the knife. "I should have trusted my intuition. I felt like there was someone watching me as I was ladling the soup, but I blew it off because I knew that the team was out here, and Chief Meyers was nearby. I'm not sure where she came from. All of a sudden I heard her voice and felt the knife digging into my back."

"She was going to use you to get away." Bruce shook his head in disgust. "This is coming from a woman who swore an oath to save lives, not end them."

"I'm glad you got away," Leah said, wrapping the blanket tighter around my shoulders.

"Me too." I chomped on the cookie. It was a gingersnap from the bakery and like the tea, it had a nice hint of spice that seemed to help awaken my senses. Between the hot tea and the hit of sugar, the quivering in my legs and hands was subsiding.

"Do you think she was working alone?" Garrett's eyes drifted to the high-top tables where Ren, Shep, and Jerry were being questioned. "Or is that why no one else has been allowed to leave?"

"I don't know. She certainly didn't seem to be in a stable mind-set. She admitted that she killed Hazel. It was basically what we suspected. Hazel realized that the data had been altered. She went to Dr. Sutton, who told her to bury the information. According to Dr. Sutton these kinds of 'glitches' happen all the time in trials."

"That's not true," Leah interjected.

"I figured as much." I chomped on another gingersnap. Feeling had returned to my fingers. "She tried to rationalize killing Hazel by claiming that many more lives would be saved with this revolutionary drug. I don't think she has any remorse, maybe other than getting caught. She was talking about going overseas, and she sounded convinced that the research was so groundbreaking that BioGold or any other number of pharmaceutical companies would still fund her."

"That is twisted." Leah's face mirrored how I felt.

I set my tea on the bar and readjusted the blanket. "She said that most trials fudge their numbers in order to make sure they maintain their funding source and then fix any issues in later rounds of testing."

Leah's mouth hung open. "This is all complete lies."

"She sounds like she might have some more serious issues going on," Bruce said. He stood behind Penny, keeping an eye on the other suspects.

Chief Meyers entered through the front. There was no sign of Dr. Sutton or the other police officers. I assumed they must be escorting Dr. Sutton to headquarters or perhaps transporting her to the nearest detention center in Wenatchee.

The Chief unzipped her khaki-fur jacket and hung on it on the rack near the door. Then she cleared her throat and motioned to one of the long community tables by the front windows. "If everyone can come join me, please." Chief Meyers approached the table and waited for everyone to follow.

We moved in that direction, as did her team of police officers and Ren, Shep, and Jerry.

200

"Take a seat. Pull up extra chairs, if necessary," Chief Meyers directed.

I wasn't sure I wanted to sit next to Jerry in particular, so I opted for the far end of the table. Garrett and Leah squished in on either side and Penny and Bruce stood a few feet away.

Chief Meyers waited until everyone was seated. She stood at the head of the table with one hand on her holster. "I don't have a lot of time, but I'd like to thank Sloan, Garrett, Leah, and Jerry for your help in apprehending Dr. Sutton."

Jerry?

Jerry had been in the loop about the stakeout?

He gave her a half salute.

"You were involved?" Leah asked, raising her eyebrows and looking at me and Garrett as if to check whether we were shocked by this revelation, too.

The chief answered for him. "We were in contact in Seattle." She gave me a half nod. "As you know, I spent a few days in Seattle working with a team of investigators there along with the research partners at the University of Washington and BioGold."

I massaged my jaw, trying to get it to pop. Jerry had been working with Chief Meyers. I couldn't believe it. That meant that Dr. Sutton was not in touch with reality. Jerry wouldn't have continued to fund her research.

"BioGold has been very cooperative in our investigation," Chief Meyers continued. "As soon as it came to Jerry's attention that the data had been altered, we had his full assistance along with that of the entire company. They turned over the entirety of their research. We had access to every file, every note document for the trial."

"I hate that it had to come to this," Jerry replied, sounding remorseful for the first time. "BioGold does not condone any of Dr. Sutton's actions, including manipulating the trial results and certainly not killing a staff member. We were not aware of

201

any of her actions and the moment that the police brought it to our attention, we offered our full cooperation. It's an absolute travesty to have this vital project be tarnished by one woman. When Chief Meyers asked if I would be willing to call a 'celebratory' meeting tonight in hopes of arresting Dr. Sutton, I immediately agreed."

Everyone was silent for a minute.

What did this mean for Ren and Shep?

I watched both of them. Ren gnawed on his fingernails and squinted at Jerry like he was trying to make sense of everything, too. Shep hung his head and pressed his index finger into the center of his forehead.

"Dr. Sutton can also add attempted murder and kidnapping to her résumé." Chief Meyers met my eyes and gave me a pained smile. "I apologize for putting you in that situation, Sloan. She escaped our grasp for a moment and used the opportunity to strike. We had the exits covered but she ducked into the kitchen unseen."

"It's okay. I'm fine." It wasn't a lie. The shaking had stopped, and the tea and cookies had settled my stomach. I had a feeling it was going to take some time to feel completely normal again, but for the moment knowing that Dr. Sutton was in police custody and that everyone I loved was safe was all the reassurance I needed.

Garrett put his hand on the small of my back. His touch sent another rush of warmth through my body.

"I can't share specifics, but if any of you have additional questions, I'll attempt to answer what I can." Chief Meyers looked around the table.

I raised my finger. "Can I ask something?"

"Go ahead." She circled her hand in a sign for me to continue.

I looked at the far end of the table where Shep and Ren were seated. "I'm confused about how you were both connected to the BioGold trial?"

"I was the nurse attached to the team," Ren answered first. "But then once Dr. Sutton realized that Hazel and I were close, I think she got worried that Hazel was going to tell me about faking the results and she had me assigned to a new team."

So he had been telling the truth all along. And Hazel had confided in him, only about a different issue—Shep.

Shep rolled his shoulders back. "I didn't have any attachment to the trial. It's kind of a long and personal story, but I needed something from Dr. Sutton." He sighed and extended his hand to Ren. "Hey, sorry, man. I had no idea that Dr. Sutton killed Hazel."

"Same, dude." Ren returned his handshake.

"Did she attack Tad, too?" I asked Chief Meyers. "We saw Shep that night wearing the same kind of scrubs that Tad mentioned his attacker had on, but then it seemed like everyone in the hospital was wearing the same scrubs."

The chief nodded. "That was what tipped us off. There are cameras throughout the hospital. Dr. Sutton was aware of their placement and did a fairly impressive job of avoiding them in the hallways, but she missed one in the laundry room when she tried to get rid of the scrubs. That's what ultimately tipped us off. That and the records from BioGold."

So it had just been a coincidence when we bumped into Shep that night.

"How is Tad doing?" Leah asked.

"As far as I know, he's improving and should be released tomorrow." Chief Meyers waited to see if there were more questions.

"What happens with the clinical trial now?" I asked.

"That will be up to BioGold." The chief gave Jerry a slight nod.

"We're not ready to give up yet. There are glimmers of promise in the research, so we'll be starting a search for a new team and with new oversight measures in place, of course. We can't let something like this happen again." Jerry shook his head solemnly. "We never anticipated that life-saving research could end up like this. You have my personal guarantee that BioGold will be permanently changing the structure of how we fund clinical trials in the future."

"Does that mean that you'll partner with a different hospital?" Ren suggested. "It might be nice if you could keep the research here and pay tribute to Hazel."

"That's a great idea." Jerry nodded and reached into his pocket. He slid a business card across the table to Ren. "We should discuss that in greater detail. We'll be looking for suggestions on other physicians we might reach out to since it sounds like you and Hazel were close. I would love to connect and brainstorm how we might keep her memory alive through future research."

There was one glaring issue that hadn't been resolved, Shep's drug use. I didn't feel comfortable bringing it up, but it needed to be addressed.

As if reading my mind, Shep spoke up. "I need everyone to know that as of tonight I'm recusing myself from my role at the hospital. I've already spoken with administration. I'm taking leave for some personal reasons and hope to return in the spring."

I had a feeling that personal reasons referred to treatment. I thought about Garrett and his first love, Halsey. Hearing that Shep was taking responsibility for his health and well-being felt like at least something positive had come out of Hazel's tragedy.

"You're all free to leave, as long as no one has any other concerns to share. Be aware that we will likely be in touch. You may be called to testify in court as well." Chief Meyers picked up her notebook.

Shep and Ren left together.

Jerry asked if he could speak with Leah for a moment.

I wondered if Dr. Sutton had spoken with him about potentially hiring Leah.

Penny and Bruce went upstairs. Garrett grabbed his coat from the back. "Let's go, Sloan."

I glanced at the clock. It was after ten. "Where are we going?"

"I'm walking you home and I don't want to hear a single word of protest." He held out his hand.

"But I don't need an escort."

He threw his index finger up, tilted his chin, and gave me his best stern look. "You've literally had a knife in your back tonight. I'm walking you home."

"When you put it like that." I reached for his hand.

He laced his hand through mine as we headed outside. The sparkling snow and twinkling lights felt strange amidst Dr. Sutton's arrest, but I was content to walk hand in hand through our peaceful village. When we got to my cottage, we stopped on the porch.

Garrett's voice was husky. "Sloan, I don't know what I would do without you."

"I feel the same."

He leaned down to kiss me. "Then let's make a pact never to find out."

"Deal."

TWENTY-SEVEN

News of Dr. Sutton's arrest spread through the village. Nitro was packed for the next few days as locals rotated through the pub to get caught up on the gossip. Tad made an appearance with a small bandage on his head and his left foot in a walking boot.

"I didn't realize you injured your leg, too," I said, while I poured him a pint.

"Neither did the doctors. They were focused on my head and the concussion." He touched the bandage on his forehead. "It wasn't until they had me get up and walk around that we realized I had a hairline fracture in my ankle. I'm in the boot for six weeks."

"How are you feeling otherwise?"

"Better." He positioned the barstool next to him to prop up his foot. "The headache is gone. It could have been much worse. I still can't get over the fact that Dr. Sutton killed Hazel. I was sure it was Jerry."

"It turned out that Jerry was assisting the police." I told him about our conversation the night of Dr. Sutton's arrest and how Chief Meyers had thanked him for his role in bringing her to justice. "Did they ever recover Hazel's data?"

"Yeah, BioGold had their own records." Tad stared at his beer. "That almost makes it worse. Hazel didn't need to die. Did you hear how Dr. Sutton did it?"

"No. I never heard specifics."

"She brought hot chocolate to the ski hill and spiked Hazel's drink. She planned to kill Hazel. It was pre-meditated. She needed to get the laptop. That's all she cared about. It's so awful. I keep wondering if there was something more I could have done. It's not like I ski." He let out a sad laugh and motioned to his graphic T-shirt, skinny jeans, and Converse sneakers. "But if I had stayed at the lodge that day, maybe I could have stopped it."

"It's not your fault, Tad." I passed him a bowl of chips. "I know how you feel, but Dr. Sutton is responsible for Hazel's death. No one else."

He took a couple of chips. "Yeah. It just sucks that I was there. It's hard not to think that maybe there was a chance that if she had come back with me, she wouldn't have been killed."

"Or you both might have," I tried to console him. "Remember, Dr. Sutton attacked you too. I don't have the sense that anything or anyone was going to deter her from trying to get that data. She had a singular mission and from my interactions with her, I don't think she had any regrets about killing Hazel."

Tad stuck his finger under the top of his cast to try to reach an itch. "Yeah, you're probably right."

"What about the flash drive? I've been wondering if it ever turned up."

"Not that I know. She lost it here, right? Did anyone find it?"

I shook my head. "No, I just keep wondering if maybe Dr. Sutton stole it from Hazel's bag the night before she killed her. Hazel was sitting in the corner over by the back patio door." I motioned to the spot. "She was panicked. We all helped her look for the flash drive but there was no sign of it. I realized later that Dr. Sutton could have taken it. She, Ren, Shep, and

Jerry were at a table in the brewery listening to the band. It seems possible that if Hazel went to the bathroom or came up to the bar to get a drink, Dr. Sutton could have used the opportunity to steal the drive. Hazel must have assumed she dropped it, but I'm guessing Dr. Sutton had it all along."

"It makes sense," Tad said, scratching his cast. "If Dr. Sutton found the data that night, then the only thing left in her way was Hazel. The timing checks out. She killed her the next day."

"Right? It all adds up, but the only lingering question I have is about Hazel's laptop bag. Garrett and I found it ditched down below the ski lifts. If Dr. Sutton had the flash drive, why would she need Hazel's laptop?"

"I can answer that." Tad gently touched the bandaged wound on his head. "Dr. Sutton wanted to make sure there was no evidence on any computer or file. That's why she went through my office and knocked me out. Here's a piece of insider IT guy info—a lot of doctors are terrified of technology. Dr. Sutton was one of them. She couldn't tell you the difference between a desktop and laptop and she had no idea how files are stored. She was super old-school. She would keep handwritten patient chart notes. A few years ago, I spent over a month teaching her how to use our digital system for chart notes. She resisted, but she didn't have a choice. The entire hospital upgraded and now everything is electronic—patient records, prescriptions, referrals."

"But because Dr. Sutton wasn't technically savvy, she thought she had to cover her digital tracks by physically taking Hazel's and your laptops?"

"She might have been book smart, but she did not know her way around a machine." Tad took his foot off the stool. "The irony is that the data is backed up to the cloud. It was there the whole time. Erasing it from Hazel's laptop or destroying her flash drive wouldn't have done Dr. Sutton much good. I guess she could have been trying to find the backup files in my office, but I don't give her that much credit. I think she really thought she was going to get away with the files and no one would ever be able to recover the data."

"That answers so many questions," I said, pausing to refill a customer's pint glass. "The night that Dr. Sutton was arrested, Chief Meyers told us that they had found the BioGold data, but I had no idea it had been so easy."

"It almost makes it worse. Hazel was so close. If only she had gone to the police."

I sighed. Tad was right and his words made me think about Alex. What other important pieces of information or life skills did I need to impart to him before he left to college? Like with Hazel, getting help and not trying to solve a problem alone.

Our conversation shifted. Tad shared that the hospital administration had already put together a volunteer committee to brainstorm a memorial for Hazel. Both he and Ren had joined the committee and BioGold had offered to fund the project. It was good to see that Tad was healing and to hear that plans for a memorial for Hazel at the hospital were in the works.

I moved on to serve other customers and do a spin through the tasting room. The Strong family was leaving later in the afternoon. It was going to seem strange and quiet not to have them at Nitro. We had been through a lot in a week, and I wasn't ready to let them go.

The afternoon chugged along. I pulled pints of obsidian stout and served hot cheese and pastrami sandwiches and chicken corn chowder. Kat sketched ideas for a spring pub crawl. We had been toying with the idea for a while and after speaking with the marketing manager at Der Keller and some other businesses in town, everyone was on board with planning an event that would attract visitors to the village in late May.

"How many stops do you think we should include?" she asked, using her finger to draw on the iPad. "And should it be themed? It might be fun if people dressed in spring costumes."

"For the love of craft beer, don't let April Ablin catch wind of that."

Kat laughed. "True. How do you feel about pink and green lederhosen?"

"Don't even." I made a slicing motion across my neck.

That made Kat laugh harder. "No costumes it is. Spring beers, different stops in the village, prizes, and gear. This should be so much fun."

Leavenworth was gorgeous in the spring with the melting runoff snow from the mountains spilling into the rivers and lakes, pastures lush with wildflowers, and long stretches of sunshine. The village came to life in the spring with vibrant blooms adorning the quaint buildings and rolling green hills. Local vendors would be selling fresh produce and handcrafted goods at the farmers market. A pub crawl would be a perfect way to capture the season.

We both froze at the distinct sound of April Ablin's sharp voice. "Ladies, ladies, what is this I hear about a pub crawl?" She sashayed up to the bar.

"What are the odds?" Kat mouthed in dismay.

"Word travels fast," I said to April, who leaned against the counter to intentionally push up her cleavage.

"A spring, or as we like to say in the village, *das Fruhling*, pub crawl, how *vunderfull*."

"How did you hear about the idea?" I motioned to Kat to close her sketchbook. We didn't need any extra input from April.

"Sloan, you *das Reh*, why would you ask a question like that?"

I loved that in April's attempt to sound condescending, she had used the wrong version of "dear," calling me a "deer" in German.

She cleared her throat and pushed up her plunging bra. "Word is already out and I want to make it very clear that the

210

chamber needs to be involved in every aspect of this event. Understood?"

"A pub crawl, why?" I wasn't about to take direction from April when it came to craft beer.

"If this is going to be a sanctioned Leavenworth event, you'll need to go through the proper channels." She pursed her lips together. They were poorly lined with hot pink lipstick that clashed with her red hair. "I would absolutely hate to have to put an end to such a delightful idea. It would be a shame if the mayor had to get involved."

Her less-than-idle-threat didn't scare me.

"Fine, April. We'll let you know once we're finished putting the itinerary together," I acquiesced. After everything that had happened the past week, I didn't have any energy left for April's antics.

"Oh, no, that's not how this works." April waved a bedazzled nail in my face. "I've called a meeting with all of the members of the chamber and city council. I expect you to be there to present your official proposal. A PowerPoint is preferred. Ten o'clock sharp. Don't be late." She tossed me a pouty, triumphant grin. "*Auf Wiedersehen.*"

She trotted out of the pub, doing a little spin when she got to the front door.

"Awesome." Kat doodled something in her sketchbook. "It will be so much fun to partner with April on the pub crawl."

"Don't worry about her. I'll worry about her, you just keep working on plans. When it comes to April Ablin it's all about working *around* her, not with her."

Kat got back to sketching an outline and map for the pub crawl, while I took another turn through the tasting room. Penny, Bruce, and Leah came downstairs with their bags shortly after April made her exit.

"I can't believe you're already leaving." I blinked back unexpected tears. I was surprised by how quickly I had gotten attached to them.

"This week has flown by." Penny wrapped me in a hug. "It's been so wonderful to get to spend time with you, Sloan."

"The feeling is entirely mutual."

"We've already decided to come visit for Maifest," Bruce said, taking two of the bags. "I need to go pull the car around. It's nice that they towed it for us and it sounds like our weather on the return trip is going to be much calmer."

He left with the bags.

Garrett took Penny to the brewery to send them home with growlers and merch.

"So, any news?" I asked Leah once we were alone.

"Jerry offered me a role on the team. He's not sure who is going to take over Dr. Sutton's role, but he did promise that there will be more oversight from the BioGold team."

"Are you leaning one way or another?"

"I'm really tempted. I asked him for a couple of weeks to decide. They're not in a hurry since they have to hire a new lead. I don't want to make a spontaneous choice and regret it, so I've decided to see how I feel once I'm in Portland. The village has been so sweet and charming, but I'm not sure making a snap decision here is the smartest move. I figure if I get home to my rainy apartment I'll either miss Leavenworth—which I'm sure I will—or I'll decide I want to do a better job of getting up this way for visits and stay in Portland."

"That's very mature."

"Garrett's rubbing off on me."

"Well, your secret is safe with me and I support whatever choice you make. As I've been telling Alex about college, you can't make a wrong decision. Either way it will work out."

"Thanks."

Penny came from the brewery with a box of beer and Nitro

swag. "I'm not sure where we're going to fit this." She set it on the bar to give me another hug.

Leah and I said our goodbyes. Garrett helped them out to the car.

I couldn't believe how much had changed since their arrival. Garrett's revelation about his past, Hazel's murder, and Alex's potential new college path.

Tomorrow he and I would take a road trip to Central Washington University. I wasn't sure where he was going to land. The one thing I knew was that I had landed in the right place. As for what was next, time would tell. Maybe Leah would move to the village. Maybe Alex would end up far away. Maybe Garrett and I would take our relationship to the next step. Hazel's death had been a reminder to live in the moment. At this moment I was happy and ready to brew up some new hoppy beers in time for the spring snowmelt.

RECIPES INSPIRED BY SLOAN

Enjoy this taste of Nitro's menu from the cozy comfort of your own kitchen. Read on for the recipes.

SLOAN'S SCHNECKEN CARAMEL STICKY BUNS

Ingredients:

For the dough:

2 packages of yeast
½ cup of warm water
1 teaspoon of sugar
1 cup of milk
1 teaspoon of salt
4 tablespoons of butter
4 cups of flour (plus more for rolling out the dough)

For the cinnamon filling:

4 tablespoons of butter
1 cup of sugar
1 tablespoon of cinnamon
1 teaspoon of cardamom

For the caramel topping:

½ cup of butter
  ½ cup of brown sugar
  ½ cup of pecans

Directions:

Preheat the oven to 425 degrees. Mix the yeast with warm water and a teaspoon of sugar and let rise for 10 minutes. While that's growing, melt the butter in the milk. Sift the flour and sugar into a large mixing bowl. Add the yeast, milk, and butter to the flour mix and knead until a dough forms and doesn't stick to the bowl. Cover with a kitchen towel and let it rise for 15 minutes.

While the dough rises, make the cinnamon filling by melting the butter over medium-low heat in a saucepan. Once the butter has melted, remove it from the heat and whisk in the brown sugar, cinnamon, and cardamom. Set aside.

Gently flour a cutting board and roll the dough into a large rectangle. Then spread the cinnamon filling equally over the dough and then roll the rectangle, like a jellyroll, along the long edge. Cut the log into 1-inch-thick slices. Grease a baking dish, arrange the rolls, cut side up in the prepared pan. Cover the pan with the kitchen towel and let rise for 15 minutes.

While the dough is rising one last time, make the caramel topping. Start by melting the butter over medium-low heat. You can use the same pan you used for the cinnamon filling. Once the butter has melted, remove it from the heat and stir in the brown sugar and pecans. Pour the caramel topping over the rolls and bake them at 425° F for 12 minutes. Allow the rolls to cool before serving. Slice and enjoy!

ROASTED BUTTERNUT SQUASH AND TORTELLINI SOUP

Ingredients:

For the roasted butternut squash:

Olive oil
    1 large butternut squash
    2 cloves of garlic
    Salt and pepper

For the soup:

1 tablespoon of olive oil
    1 white onion
    4 to 5 celery stalks
    12 to15 baby carrots
    4 cloves garlic
    1 small bunch of fresh herbs—Sloan uses parsley, thyme, and oregano
    4 Italian chicken sausages (grilled and diced)
    1 teaspoon of pepper
    1 teaspoon of salt

32 ounces of vegetable stock or chicken stock
Butternut squash blend
1 teaspoon of pepper
1 teaspoon of salt
2 cups of cheese tortellini
Heavy cream

Directions:

For the roasted butternut squash:

Preheat the oven to 400° F. Line a baking sheet with parchment paper and drizzle with olive oil. Peel, core, and deseed the butternut squash. Then cut it into small half-inch pieces. Place on baking sheet. Finely chop the garlic cloves and sprinkle over the butternut squash. Drizzle with more olive oil and season with salt and pepper to taste. Bake at 400° F for thirty minutes. Remove from the oven and allow to cool. Once the squash has cooled, blend in a food processor or blender until it's smooth and creamy.

For the soup:

Add a healthy glug of olive oil to a soup pot, and heat on medium-low. Chop onion, celery, and carrots. Sauté in olive oil until onions become translucent, about five minutes. Dice garlic. Add to the veggie mix. Then add fresh herbs, grilled chicken sausages, salt, and pepper. Stir well. Cover with vegetable or chicken stalk and blended butternut squash. Bring the soup to a gentle boil. Turn the heat low, cover, and simmer for thirty minutes. Add a healthy splash of cream. Serve hot with grated Parmesan cheese and crusty bread.

CHOCOLATE PEANUT
BUTTER PRETZEL BARS

Ingredients:

For the crust:

2 cups of pretzels

½ cup of butter (melted)

½ cup of brown sugar

For the filling:

2 tablespoons of butter

1 tablespoon of heavy cream

1 cup of milk chocolate chunks

1 cup of dark chocolate chunks

1 tablespoon of vanilla extract or 1 teaspoon of vanilla bean paste

1 teaspoon of salt

1 healthy splash of chocolate stout (if desired)

2 tablespoons of sugar

1 cup of heavy cream

For the peanut topping:

½ cup of butter (melted)

½ cup of brown sugar

2 cups of peanuts

1 cup of oats

1 cup of shredded coconut

Directions:

Preheat the oven to 350º F. Place pretzels in a food processor or blender and pulverize them into small fine pieces (but not a powder). Mix them with melted butter and brown sugar and then press them into a greased square baking dish to form a crust. Bake at 350º F for 10 minutes, then remove from the oven and allow the crust to cool.

While the crust is cooling, start on the filling by heating butter and heavy cream in a saucepan over medium-low heat. Slowly add in the milk chocolate and dark chocolate chunks, stirring constantly. Whisk in vanilla extract (or paste) and salt as the chocolate melts. If desired, add in a healthy splash of your favorite chocolate stout. When the chocolate is silky and smooth, remove it from the heat. In a separate mixing bowl (or in an electric mixer), whip the remaining heavy cream and 2 tablespoons of sugar until soft peaks begin to form. Gently fold the chocolate mixture with the whipped cream in small batches, ½ cup at a time. Once the whipped cream and chocolate have developed a mousse, set it in the refrigerator to chill.

Add melted butter, brown sugar, chopped peanuts, oats, and shredded coconut in another mixing bowl. Toss together and then place on a parchment-lined baking sheet and bake for 10 to 15 minutes or until the nut mixture has caramelized a golden-brown color. Remove from oven and allow to cool.

Remove the mousse from the refrigerator and spread it evenly over the cooled pretzel crust. Break up the caramelized peanuts into small pieces and sprinkle over the mousse. Chill in the fridge for another 30 minutes, then slice and serve cold. These would pair perfectly with Nitro's Obsidian IPA.

GOULASH SOUP

Ingredients:

6 slices bacon, chopped

3 pounds boneless chuck, trimmed and cut into 1/2-inch cubes

4 white onions

2 red peppers

4 Yukon gold potatoes

3 cloves of garlic

3 tablespoons of paprika

1 teaspoon of caraway seeds

1 teaspoon of salt

1 teaspoon of pepper

1/4 cup of flour

1/2 cup of stout beer

1 can of tomato paste

6 cups of beef broth

Directions:

In a Dutch oven or large stockpot, cook bacon over medium heat. Once it is crisp, remove it from the pan and allow it to cool. Drain bacon fat, reserving 1 to 2 tablespoons, and then reduce the heat to low.

Chop onions, peppers, and peeled potatoes, then add to the pan, stirring, until the veggies turn golden brown. Add garlic, paprika, caraway seeds, salt, pepper, and flour and cook, stirring continuously, for 2 minutes. Whisk in stout and tomato paste and cook, whisking, for 1 minute. (Mixture will be very thick.) Stir in beef broth, chuck, and chopped bacon, and bring to a boil. Once the soup has reached a boil, cover it with a lid, and turn the heat to low. Allow the soup to simmer for about 30 minutes.

SLOAN'S TOUR OF LEAVENWORTH

Break out your lederhosen. We're traveling to Sloan's alpine village and beloved hometown of Leavenworth, Washington, where the mountains are coated with a fresh layer of snow, Front Street is bustling with Bavarian festivals and food, and the beer is always flowing. Meander the cobblestone streets as you nosh on a giant pretzel and take in the sounds of a polka band playing a German waltz in the gazebo. The Sloan Krause Mysteries might be a work of fiction, but the charming town nestled in the Northern Cascades is entirely real and well worth a visit.

Leavenworth is an idyllic destination that will leave you feeling like you've stepped into a fairy tale. Beyond its charming architecture and delicious food, Leavenworth is also an outdoor lover's paradise. Surrounded by stunning alps, Sloan's village offers a wide range of outdoor activities for every season. In the winter, hit the slopes at the Ski Hill or snowshoe through miles and miles of backcountry trails. In the summer, take a scenic hike to a nearby waterfall or raft on the Wenatchee River and stop at Blackbird Island for a picnic lunch.

Leavenworth is also home to numerous festivals throughout the year, including the famed Oktoberfest, where the entire village gets in the spirit with a parade along Front Street, beer tents, music, traditional dances, and German pastries galore. If you can't visit for Oktoberfest, not to worry because there are a plethora of other events throughout the year, like the Autumn Leaf Festival, Maifest, and the Christmas Lighting Festival, which transform the town into a winter wonderland.

Sloan's guide to visiting will give you everything you need for a bookish adventure. With its charming architecture, delicious food, stunning natural beauty, and vibrant culture, this Bavarian-style village will surely capture your heart and leave you with unforgettable memories.

Prost!

Stop One – Icicle Brewing

Looking for a taste of Bavaria or want to bump into Otto and Ursula? Head to Icicle Brewing, the inspiration for Der Keller. You'll feel like you're in the German countryside in this classic pub that brews up some of the best beers in the Pacific Northwest. As soon as you step inside, you'll be transported to a cozy German tavern with rustic decor, dim lighting, and the warm, welcoming aroma of schnitzel and sauerbraten.

Take a seat at the bar or snag a table on the outdoor patio and prepare to be transported to the heart of Bavaria. Icicle's menu is full of traditional German dishes and some PNW favorites, like their classic tomato soup and grilled cheese— perfect for a snowy winter's evening. The outdoor patio is the best spot to sip a frothy pint of Icicle's Bootjack IPA, soak up the mountain air, and keep your eye out for any nefarious activity in the village. With its friendly atmosphere, delectable food, and extensive beer selection, Icicle is a must-visit for any foodie or beer lover. What's even better is that Pam Brulotte, one of Icicle's owners, is also the inspiration for Sloan. She's been helping to elevate women in the craft for over a decade and will make you feel like part of the family.

Stop Two – Blewett Brewing

Sometimes the lines between fiction and reality get blurred, which is definitely the case for Blewett Brewing, which opened a few years after I started writing the Sloan Krause series. I happened to stumble upon the new nanobrewery and had to pinch myself because it felt and looked so much like my vision of Nitro, complete with an open viewing area to the brewery and young brewers who are constantly creating new flavor profiles.

The brewery specializes in Pacific Northwest beers, unique hoppy ales, and wood-fired pizzas. Located just a few blocks off Front Street (much like Nitro), this cozy spot is a hidden gem well worth visiting. Inside, you'll find a warm and inviting atmosphere, complete with rustic wood accents, comfortable seating, and friendly staff. The brewery features a rotating selection of craft beers, including hoppy ales, stouts, and lagers, all brewed in-house. But, hey, who knows? Garrett might just be working in the back and need a taste tester.

Stop Three – A Book For All Seasons

The first place I find whenever I travel is the local bookstore, and I promise A Book For All Seasons will not disappoint. Plus, you'll need some vacation reading for your Leavenworth getaway. Make sure to go to Sloan's favorite bookshop during your stay. This charming independent bookstore is located right in the heart of the village and offers a cozy atmosphere where you can browse a wide selection of books and bookish treasures.

A Book For All Seasons' welcoming staff is always happy to

help you find the perfect book. They host a variety of author events and signings (hey, like yours truly), and their stacks of books and reading material are thoughtfully curated. You're sure to find something that piques your interest. Whether you're looking for a thrilling mystery, a thought-provoking memoir, or a beautiful coffee table book of the Enchantment Mountains, A Book For All Seasons is the place to indulge your literary passions. Fun fact: Chief Meyers often unwinds by perusing the shelves at A Book For All Seasons for her next romantic read. Be sure to say hi.

Stop Four – München Haus

For a truly authentic Bavarian experience in Leavenworth, make sure to visit München Haus, *the* place in town to try an authentic German-style sausage. You'll smell it before you see it. When Sloan is walking to Nitro, especially during lunchtime, the mouthwatering aroma of sizzling bratwurst, the sound of happy diners chatting, and the vibrant colors of the outdoor seating area immediately draw her in.

München Haus offers various sausages, from classic bratwurst to unique and creative options like elk and wild boar. I mean, when in Leavenworth, why not? The food is served in generous portions, and you'll love pairing your sausage with a cold beer from their extensive selection of local and international brews. The outdoor seating area with its fire-places is a great spot to enjoy your meal and take in the lively atmosphere of the village, or you can take your brat to go and wander along Front Street while munching on a German dog. München Haus might just be the next best thing to actually being in Munich.

Stop Five – Enzian Inn

If you plan to stay for the weekend, the Enzian is a dreamy getaway with its baroque architecture, massive fireplace, pools, guest suites, and breakfast. Oh, the breakfast. The breakfast. More on that in a minute.

But first, let's step into the lobby, where you'll feel like you've been transported to the alps with its intricate wood carvings, stone fireplace, and Bavarian décor. The Enzian Inn offers a wide range of accommodations, from comfortable guest rooms to luxurious suites, each designed to evoke the rustic charm of a Bavarian lodge. Back to breakfast, though. The Enzian's legendary breakfast buffet is a highlight, offering a delicious selection of pastries that taste like they were hand-made by Ursula herself. After a day of exploring the village or hiking in the nearby mountains, take a refreshing dip in the hotel's indoor pool, or relax in the outdoor hot tub. The hotel's grounds are beautifully landscaped and offer plenty of opportunities for a leisurely stroll, complete with views of the stunning Cascade Mountains. If you don't have time for a stay, that's okay, but be sure to start your day at the Enzian. You'll be greeted with a traditional morning alphorn serenade—the quintessential Leavenworth experience.

Stop Six – Nutcracker Museum

Yep, it's real. This one isn't fiction. There is indeed a one-of-a-kind Nutcracker Museum in Leavenworth. This quirky and fascinating museum celebrates the history and artistry of the beloved holiday figurines. You'll be amazed by the sheer number and variety of nutcrackers on display, from classic German styles to modern and whimsical designs.

The museum's collection includes over 7,000 nutcrackers from around the world, each carefully curated and displayed uniquely and creatively. You'll learn about the history of nutcrackers, their role in European folklore, and the many different materials and designs used to create them over the years. The museum is housed in a charming, old-world building that adds to the overall charm and character of the experience. Whether you're a fan of the Nutcracker ballet, a collector of holiday decor, or simply on the hunt for new and inventive murder weapons, be sure to check this one out.

Stop Seven – The Ski Hill and Lodge

Whether you visit in the dead of winter or during the spring when the hills are alive with wildflowers, the Ski Hill and Lodge are a perfect spot to stretch your legs and connect with nature.

For outdoor enthusiasts looking for a scenic and exciting destination in Leavenworth, look no further than Ski Hill and Lodge, a premier winter and summer recreation spot that offers a wide range of activities and adventures. In the winter, hit the slopes and enjoy some of the region's best cross-country skiing, snowshoeing, and tubing, all set against the stunning backdrop of the Cascade Mountains. You'll love the exhilarating runs, beautifully groomed trails, and the lodge, where you can warm up with a cup of hot cocoa or a pint of Nitro's dark chocolate stout.

In the summer, Ski Hill and Lodge become a paradise for hikers, mountain bikers, and outdoor adventurers. The lush alpine setting provides the perfect backdrop for a wide range of outdoor activities, from scenic hikes to thrilling downhill mountain biking. Take in the stunning views of the surrounding mountains, breathe in the fresh alpine air, and immerse yourself in nature.

I hope you've enjoyed this tour of Sloan's Leavenworth. If you visit in real life, send me your pics and have a pint!

Cheers to bookish adventures.

ACKNOWLEDGMENTS

It really does take a village to write a book, and I'm so grateful to my village. It feels a lot like my own version of Leavenworth, minus any pop-in visits by April Ablin, thank goodness.

Thanks to Kitty Wong for your cover illustration. You brought the Ski Hill and lodge to life in ways I could never have imagined. It was a delight to partner with you and be a witness to your creative process, from the initial pencil sketches to the final cover. There's something particularly special about working with an artist from Hong Kong and knowing that Sloan has made her way to your side of the world. Now we need her (and me) to come for a beerish tour of the city.

On the note of covers, I have to give a special shoutout to the Tech Guy, also known as Gordy Seeley, my real-life partner-in-crime and the guy who helps with all the tech behind the scenes. Like, for taking Kitty Wong's illustration and doing the final cover design—adding in the title, back cover copy, spine, barcodes, and the less glamorous yet equally important elements that make a book a book. The same goes for the interior layout. I write the words, and you make them look pretty; thank you a million times for that and much more.

To Raina Glazener, where would this mystery be without your eagle eyes? Let me tell you, probably littered with minor errors and errant commas. Massive gratitude for your stellar copy-editing skills and insight into places where the book needed a little extra blood splatter. Okay, sure, this is a cozy, so maybe not so much with the splatter, but there is no one as talented or as thorough as Raina in the business, and I'm so thrilled to have you in my village.

After reading this, Melissa Makarewicz might become your favorite person because she's the genius behind Sloan's bonus content and stories. Melissa runs The Literary Assistant, and when we teamed up last fall, she pushed me to think outside of the box (or, in this case, the brewery) when it came to Sloan. She encouraged me to write bonus short stories and crossovers. So if you aren't a newsletter subscriber, get on the list because, thanks to Melissa, I've written some extra shorts for newsletter subscribers. Want Sloan's drink and food pairings on social media or to know what Nitro's planning for their spring line? Melissa's clever prompts have encouraged me to continue to build Sloan's world, and there's more coming.

And last, but certainly not least—you. As I mentioned in the dedication, this book wouldn't exist without you. Thank you for being a reader. I know it sounds cheesy, but I fully believe that books make the world a better place, so here's to saving the world one book at a time.

READ ON FOR AN EXCERPT FROM...

A BREW TO A KILL

A new Sloan Mystery short
Coming in May 2023!

A BREW TO A KILL

CHAPTER ONE

The aroma of mosaic hops and rose petals wafted from the brewery. Spring was in full bloom in Leavenworth, Washington, where Garrett Strong, my brewing partner at Nitro, and I were putting the finishing touches on our spring line of Pacific Northwest beers. Our rose-hips and lemon lager was an update from a beer we had brewed last year, and our pear and apple IPA was a new addition. The fruit-forward brew was layered with local, organic produce, Yakima valley hops, and a touch of vanilla for a sweet finish.

"Sloan, how are we doing for time?" Garrett asked as he climbed down from the ladder attached to one of the brite tanks.

"We should head over to the Festhall soon. Maybe twenty minutes," I replied.

Garrett tugged a pair of chemistry goggles from his head. "Perfect. That gives me time to change and steal two of your white velvet cookies before we go."

"I'll check in with Kat to make sure everything is good with the tasting room and meet you in the kitchen to load up in a few." I left him to get ready and went to the front.

A long distressed wood bar with dozens of taps divided the

brewing area, commercial kitchen, and our shared office in the back of the building with the tasting room in the front. Every time I walked into the bright space with exposed ceilings and bright windows that looked out onto Leavenworth's cobblestone streets, I couldn't help but smile. I was so lucky to be living my dream.

"Hey, Sloan," Kat said, greeting me with a dimpled grin as she pointed to the window. "Can you believe how gorgeous it is this morning? It's going to be perfect weather for the farmer's market."

I stole a glance at the tangerine light spilling through the rustic wood-paned windows. Today was the official kickoff festival for the return of the farmer's market season. During the winter months the market went on hiatus, but now that the hills were lush with emerald green grass and rows and rows of pretty pink cherry blossoms, I couldn't wait to get back in the swing of market weekends.

We had decided to set up a booth for the kickoff festivities where we would share samples of our spring beers and sweet pairings. Kat and I had baked batches of white velvet cutout cookies in the shape of hop cones and frosted them with a citrus royal icing with a super secret ingredient—a splash of our signature citrus IPA. In addition to the ode-to-beer cookies, we opted for rhubarb-filled crumbles and shortbread.

"I know. The weather gods are on our side this weekend," I told Kat. "How are things going with prep for the day? Do you need anything before we take off?"

"Nope. I'm all set. It should be pretty chill today since everyone will be at the market. Look at this, though." She reached for her phone and held her screen for me to see. "I posted our daily special and the fact that we'll have a booth at the market on social a little while ago, and we got a message from a travel influencer who's in town. He's huge. He has over a million followers. A brew with a view, do you know him?"

I glanced at the screen and shook my head.

"Well, he's barely of legal drinking age. I think he's in his early twenties. His name is Josh, and he does these insane hikes and then shoots videos and pics of beer. He slid into our DMs to ask if we could give him some cans. He's going to hike Dragontail Peak tomorrow and feature Nitro."

"Sure. Yeah."

"This could be huge for us. A lot of Josh's videos go viral." Kat clicked off her phone. "The chance at a couple of million beer lovers seeing Nitro at the top of a peak is worth a six-pack or two, right?"

"Without a doubt." I was thrilled that Kat had happened upon Leavenworth while on a personal quest to meet her idol during Oktoberfest a few years ago. The meetup with her celebrity crush hadn't gone as she had planned, but sometimes fate has a way of putting the right person in your path at the right time. That was true for Kat. She had become an integral part of Nitro's team and part of my extended family.

"I'll hook him up," Kat promised. "You'll probably see him at the market. He has the kind of personality that's hard to miss."

"I know the type. April Ablin comes to mind." I chucked and made a funny face.

"Exactly." Kat snapped and shot her finger at me. "But, hey, if it brings more beer tourists to the village, why not?"

"Why not," I agreed.

Garrett entered the tasting room, pushing a cart with cases of our beers. "Ready to go sling some spring ales, Sloan?"

"That's a mouthful, but yes."

We said goodbye to Kat and made our way along Front Street. The village looked like a watercolor painting with pink and yellow geraniums cascading from window boxes on the half-timbered buildings. Blue gingham checked bunting wrapped around the gazebo fluttering in the slight breeze.

Sunlight drenched the cobblestone streets and kissed the top of the mountain ranges that surrounded the village.

The Festhall was located at the far end of Front Street across from Der Keller. The Der Keller empire continued to expand. My ex-husband Mac had recently taken over operations, a move I had been nervous about. Not because he was dangerous but because Mac tended to overspend, overcommit, over-embellish, over everything. Otto and Ursula, Mac's parents, had divided shares of their beloved business to Mac, Hans, and me, so they could scale back and enjoy their retirement years. At first, I was convinced we were headed for disaster, but to my surprise and delight, Mac had focused on personal growth since our split. He had stepped into his new role with a focus and determination I had never experienced when we were married.

Der Keller was thriving under his leadership, allowing Hans and me the freedom to offer insight into the brewery's future without constantly reigning Mac in.

"It's already hopping," Garrett noted as we approached the empty lot across from the Festhall, where the market setup was in full swing.

White vendor tents in neat rows stretched from one end of the lot to the other. It looked as if every farmer, grower, and crafter from the Wenatchee Valley was ready to kick off the season. There was something for everyone—produce, flowers, honey, candles, pastries, bread, wine, and food trucks.

"It's going to be a full market." I glanced around for our tent. "It looks like we're next to Weber and Annabelle." I pointed to a farm stand a few booths away.

Garrett maneuver the beer cart past other vendors unpacking truckloads of tulips and daisies. Then, he went straight to work setting up our Nitro booth with his usual efficiency, unpacking crates of our new spring ales and tasting glasses. I set out platters of my cookies with little notes Kat had designed for each offering.

We also put out beer merch, stickers, hoodies, hats, and coasters. Canning our beer was a relatively new option. Since we only produced small batches, we didn't have much extra to spare, but Garrett had scored an inexpensive canning system at a beer convention a few months ago, and we decided to take the plunge. We took advantage of the slower winter months to ramp up canning to sell six-packs at the market and to guests who wanted to bring home a taste of Leavenworth. I was excited to see the community respond to our latest endeavor and had a feeling that today's stock might not last long.

By the time our booth was prepped and ready to serve thirsty shoppers, a polka band paraded through the tents announcing the market's official opening. The mayor followed them, complete in Kelly green lederhosen with black suspenders and a felt hat. After his short welcome speech, he turned the microphone over to my nemesis April Ablin.

April was a real estate agent and the self-appointed queen of the village and all things German. In true April fashion, she was dressed in a cotton candy pink dirndl. With two milkmaid-style braids and hot pink lipstick. "Gluten, oh, oh, sorry, I meant Guten Morgan."

She waited for applause.

Someone offered a tepid clap.

"Thank you, thank you." April bowed and then fanned her face. "I'm so touched by your warm welcome and thrilled to be the guest of honor to cut the ribbon for this year's farmer's market."

"Doesn't she cut it every year?" Garrett whispered.

"I'm sure she buys the ribbon herself."

He laughed.

April prattled on about Leavenworth's rich history, our Bavarian culture, and the upcoming Maifest. I wasn't sure who she thought her target audience was because, aside from a handful of tourists, everyone else had lived in the village longer than April.

I tuned her out and scanned the crowd of familiar faces. A group of young, fresh-faced backpackers congregated at Weber and Annabelle's farm booth. They didn't look much older than Alex, my soon-to-be college student. And one of them, who I assumed must be Josh, the beer influencer, given his logo hat, T-shirt, and backpack, looked like he was about to go head-to-head with Weber.

Annabelle yanked Weber's flannel to hold him back as Josh took a swing.

What was going on?

"Get out of here. I don't want to see you anywhere near my booth, my farm, or my *wife*," Weber practically spit in Josh's face. "That's an order."

"It's a free world, man. Chill out." Josh glanced at his friends for moral support. "We're here to climb and spend money in your town. Your energy is not matching the vibe."

Weber lunged at him. "Get out of here—now."

"It's cool. It's cool. We were only trying to help you out, man. Take a few produce pics and post them on social. Your wife has a perfect, wholesome aesthetic. That's all. No need for you to go all patriarchy on us." Josh shrugged in a way that made it clear he was trying to maintain a casual appearance about the argument, but I could tell from his balled-up fists and clenched jaw that there was more going on.

"This is your last chance. Walk away now." Weber clutched a pear in one hand and pointed toward the end of the market with the other.

"Okay, relax." Josh pressed his hands out in an attempt to calm Weber down.

It didn't work.

Weber squeezed the pear so tight it smashed in his hand and dripped down his flannel. He dropped it on the ground and went after Josh, who took off in a sprint. "That's right, you better run. Stay far away from me because if I see you here again, you will get what's coming."

Chatter stopped. People turned to see what was causing the commotion as Josh ran past Der Keller with his friends following him. Even April paused her un-commissioned speech.

"Keep running," Weber hollered.

Annabelle shrunk behind him, her cheeks flaming as red as the baskets of strawberries lining their booth. Her mortification was palpable. She tried whispering and tugging on Weber's sleeve, but his fierce gaze was focused solely on Josh.

I didn't know Weber well, but he and Annabelle had been coming to the farmer's market with their organic produce for years. They were always personable and eager to talk about what was in season on their farm. It seemed out of character for him to attempt to attack and threaten Josh. But then again, I wasn't going to jump to any conclusions. I had no idea what had transpired between them before their altercation.

"Attentionion, Attentionion." April made up a word that didn't even sound German as she tapped the microphone. "It's time for our ribbon cutting. If you would be so kind as to count down from ten with me, I'll cut the ribbon, and the market will officially be open for business.

She signaled the band to continue and wielded a massive pair of scissors.

I was eager to check out the other vendors and share Nitro samples. The start of the market was supposed to be a fun and festive occasion, but I couldn't shake the feeling that something was amiss.

ABOUT THE AUTHOR

I'm a voracious storyteller and a lover of words and all things bookish. I believe that stories have the ability to transport and transform us. With over twenty-five published novels and counting, my goal is to tell stories that provide points of connection, escape, and understanding.

I love inhabiting someone else's skin through the pages of a book and am passionate about helping writers find their unique storytelling lens. As a writing teacher and coach, I guide writers in crafting the story they've always wanted to tell while navigating the path to publication that's right for them.

With more than 300,000 copies in print, my work has been published in hardcover, mass market paperback, audiobook, e-book, and translated internationally. I write multiple series for both Macmillan (St. Martin's Press & Minotaur Books) and Kensington Publishing—such as The Bakeshop Mystery Series and Sloan Krause Mysteries—and also publish my own novels

—like Lost Coast Literary—through my publishing company, Sweet Lemon Press.

Now living in sunny California, I spent most of my life in the Pacific Northwest. My love for the region runs deep. Hence why many of my books are set there. From the Shakespearean hamlet of Ashland, Oregon to the Bavarian village of Leavenworth, Washington to the hipster mecca of Portland, Oregon and a variety of other stunning outdoor locales, the Pacific Northwest is a backdrop for many of my books and almost becomes another character in each series.

When not writing, you can find me testing pastry recipes in my home kitchen or at one of the many famed coffeehouse or brewpubs nearby. You'll also find me outside exploring hiking trails and trying to burn off calories consumed in the name of "research".

I love hearing from readers and connecting on social media. Be sure to follow me to learn about my writing process, upcoming books, special events, giveaways, and more! Also, sign up for my e-mail newsletter to stay up to date on new releases, appearances, and exclusive content & recipes.

Come on a storyventure with me!

facebook.com/elliealexanderauthor

twitter.com/ellielovesbooks

instagram.com/ellie_alexander

youtube.com/elliealexanderauthor

tiktok.com/@elliealexanderauthor

pinterest.com/elliealexanderauthor

goodreads.com/elliealexanderauthor

bookbub.com/authors/ellie-alexander

amazon.com/author/elliealexander

ELLIE ALEXANDER'S AUTHOR ACADEMY

COURSES AND COACHING TO HELP ASPIRING
AUTHORS WRITE, PITCH, AND MARKET THEIR
BOOKS ON THE WAY TOWARD REALIZING
THEIR DREAMS OF BECOMING PUBLISHED

Are you struggling with where to start when it comes to writing? Or maybe you've gotten partway through a draft and don't know what comes next? Perhaps you've finished a book and need help navigating the path to publication.

I love teaching and sharing the vast amount of knowledge that I've acquired publishing 29 books and counting. I've been in your shoes, and I have stacks and stacks of unfinished, terrible, horrible, no good first drafts that will never see the light of day. I've taken everything I've learned (the good and the bad) and transformed it into a mystery series masterclass. My comprehensive course takes the mystery out of how to craft, edit, and publish a novel with step-by-step videos, tangible assignments and activities, and an engaged and activity private community of writers just like you who will help cheer you on as you pound out that word count.

You can write that novel! It's time to stop dreaming about finishing the book that's been taking up space in your head and to start realizing your dream! I'm so excited to help guide and champion you, and can't wait to see your book on the shelves!

Sign Up Today!